I0633001

THIS BOY'S WAR

THIS Boy's WAR

A NOVEL

ARNOLD GROSSMAN

Logis Books
Denver, Colorado

ALSO BY ARNOLD GROSSMAN

1988, A Novel of Politics

A California Conspiracy

One Nation Under Guns,
An American Epidemic

The Welcome

Going Together

The Boat Builder

Copyright 2018 © by Arnold Grossman

All rights reserved. No portion of this book may be reproduced
without permission of the publisher.

ISBN: 978-1-7339823-0-6

This is a work of fiction. All of the characters, organizations and events portrayed in
the novel are either products of the author's imagination or are used fictitiously.

Printed in The United States of America
Book Design: Rudy Ramos

For information, contact: **arngross@msn.com**

For Nina, Zoey, Adin, Leah and Michaela
Grandest children All

CHAPTER

1

How did I get here, lying on the cold wet sand that smells like a bunch of toilets at school that didn't get flushed and blood and sea water and exploded gun powder all mixed together?

I'm pressing my face into the sand, as if it could open up and get me out of here to someplace else, like a cave maybe. Fat chance.

Ice-cold waves of water are running up and trickling over my feet, but I'm not going to try to move them or anything else on my body. I have to look like a corpse, not a thirteen-year-old Jewish kid who's still alive in an army uniform that's way too big. The Germans wouldn't shoot at a dead body. At least I don't think they would.

I feel like I'm going to throw up, but I'd probably drown in my own vomit, which would be disgusting. I guess I'm still seasick from the ride in the landing craft that got me here. It stopped all of a sudden a little ways from the beach, and just about everyone fell over when it did. Then the big door on the front fell into the water that we were supposed to jump into. Actually I was pushed into it by someone behind me, like what used to happen at the lake in summer camp, but this time it wasn't another kid doing the pushing. It was an officer in the United States Army.

I started wading to the shore and looked up at the sky. It was covered totally by black puffs of smoke. And the noise was loud enough it could make me deaf with the bombs exploding, machine guns shooting at everybody and airplanes flying real low over the beach, if you could call it a beach, which I can't. Beaches are where you go with your family to swim and get sunburned, not where people are trying to kill everybody else.

I saw the first dead person in my life before I even got on the sand. It was a soldier, floating like he was looking down into the water. But he wasn't seeing anything anymore.

There was blood all around him, making red circles that kept getting bigger. Then I saw more dead people, doing the same thing, floating with their arms out like they wanted to fly away, which is what I wanted to do.

It was probably the craziest thing any kid in the whole world ever did that got me here, to France and a place called Normandy on June sixth, nineteen-forty-four. I found out they called it D-Day, but I don't know what it means. Death Day? And the sand I'm on is called Omaha Beach, which seems strange. Omaha is in Nebraska, I'm pretty sure. There are farms there. No ocean, no beaches and no dead people everywhere you look.

Anyway, here I am, just a kid named Saperstein who should be home eating his mother's chocolate cake after school instead of swallowing sea water with blood and urine and poop in it. And it all started a few months ago when a brick crashed through a window in the house where I live, like one of those bombs that keep dropping on this beach, maybe not as loud, but it felt that way. It was something I'll never, ever forget, and really don't want to. There was a paper note stuck on it, saying, "Jews get out." Guess it was our welcome wagon to a place we weren't so welcome, in Teanec. New Jersey.

It has to be the real hell, this place I ended up in, not the one with a devil in a black cape holding a pitch fork down in the middle of the earth someplace. It's right here, in France, on the sand, at the edge of the English Channel that probably will never get clean again from what war put into it.

I'm thinking what I was doing not so long before I ended up here. I was celebrating my bar mitzvah. That's where the rabbi told me, "Today you are a man." But I wasn't. I was still a kid who thought the most important things in the world were whether the New York Giants would win the pennant and maybe even the World Series and whether Pam Kaufman would let me get to second, or maybe third base with her on a hay ride. If the rabbi would be here today, I have a feeling he'd bend over and say, "Saperstein, I made a mistake. You weren't a man when you read from the Torah. But today you really are one. So get your head out of that sand and go do what men do. You'll make everybody back home proud of you. But clean your face first."

I actually could feel his hand on my shoulder, gripping it tight and turning me over. When I looked up through the sand in my eyes I couldn't make out the rabbi's face, or his black hat. Instead I saw a man with a helmet on his head and sergeant stripes on his green uniform staring down at me. He yelled out to somebody, "This one's alive. I don't know if he's been hit."

"Jesus Christ, they're taking them that young now?" he said to another face with a helmet staring down at me.

"You O.K. soldier?" the other face asked me.

"I think so," was all I could say.

"Well if you are, you'd better get your butt off this beach while you still can. Where's your unit?"

I admitted I didn't know.

"Which one is it?"

"Fourth Ranger Division."

The two faces looked at each other, then back at me.

"You're a Ranger?" said one of them, like he didn't believe it.

"Well, sort of."

"Kid, there's no such thing as a sort-of Ranger. You are or you aren't one. And if you are one, you'd best get against that cliff over there," said the sergeant, pointing to a group of soldiers all huddled together against this wall of dirt that went straight up for probably a hundred feet to a flat place on top.

I picked myself up and nodded at the soldiers, who just kept staring at me in a very strange way, and I bent down and started running to where they were pointing.

"Hey, you, wait," the sergeant yelled at me.

I stopped and looked back at him.

"Where's your rifle?

"I don't have one."

"You're a Ranger and you don't have a piece? What did you think you were going to kill krauts with?"

"I'm not going to kill anybody."

Before he could answer me, there was a real loud whistling sound getting closer and closer. Then it stopped and a bunch of beach between me and the two soldiers went flying up in the air and then about a ton of sand came down in a big cloud and it knocked me off my feet. When it stopped coming down, I saw the soldiers crouched and running in the other direction.

"Get the hell over to that cliff before you get blown to hell," the sergeant yelled back over his shoulder.

I started to get up again, but then something else came down from the sky, something small. It almost hit me. At first I thought maybe it was a seashell the way it was curved and had lines in it. But it had blood on it too. I guess I didn't want to believe what I thought it was, an ear. A human one. I picked it up and held it in my hand. It was warm. And it made me feel like crying for whoever just lost it. But instead, I did what seemed like the right thing to do. I bent down and dug a hole in the sand with my hands. I put the warm ear in it and then covered it up and built a little mound on top of it. I remembered the small American flag I carried with me since I left home, for good luck and to let people know what side I was on. I stuck in the mound and thought I should say a prayer for when they bury people, even though this was only part of a person. But I was shaking too much to remember the prayer, so I just made a salute to the flag and to the ear underneath it, making a wish that whoever lost it was O.K. without it.

Then another bunch of sand blew up pretty close again, and that made me think the next ear, or arm, or just about anything that came down could be mine and I ran as fast as I could toward the Rangers at the cliff. I thought about the words you always heard in stores when there was no meat to buy, or at home when I asked why we couldn't go for a Sunday drive because there was no gas for the car: "Don't you know there's a war on?"

Well, I guess now I do know there's a war on and what it looks like, how it smells and what it does to people. I also finally know the answer to my question of why I ended up in the middle of one.

As crazy as it sounds, after all the things that were happening to me and my family made me feel like it really was all my fault, like this gang of bullies kept telling me, that if it wasn't for people like me, Hitler wouldn't be killing our boys over here. I guess if you hear something enough times you'll probably believe it, like I did.

That's when I decided I'd better try and do something over here. That's why I'm here. With a story to tell about it all, one that's really pretty hard to believe.

Even for me. Specially for me.

CHAPTER
2

It was one of those family Sunday nights we always had, after the usual roasted chicken dinner. We were sitting in the living room, my parents, my brother, Stanley, and me, listening to the Jack Benny show on the radio. All of a sudden there was an awful, huge crash, the sound of glass shattering and then a thump of something hitting the floor hard. It was like what I thought was a bomb hitting us, from a German plane maybe attacking New Jersey

Of course, everyone turned and looked at me at first, like I broke something. But then my mother put her hand over her mouth and pointed to a bunch of glass on the floor near the front window and a brick sitting in the middle of it. My father jumped up to look outside, but I guess he didn't see anything.

"Oh, my God," my mother finally said. She pulled my head against her, like she was going to protect me from what would come next. She didn't do that with my brother. I guess she knew he could take care of himself.

My father looked around at us. "Anybody hurt?" We all just shook our heads. Then he picked up the brick, which had a piece of paper wrapped around it. He read it, and shook his head slowly back and forth.

"What is it?" my mother asked. "What does it say?"

My father didn't say anything, but walked over and handed her the paper, which she stared at and said again, "Oh, my God." And, "Who would do such a thing?" The paper was shaking in her hand. She started crying. It was something I never saw before, except at my grandfather's funeral, but that was sad crying and this was scared crying. There's a difference. It made me feel like covering *her* head, but, well, you don't do that.

My brother got up and took the paper out of her hands. You could tell he was all steamed up. He's three years older than me and has a real temper.

"Those lousy bastards," he said. And he went to the front door and tore it open.

"Where do you think you're going?" my father said.

"To shove this thing up somebody's ass."

"Don't talk like that in the house," my mother said. Which was kind of strange, I mean when someone just smashed our window with a brick, which could have split someone's head open, she was worried about swearing in the house.

"You're not going anywhere," my father said, the way you knew he really meant it. My brother got all red in the face and started the puffing he usually does when he's ready to punch somebody, or a wall.

I couldn't stand not knowing what the note said, so I asked my brother what was on it before he went out to shove it somewhere. He just tossed it in my lap. I looked down at the big, black letters that said, *JEWS GET OUT* and underneath, *THE BLACK CAT GANG.*

"Shut the door," my father said, which my brother did, hard enough that it made glasses rattle in the china cabinet.

"But somebody's gotta pay for this," Stanley said.

"No," my mother chimed in. "Don't let him go out there," she said to my father.

"Don't worry. He's staying put."

"God knows who could be waiting for him," she said. "A Black Cat Gang. A bunch of hoodlums."

I don't know if I'd call the people who smash our window and tell us to get out of town a bunch of hoodlums, like my mother said. To me, hoodlums are gangsters with names like Baby Face, Pretty Boy or Dutch, who go around with machine guns robbing banks, not throwing bricks through windows of Jewish houses.

But I found out soon enough there really was a bunch of high school kids who called themselves the Black Cat Gang. Where they got a name like that beats me. They weren't interested in robbing anything, at least not that I ever knew of. They just wanted to do one thing, and that was to make life really awful for anyone with a name like mine, David Saperstein, and to try and scare any families like ours who moved to Teaneck into packing up and getting out of town. It didn't work. No family I heard of had to pack up and leave town, at least not for being Jewish and scared. My mother did think about it after that night with the rock and the note, though, but she got over it in a hurry, mostly because of our next door neighbors on both sides. They were gentiles, like about ninety-nine and forty-four-one-hundreths per cent of everybody in Teaneck. They heard about what happened to us and came over with cookies and cakes and told us they really wanted us next door to them, and would do anything to make sure we didn't think of leaving. I thought about telling them if they kept bringing the cookies and cakes, that would help us stay, but I didn't.

For a couple of weeks or so, things stayed normal. My father spent a lot of time telling us everything was going to be O.K. We had neighbors who wanted us there, and the police were going to keep an eye out, whatever that meant, just in case. They came to the house the night after the brick thing happened and were pretty nice to us. I told them we had a friend on the New York police force and wondered if they knew him. That was pretty dumb, I know. My dad thought so too. He gave me one of those looks, where he lowers his eyelids as a signal to stop, and I did. He must have thought I was going to mention the Double Bubblegum Sol gave me for my Bar Mitzvah. It was something nobody could get, Bubblegum, because of the war. It was something about needing the rubber to make tires for all the jeeps over there. I also heard it was just because soldiers like to chew Bubblegum when they're in the trenches, to calm them down, the way baseball players chew tobacco.

You could tell things were getting better after awhile, when my mother started knitting again, which probably meant she was calming down. She never knitted when she was upset. Instead she would stay in the kitchen and bake bread, like she did in the couple of days after "it" happened (she never used the words brick or Black Cat Gang, like maybe not saying them would keep "it" from happening again). She would spend most of the day rolling dough, pounding it, pinching it, braiding it, and then baking it into her famous loaves of challah bread. Then she'd hand them out to the neighbors who brought us the cookies and cakes. I don't know what they did with all that bread, besides bringing us some more of their stuff. My brother, who always has something funny to say, or at least he thinks he does, said, "With all this baking going on, maybe we should change our name to Pillsbury. Probably safer here than Saperstein." All my mother did was stare at him, like she didn't know what he meant, but I knew she did.

Then it happened again, a few weeks later. Not a smashed window. Worse this time.

It was Halloween, when little kids go out in costumes from the Five and Ten, doing trick or treat for candy, and older kids, like me, do just the trick part. Only we called it door-belling, when you ring the bell and do something mostly stupid, like tying a rope from the handle on the door to something so people can't open it. Or, worse, leaning something bad against the door, ringing and running into the bushes to watch a milk bottle spill over into the house with what looked like pee, but was really just ginger ale.

Anyway, it was just another Halloween and it was a school night, so I had to be home by nine, even though I was now a man. Just kidding. My parents weren't. It was still nine, they said.

Three of my friends wanted to walk me home, probably to let me know that they were on my side. We stopped to talk about the stuff we did around the corner from my house. One of the kids, Gordon, said, "What's that smoke?" You could smell it, sort of like a campfire burning.

We turned down Grenville Avenue and saw a bunch of people standing in the street, watching something. "Hey, David, your house is on fire," another friend, Roger yelled out.

"Very funny," I yelled back. Roger was always doing that kind of stuff, just to see what he could make us believe, like when he came out of his house once and told me my mother called to tell me Mr. Baumgartner's German shepherd ate my cocker spaniel. I believed him and ran all the way home and yelled at my mother, "That German guy let his German dog eat Rusty?" She just looked at me and slowly shook her head.

But I moved down the street to get a closer look. I also heard a lot of people talking loud to each other. I could see flames that looked like they were coming from the front door. And I ran as fast as I could to get there. When I got closer, I could see the fire wasn't in the house, but on the sides of the door and on top of it, like it was trying to get inside.

My father was holding a green garden hose and squirting water on the fire, but it didn't seem to be doing much good. My brother threw a garbage can of water at it, too. My mother saw me coming. She was crying again and she grabbed me, like to protect me from the fire, which wasn't all that big, but she must have thought it was going to be.

"Look what they did, David." she said. "Now they're trying to burn our house down."

"Who is?" I said, with actually a pretty good idea of who she meant. I wiggled out of her arms and she tried to stop me from getting closer to the house, but she couldn't. Then I saw probably the scariest thing ever, in the middle of the white door. It was a swastika, in black paint, and the fire was like a big ring all around it. It looked like a red, white and black Nazi flag, the most awful thing I ever saw, and I ended up dreaming about it almost every night, at least when I wasn't dreaming about the Giants getting into the World Series.

My friends caught up with me and stood there watching, real quiet, and I think real scared, like I was.

Gordon started to say something but got drowned out by a loud siren that just kept getting louder. It was a fire engine headed for the house. Then another one came right behind it. They both stopped and a bunch of firemen in shiny black raincoats and helmets started pulling thick white hoses out of the red trucks, and saying things like, "Stand back, everybody. We'll take care of this." And, "Anybody hurt?" Nobody answered. People just shook their heads, and stared at our house.

"What the hell is this?" Gordon asked.

"The Welcome Wagon," Roger answered, and he wasn't trying to be funny like he usually does.

"Yeah, trick or treat," Gordon said, like he was disgusted, and probably pretty scared, too, maybe because he was the only other Jewish kid in our crowd.

I guess it was right there, looking at our burning front door, watching the fireman put the whole thing out in just a couple of seconds, that I made up my mind. There was a war on, everybody knew that. It's what we heard every time we turned on the radio, when my father tried to buy stuff that was rationed, like gas or tires for the car, even when my mother asked if there was any sugar at the grocer's. There's a war on. But before that night, the war was always "over there." Now it was here, on Grenville Avenue in Teaneck, New Jersey. And I had to find something to do about it. The question was what.

CHAPTER

3

I can still smell the smoke and see the black paint and the ring of fire around the front door. Probably, I never will forget it. Wouldn't you if somebody hated you enough to set your house on fire?

And just to make sure I didn't forget it, some kids at school got into following me home a lot ever since the Halloween night and making any kind of trouble they could for me. It got to be that every time the last bell rang at school at three-fifteen, I'd start trying to figure out how to keep from running into them or, actually, them from running into me. I was pretty sure who they were: the Black Cat Gang, but I couldn't prove it, at least not yet.

One time, and it was a pretty bad time, they saw me on a Saturday morning coming out of the house on Queen Anne Road that was made into the synagogue where I went to Hebrew school. I had to keep going for a couple of months on *Shabbas* (that's Sabbath for us) after my bar mitzvah, I guess to prove I took the man thing seriously and didn't do it all just for the party and the presents.

"Hey, Jewboy, what's in that blue book you always try to hide?" one of the gang asked.

I guess my answer wasn't a very good one.

"Nothin' much."

All of a sudden there was a circle of them, all bigger and older than me, taking turns trying to pull the paper-covered book with Hebrew letters on the front out of my hands. Finally one of them got a tight hold of it and yanked. I wouldn't let go, so he had to settle for about half of the book that he ripped away. I tried not to cry, but that didn't work. Besides being scared as hell of what they were going to do to me next, I actually was madder about what that kid did to the workbook. My teacher at the synagogue once bawled out a kid who had a book with the cover missing and said it was a sin to do anything to a book that had the name God in it. It was like tearing off His clothes, which has to be just about the worst thing you could do to Him. I also learned that you never, ever refer to Him with a small "h," and I had to stay after on the day I did that and write His name with a capital letter about five hundred times, until the chalk ran out.

"That's a sin you just did," I yelled at the kid who was holding the ripped off part of the book and smiling a really ugly smile, staring at the pages. I either wanted lightning to come out of the sky and fry him to a crisp, which didn't happen of course, or break his stupid nose, which also didn't happen.

"Hey," he said to his buddies, still with that stupid smile, "The Jewboy says I'm a sinner. Look who's talking. He killed Christ."

"No I didn't."

"Yes you did."

I wanted to say it was impossible. I'm only thirteen. I obviously wasn't there. Good thing I didn't say it though.

"And now look what all you Jews are doing." I couldn't figure out what all of us had done now. I just stared at him thinking I maybe should run. But the rest of them, I think there were four, were watching me too close to try that.

"That war that's going on, killing our soldiers. It's your fault, you know that don't you Saperstein?"

"Yeah," chimed in another kid, a really big one. "If it wasn't for the Jews, there wouldn't be a Hitler killing our boys over there."

Now that I really didn't get. I mean everybody knows that the Germans are beating up and killing Jews like crazy, not the other way around. We heard about people, even little kids, getting put on trains and in camps, even gassed. It's our fault?

The one who took my book, Eric, I heard them call him, said, "Look at this stuff. What is it, Jew language?"

"It's Hebrew," I said.

"Yeah? Same thing, isn't it?" I shrugged, because I didn't actually know. "Well, read it to me." He shoved the torn book practically in my face. I wouldn't take the pages back. It was a sin, what he did. I didn't want that to be my fault, too, on top of everything else.

"Come on," another kid said. "He's just gonna stand there and piss in his pants. Let's go." He came close to me. "Nobody wants you here, don't you know that, Jewboy?"

"Where?" was all I could think to say, as if he meant on that on the sidewalk on Queen Anne Road, which I knew wasn't what he meant, and that probably made him madder.

"In our town. Our school."

"Yeah, in our country, either," said a kid I never saw before, older than the rest, and just as mean looking. He said, "My father's over there getting shot at. And for what? To protect the Jews that started it all. What about your old man? Is he in the Army?"

I just shook my head.

"Of course not," said the older kid. "Probably a draft dodger on top of everything else."

"He can't," I said.

"Can't what?"

"Go in the army. He's too old."

"Sure, I'll bet. Probably lies about his age."

All of a sudden, I wasn't as scared as before. What did it was what he said about my father, who would never lie about anything. He felt bad all the time about being too old to join up. I even heard him tell my mother once that maybe he should fudge about how old he really was and say he was younger to get in the Army. She told him that would make him a liar, maybe even get him in trouble. "What do we tell the children about lying?"

I could feel this shaking all over, and I didn't care what these kids were going to do to me. I tasted this awful, burning stuff that came up in my throat that was maybe going to make me throw up. And I dropped what was left of the book on the ground without realizing that was a sin, too, when I made a fist with both hands.

"You're a liar, a dirty rotten liar," I said to the older kid. No, I shouted it. "My father isn't a liar like you. Take it back, you damn son-of-a-bitch." Then I got real close to him and saw his eyes shoot around, looking at the other kids, like he didn't know what to do, or what I was going to do. He must have figured he was looking pretty bad to his friends, so he grabbed my jacket and said, "Oh, yeah, Jewboy? I'm not taking anything back, you little piece of dog shit."

He got so close to my face I could smell something like fried bacon. He held up a fist that was looking very big. I got ready to feel it crunch into my mouth or my nose, and to taste the blood, like metal, that would get mixed in with the stuff from my stomach, and closed my eyes.

But then I heard something, something loud. It was a horn, from a car, once, twice then three times. I opened my eyes, and the fist was still there, but the kid wasn't looking at me. Neither were the others. I turned just enough to see the car. Not just any one. Our car, with the gas ration stickers on the window, with the door open and my father leaning out of it.

"What's going on here, boys?" he said loud enough for all of us to hear. The way he asked the question, it made him sound like he knew exactly what was going on, and didn't like it.

"Who's asking?" said the one who was ready to punch me.

"I think you'd better let go of that boy."

He did lower his fist, but still hung on to my jacket. "Who is that guy?" he asked his friends.

One of them said, "It's his old man."

"You sure?" asked another. "How do you know?"

"I know, that's all."

My father got out of the car and started coming toward us.

"Come on. Let's get out of here," the one that was Eric said.

Finally the one waiting to punch me got real close again and said, "Just watch yourself, Jewboy. You're not always gonna have your old man around to protect your ass."

And that was that. They took off, not actually running, but walking pretty fast, like they didn't want to still be standing around me when my father got there.

"You O.K., son?" he asked, looking me over, I guess for blood or missing teeth or anything like that.

"Yeah," I said. "I'm O.K. How come you were here?"

"I was on the way home from synagogue and happened to see you and those kids."

I forgot that he goes every Saturday morning to say kaddish (that's the prayer for dead people) for my grandfather.

He didn't see the torn half of the book on the ground. He just put his hand on my shoulder and said, "Come on, son. Let's get you home."

I stopped and asked him, "Do you think maybe we shouldn't tell Mom what happened to me?"

"Do you think we shouldn't?"

I just shrugged my shoulders and thought about something somebody once said, I think it was my uncle Jack, that us Jews have a way of answering a question with a question. I saw what he meant.

"I guess I got here just in time," my father said. "You looked ready to take that bigger boy on."

"More like he was going to take *me* on. But I didn't care."

He gave me one of those looks, like when I did something that maybe I shouldn't have done, but that he was kind of glad I did, a man to man thing, if you know what I mean.

I was still shaking on the way home. And I got to thinking about what I said after the Halloween fire and swastika on the door. I didn't know what to do then.

Now I did.

CHAPTER

4

It definitely smelled of war that place, oily. Uncle Sam's Eighth Avenue Army-Navy Surplus Store it was called. I guess the smell came from all the guns there, which always seemed to be getting oiled. It could have been the piles of green ponchos too, which had some kind of stuff to make them water-proof for fighting in the rain. I had one in summer camp, and it smelled like that. So did the tent we slept in. There was another smell that reminded me of my grandmother's apartment. Moth balls.

I was looking around for uniforms and up near the ceiling there was this big poster that scared the crap out of me. It was a picture of Hitler, looking straight down on me, like he found himself a Jewish kid to kill. But what he was really doing in the picture was stamping his big, black boot down on top of an American ship out in the ocean. Underneath him it said *LOOSE LIPS SINK SHIPS!* It's a pretty scary thing to think about, the enemy hearing what people talk about, like Navy ships in the Hudson River or Army trucks out on the highway. I wasn't even supposed to brag to kids that my two uncles were driving tanks somewhere . That's why there was a flag in our front window, red and white with two blue stars, which meant they were "over there." We prayed a lot the stars would never be gold instead. That would say my uncles weren't coming home.

"Lookin' for something, kid?" It was almost like Hitler up there on the poster was talking to me. But it was somebody behind me. American, not German. I turned around and saw this big guy with a cigar butt sticking out of his mouth. He needed a shave and his shirt buttons over his big stomach looked like they were going to pop. He just kept staring down at me, like he wasn't too happy about seeing me.

"I was hoping to get a uniform." My own voice sounded higher than usual to me.

"A scout uniform?"

"No. An army uniform."

"We got a whole store full of 'em. What kind you want?"

"American," I said.

"I didn't think you wanted a kraut or Jap one. Whaddya want? Dress, summer, winter?

"A battle uniform." I could feel my face getting all red. "Fatigues?"

"Fatigues?" he said, like he was making fun of me. "They didn't wear no fatigues in World War One."

"I'm thinking of World War Two."

"Everybody's thinking about it kid, about World War Two. Don't you know that?" He was starting to look suspicious. Maybe he thought I had loose lips.

I pulled this picture out of my pocket. It was a folded up cover of *True Combat Magazine*. I showed it to him. "I want to buy the kind of uniform the Army's wearing over in Europe. Like this." There was this soldier with huge muscles showing through his fatigues, and with a knife in his teeth. He had a grenade in one hand and a .45 automatic in the other, and was jumping across a ditch to chase a scared German soldier who was trying to get away.

The big guy looked like he was getting mad now. "Look, kid, you can't come in here expectin' to buy the same uniform our boys are wearing over there. It ain't patriotic to imitate a real soldier. Don't you know there's a war on, for chrissake?"

All of a sudden I had this urge to pee, which sometimes happens when I think something really bad is going to happen to me. It would be real disaster leaving a puddle on the grimy linoleum floor. So I figured the whole thing, this trip to the surplus store, was a bad idea. I started walking away from the man who just kept staring at me. On the way past a bunch of hunting knives, like the one the soldier in the picture had in his mouth, I heard that voice again.

"Hey!"

I really had to get out of there.

"Come back here, kid."

I didn't know if I should make a break for it, out onto Eighth Avenue and hope to get lost in the Saturday afternoon Manhattan crowds. But I was frozen like ice. I didn't want the guy coming after me, yelling something like, "Grab that kid. He's trying to impersonate a soldier."

I couldn't believe I actually did something this stupid, getting into a mess like that. I closed my eyes and said, *Please, God, get me out of this store alive, and I'd seriously consider not trying to help win World War Two. It'd even be O.K. if you make the Giants lose three in a row to the Dodgers, if you'll just get me out in one piece.*

"Is this what you're lookin' for kid?"

The man with the big stomach and little cigar seemed to pop out of the pile of green wool pants that went all the way up to the ceiling. He was holding a pair of olive-drab fatigues that looked pretty real to me.

"These things might be small enough to fit you," he said, pushing them at me. "Wanna try 'em on?"

I took the fatigues, a jacket and pants that went together, and smelled them.

"Whaddya think, somebody crapped in them or somethin'?"

"No, I didn't think that." The truth was, I liked the smell. It wasn't oil. Or moth balls, either, but like new tablecloths, just like in my father's textile factory in Union City. My parents always called it "the place," never a factory. Guess it sounded better. Anyway, the fatigues had the same fresh smell, and made me wish I was at "the place" instead of where I was.

"You mean it's O.K. to wear these?"

The man nodded. "Why not?" he growled.

"With the war on?"

"Hey, kid, don't take everything so serious. Can't you tell I'm jokin'?"

Not really. I mean there wasn't much to laugh at when you feel like you're trapped in some kind of prison with a picture of Hitler on the wall and a guy with a cigar and hands big enough to pound you through the linoleum into a torture chamber downstairs.

I lied. "Oh, sure, I knew you were kidding."

"Know why they're small enough to fit you?" he said. "They're for WACs."

I almost let the fatigues fall on the floor. What if somebody found out I was wearing a woman's uniform? Great, just what I needed. The Black Cat guys would love that one. I'd be a Jew*girl* that caused the war. I put my face in the jacket and smelled. The big guy watched me do it.

"You think they're gonna smell like a woman? They're brand new. Besides, you should consider yourself lucky. I can't get men's uniforms. But the people who made these things made too many for the WACs."

All of a sudden I pictured women in white brassieres and panties slipping into the fatigues I was holding. It got my mind off the scary big guy and now I saw a whole squad of WACs all lined up and wearing the same jackets, tight jackets that looked like the buttons were going to pop off around their breasts. I hoped the guy who kept watching me wasn't looking down below my belt. I held the jacket in front of me, the way I hold my books sometimes when I have to stand up on the bus with an embarrassing bulge.

"Well, make up your mind. You want 'em?"

"Yes, I do. I want them," I said.

"They button on the opposite side. But don't worry. Nobody's gonna notice. Whaddya want the uniform for, anyway? It's, what, six months to Halloween yet?"

"Well, I just want to make sure I have them in plenty of time. Do you have any helmets?"

He nodded and pointed to a dusty display of steel helmets on the wall behind him. There was one that had a pointed top, the kind that sometimes has horns on it, an English air-raid warden's helmet, a couple that must have been from World War One, a couple of firemen's helmets and one that gave me goose pimples. It definitely was a German helmet, and I couldn't stop staring at it.

"It's not for sale."

"Is it really, you know... from..."

"Came off a dead kraut. My nephew brought it home. It's even got some dried kraut blood in it."

"Did he shoot him, your nephew?"

"You kiddin'? He found it on the side of a road. The kraut was killed in a car wreck in France. No, that kid wouldn't shoot anything. Hates guns. He's a ballet dancer. He's a little — " He did this swishing thing with his hands and made his bushy eyebrows go up and down, which really looked dumb. "Know what I mean?"

I knew what he meant, but I acted like I didn't and just shrugged. I've got a cousin who dances in ballet and a lot of kids do that same swishing thing when they talk about him, which I don't like. He can't help it. Some kids are good at sports, but they can't do what he does.

"You don't have an American helmet?" I asked him, and was hoping he wouldn't ask me again if I didn't know there was a war on.

He stared at me like he was wondering if I was a dancer. Then he jerked his head to the side and looked real serious and said, "Come on with me."

I didn't like the way he was looking at me and wondered where he wanted to take me. I figured if I ran like hell I could get out of the store before he could catch me, but I made myself keep standing there.

"Hey, kid, I ain't got all day. You want a helmet or not?"

"Yeah, I guess I do."

He kind of rolled his big body down the aisle, between pea coats and arctic white ski parkas. I figured if I wasn't going to make a break for it out of the store, I'd better follow him. Every step he took made the floor creak, but not my steps.

He turned a corner at the end of a row of black and red flannel mackinaw coats and then stopped in front of a door with a sign on it: "PRIVATE. KEEP OUT OR ELSE. THIS MEANS YOU." He opened the big door that creaked like the floor. He went into a dark room inside and waited for me to go on in too.

I couldn't see anything. But I could smell two things: the stale cigar butt in the big man's mouth, and metal. When the light bulb hanging from the ceiling came on, I could see all kinds of metal stuff, stacked on shelves and even in piles on the floor. It looked like I was in an armory or an ammo depot. There were all kinds of machines, and I couldn't figure out what they were for. They had a lot of grease on them. Then I saw stacks of rifles, with U.S.A. burned into the wooden part. I almost tripped over a machine gun on the floor that was missing one of the legs and was tilted over. It had to weigh more than I do.

"That what you lookin' for, kid?" The guy almost looked like he was going to smile, but he didn't actually. He was pointing at a stack of maybe twenty or thirty green army helmets. The real thing.

"Yes, sir, that's it." I had this picture of me standing at attention in a brand new infantry helmet and a pair of official fatigues, even though they were for women, which I figured nobody would notice, unless they saw they buttoned the wrong way.

He picked a helmet off the pile and tossed it to me. Lucky for me my position was catcher, and I didn't drop it. It felt good in my hands. Solid steel. Heavy. I put it on, and it came down over my eyes. I knew I'd have to put some newspaper inside.

"O.K. Private....what's your name kid?"

"Saperstein."

"Private Saperstein Sounds strange."

"Why?"

"Well, you know, it's just different. Don't get me wrong. I got nothin' against your people."

"Are some of your best friends Jews?" I asked him.

"Yeah. Matter of fact, I do a lot of business with 'em. You know, they're big in the clothing business. Just take a look at all the clothes I sell. Most of it's made by your people."

"Right. my people. Some of *my* best friends are gentiles." I don't know what made me say something like that, or where I got the guts. He didn't either, I guess, because his eyes got narrower and he just stared at me.

About ten minutes later I was standing outside of Uncle Sam's Army-Navy Surplus Store on Eighth Avenue, holding two brown paper bags. One of them, the heavier one, had the genuine U.S. Army-issue helmet, size small. There was a canteen too, covered in green cloth, and a belt the same color. That's where you hook your canteen if you're in the Army. And the last thing I bought was a pair of used combat-style boots, size eight, the smallest ones they had. Something else that probably needed newspaper. In the other bag I had the fatigue uniform, the only thing that really fit me. The whole works cost me twenty-four dollars and nineteen cents. I took thirty dollars with me, which was everything I saved from baby-sitting for twenty-five cents an hour. So I still had five dollars and eighty-one cents. I need forty cents for a subway and bus ride back home. And I could still get a hot dog at the Port Authority bus station, which I could almost taste just thinking about it. I could also hear my mother if she knew I was even thinking about putting something so dangerous in my stomach. A non-kosher (*tref*, they call it) hot dog didn't give kids polio, but she was sure it would do something really bad to you.

I bought the red-hot of my dreams anyway when I got to the steam cart in front of the terminal. The guy who sold it to me looked like he could have been related to the owner of the surplus store. He scowled. It's kind of a New York thing.

"Kraut?" the guy asked, pointing to a pot of hot sauerkraut.

I remembered with the store guy said about the dead kraut his nephew took the bloody helmet from. Yuck.

"Kraut?" the hot dog guy said again, louder.

"No, thanks," I said. It seemed unpatriotic to eat something called that, when there was a war on over there.

I took a deep whiff of my hot dog before the first bite, and I could imagine I was at opening day at the Polo Grounds again, with all the smells of baseball – franks, mustard, roasting peanuts and beer. Even the cotton candy had a smell, something sweet.

I ate the dog very slowly. You don't just gobble down something straight from heaven. When I was finished, I felt a lot better about everything I just did at the surplus store and was ready to head home on an Orange and Black bus. It almost felt like I was reporting to the Army for duty. And with this secret plan I had, I didn't even have to go to basic training.

Not bad, when you think about it.

I always wonder what's going on over my head when I'm in the Lincoln Tunnel under the Hudson River. This time I thought about the ships that were up there, the kind that loose lips can sink, like the poster said. Before the war they were cruise liners, like the Queen Elizabeth. Now they're troop ships. Last week when my parents took my brother and me to Brooklyn to visit relatives, we passed three of the big ones on the West Side Highway. There was a gray wood fence all along the road so nobody could see the ships, except for the tops of their smoke stacks that stuck up.

"That's a three-stacker," my father said when we went past. "Has to be the Queen, getting ready to take a whole lot of our boys over there."

The bus slowed down and then stopped because I guess there was too much traffic in the tunnel, at least I hoped that's all it was. I had this awful picture of what would happen if enemy agents knew about the Queen and where it was going, filled with soldiers. If they bombed it right then, when I was in the tunnel, it would probably tear a hole in the ceiling and I'd drown with everyone on the ship. I can't help it when I get those scary ideas. Good thing the bus started moving again and got out of the tunnel pretty quick.

I reached down under my feet to touch the stuff I bought. And I tried to picture me wearing it all and walking up the gangway with all those real soldiers. "Private Saperstein, reporting for duty," is what I thought I'd say. Or maybe just nothing, which would probably be better, seeing as how I wasn't supposed to be there.

CHAPTER 5

"All right, men, this is your chance to prove yourselves." He always called us men, Mr. Velardi, the junior high gym teacher, did. He was a short, kind of plump guy with black curly hair. Nobody ever saw him smile. It was like his face got frozen one day with his mouth pointing down and one bushy eyebrow turned up.

"This is serious business, getting in the best possible shape. You never know when you're going to be called on to prove your mettle, to show what you've got, to tell the world you have the heart to accomplish any mission."

Most of the kids didn't know what mettle was. (I only did because I looked it up). They thought he meant metal. That's why some of the kids in the back of the gym, where he couldn't see them, would salute and say stuff like, "Yes sir, Sergeant Metal Balls," like they were being cool, but they really weren't.

"Did I hear something?" Mr. Velardi would say, looking at the back of the gym and kind of closing one eye. "Somebody have something to say?" Nobody did, of course. "Somebody maybe thinks something's funny? Maybe that somebody doesn't realize there's a war on. And that people just a few years older than you are overseas, already wearing uniforms, getting ready to fight for their country, defending it against people who want to destroy it. You think any of them are making jokes out of their training? Think about that. Are you ready to do what you've got to do if your country calls on you?"

I couldn't help wondering if he was talking to me. But how would he know? *Oh my God, my parents. No, they couldn't have told him what happened at dinner, could they?*

"Saperstein!" Mr. Velardi shouted, and when he did, it made the gym windows rattle against the wire mesh on the outside.

"Yes, sir?"

"If you can tear yourself away from your daydreams, take your position on rope number one."

I figured out long ago you do what Mr. Velardi says if you don't want to end up trying to do fifty pushups. I beat it over to the climbing rope that started about two feet off the shiny gym floor and went up to the ceiling. When I got to the rope the last two people I wanted to see were standing next to it, Donnie Schoo and Walter Grassfield, two ninth graders and members of the Black Cats. They stood there with big sneers on their faces and their arms folded like they were daring me to say or do anything. I figured they were just waiting to watch me climb to the ceiling and wishing I'd fall back down and break my butt.

"Well now, how high is the little Jewboy going to climb today?" Schoo said. Actually, he hissed.

"Yeah, and how fast?" said Grassfield.

I tried to ignore both of them, but that wasn't going to work. How do you ignore two guys who don't want you in Teaneck High, or anywhere else, except maybe in an oven somewhere.

"Cat got your hymie tongue? A black cat maybe?" Schoo said to me.

"Maybe the cat'll get your pecker, too," said Grassfield.

Now that made me almost as mad as I was scared. "At least I've got a pecker" was all I could think to say.

"Ooh, hear that?" said Schoo, waving his hands. "He doesn't think we have peckers."

"Maybe we should prove we do. We could piss on his face, maybe."

"I wouldn't if I were you," I said. "I have a feeling Mr. Velardi wouldn't like that."

"O.K. Saperstein, let's see what you can do," Mr. Velardi shouted out at me from across the gym, holding the stopwatch he always had around his neck.

I grabbed the rough brown rope that smelled a little like the army and navy store, oily. It has these sharp prickly things all over it. You shouldn't slip and slide back down, unless you want your thighs to look like they came out of a meat grinder.

"Go ahead, Jewboy, show the teacher how good you are. But watch your little weenie," Schoo said.

I wrapped my skinny hairless legs around the rope and grabbed the bottom with my Keds. I shimmied up a few feet and stopped to look back at the two guys waiting for me to do something wrong and wished I could fall from the top and land on both their stupid heads. And I wouldn't mind the hamburger thighs either. Schoo grabbed the bottom of the rope and started moving up it. It wasn't just that he was climbing behind me that sent an air raid alarm off in my belly. It was the shiny blade of an open switch-blade knife he was holding with his teeth.

Schoo said, "You better climb like you never climbed before. If I catch your sorry ass, Saperstein, I'm going to cut your little pecker off, so help me."

That did it for me, all right. I dug my feet in and wrapped my hands around the rope like a vise. And I just started lunging up, one huge pull after the other, faster than I ever climbed a rope, or anything, in my life. Finally I saw the ceiling lights coming closer, and then I heard Grassfield down on the floor.

"Come on, Schoo. The little bastard's getting away from you."

Schoo tried to catch up to me, but he couldn't. He was huffing and grunting like a pig when he saw I was a good twenty feet higher than him. I just shut my eyes and managed to get up to the ceiling. When I got there I looked down and saw Mr. Velardi trotting over to the bottom of the rope that just twisted around and around like a snake.

"Saperstein!" he shouted.

What did I do wrong now?

"You just broke a junior high school record," Mr. Velardi said, looking down at his stop watch. "How did you learn to climb a rope like that?"

Then he yelled up to Schoo, "Hey, you going to stay up there all day?" And that made Schoo make a really big mistake. He opened his mouth to say something, and the knife fell all the way down to the floor, and to Mr. Velardi. With a sickening sounding *thwunk*, the thing landed at attention, sticking right into Mr.Velardi's canvas gym shoe and the big toe of his right foot.

Mr. Velardi was speechless, which is pretty unusual for him. He just stared down at the knife and this red blot that started growing around it on the white canvas of his shoe.

• • •

So, there we were sitting in a circle in the school office, me, Schoo, Grassfield and Mr. Velardi and Miss Vale, the junior high principal. She's a pretty nice lady, but don't let that fool you. She can glare at you, the way my father sometimes does, and make you feel like you're getting smaller. And she was glaring, all right, not saying anything, first at Schoo and then at Grassfield, and then down at Mr. Velardi's foot, which didn't have a sneaker on it anymore, but a brown bandage wrapped around it.

After a long time, Miss Vale finally said something. "All right, who's going to tell me what happened in the gym?"

Nobody was interested in going first, I guess. We all just looked down at our own hands, or at the bandaged foot.

"Mr. Velardi?" she said, with one eyebrow getting a lot higher than the other. I never could do that.

He winced and turned around in his chair and stared at Schoo.

"Are you all right?" Miss Vale asked. He nodded, but with a sad kind of look. "Where did the knife come from?"

He gave Schoo a look that could have burned through a brick wall and said, "Schoo," which sounded kind of funny, like shoe, where the knife landed, in his shoe.

"Is that right, Herbert? Did you throw the knife?"

His eyes widened. "I didn't throw any knife."

Miss Vale looked back at Mr. Velardi, her head cocked. More silence.

"Mr. Velardi says you did. Are you saying it's untrue?" she asked.

"I'm saying I didn't *throw* a knife." More silence still. He squirmed in his seat. Finally, he said, barely audibly, "I dropped it. O.K? I dropped the knife. It was an accident."

"You dropped an open knife from up on a rope? You were holding it in your hand, and it just dropped out and fell to the floor — to Mr. Velardi's foot?"

His answer was too soft for anyone in the room to hear. It sounded something like *inteeeff*.

"What did you say, Herbert?"

He took a deep breath. "It wasn't in my hand. It was in my teeth." As if that wouldn't be as bad as holding it in his hand.

Miss Vale nodded slowly and spoke, not raising her voice. "You were climbing a rope in gym class with an open knife in your teeth. Can you tell us why?"

Schoo looked at Grassfield, like he was asking for some help, but he didn't get any. Grassfield just looked down at his hands.

"I think he was chasing Saperstein," Mr. Velardi said.

She turned to me. "Is that right? Was Herbert chasing you up the rope?"

"I guess so."

"Were you chasing him?" she asked Schoo. He shrugged.

Mr. Velardi said, "What we have here, Miss Vale, is Saperstein, a boy who has now broken the school record for rope climbing." She looked at him like he had said something crazy, talking about my record rope-climbing time, when he just had a knife stuck in his foot.

"But the important thing is, why he broke the record," he said and looked over at me. "Does this boy strike you as some kind of super athlete?"

"Excuse me, but what's the point?" She asked, starting to look pretty impatient.

"The point is, these kids scared him into climbing that rope in record time. I mean, he scurried up there like a monkey."

Now Miss Vale was getting kind of agitated, like she did the time I got caught with a couple of other kids disappearing from the back of English class through a trap door in the floor into the old tunnels under the school. It really threw the teacher for a loop when she tried to figure out how we got out of the room.

Miss Vale looked at me and said, "Is that true? Have these boys been chasing you?"

That was enough to make me feel pretty awful in the stomach. I mean, how was I supposed to tell the truth without getting my butt kicked later on by the kids who were doing the chasing? I fired off a quick little prayer to God: *Please don't let me throw up here in the principal's office.* Finally I took a deep breath and nodded, like maybe it would be the same as saying they did it, without them hearing me say it. Fat chance of that.

"Why were they chasing you?" she asked.

"Because I'm — " the next word got stuck down under my throat somewhere. I just couldn't say it.

"Because he's Jewish," Mr. Velardi said.

Even though that wasn't exactly a surprise to anyone sitting there, it still was one of those drop-a-turd-in-the-punchbowl things. Everybody got quiet and stared at me, like I was the bowl. Or probably the turd.

Finally, Miss Vale asked me, "What do you have to say to that?"

I could feel my face getting really hot and I started sweating. And all I could think to say was, "Nothing."

"You have nothing to say about what these boys were doing to you?"

"I guess not." Which wasn't true. But I wasn't going to have Mr.Velardi with me when I walked home from school, or anywhere else, now was I?

Miss Vale kept looking at me. Maybe she was thinking my face was so red it was going to catch on fire, which it actually felt like. Then she looked over at Mr. Velardi and said, "Perhaps you should go to the hospital."

He shook his head. "It's just a scratch. Or, well, a puncture." Which made him sound like a dog-face hero in a *True Combat* story, wounded, but telling his squad leader that it only hurt when he laughed.

• • •

My walk home from school that afternoon was scarier than it ever had been before. Miss Vale said she would drive me, but that was the last thing in the world I needed. It would have been my luck to be seen riding in her car by half the school. So I made up some excuse about having to stop and pick something up at the store for my mother and told her I'd be O.K.

Now wouldn't you think that after what happened in the gym, and how just about everybody in school heard about it, those morons would have left me alone? Guess again. I was almost home, taking a shortcut through a field where there's a pond with a bunch of tall cat tails and skunk cabbage growing around it. I thought I heard a snicker from somewhere in the weeds, and all of a sudden I was thinking how I should have taken the ride with Miss Vale.

I started walking faster, heading for the street. I heard another snicker, and then a big, ugly laugh. I thought I was going to throw up everything inside of me when I saw three ninth-grade kids walk out of the weeds come at me. I knew who they were, and what they wanted: Me, for getting their stupid friends, Schoo and Grassfield, in trouble.

"Well, if it isn't the world-champion climber, the little Jewboy monkey," sneered one of them, a kid with a huge, fat body and a small head. He had a buzz cut that made him look like a porcupine was sitting on his shoulders.

Another kid shouted, "Hey, Saperstein." It was Kenny Schaklee, a short, wiry guy who was a star wrestler on the varsity team. He pinned me once in about twenty seconds in an intra-mural match. Just what I needed, as if nearly getting my thing sliced off wasn't enough.

"I'm talking to you Saperstein," Schaklee said. "Hey, you think you're as good a wrestler as a rope-climber?"

"Nah, Jewboy monkeys can only run up ropes. They're too chicken-shit to wrestle, isn't that right, Saperstein?" said the fat one with the porcupine on his head.

The third kid didn't say anything. He just kept grinning. I didn't know him, but I had a feeling he was Tony Ferraro, the starting center on the football team, who was thrown out of three games for punching guys on the other team. He had a nickname, The Dentist, because he really needed one for the buck teeth that stuck out so far he couldn't close his lips. Some kids thought the name was for all the teeth they say he knocked out on the other teams, but I don't think so.

It was pretty clear the only thing I could do was try to walk the last three blocks home, the longest blocks in the world, without losing any teeth or other parts of me.

Just when I thought there was a chance I might actually make it to the house, I felt a hand grab my shoulder from in back of me. I knew right away it had to be The Dentist.

And then all of a sudden I got as mad as I was scared. I felt it cooking inside of me.

Even though I knew I didn't have a chance in a fight with this bigger, older bully of a kid, I looked him in the eyes and all of a sudden I wanted to smash a fist into those two buck teeth of his.

"Leave me alone," I shouted at him.

He grabbed me even tighter. "Why should I? Give me a reason to leave you alone."

I had this quick flash of me walking into the house with blood gushing from my nose, teeth missing, and two black eyes. Still, I clenched my fists, ready to go at him, ready to die if I had to.

The next thing I heard was, "Because I said so." It sounded like somebody else other than the three kids who jumped me. It was coming from behind them.

Then I saw who it was, a tenth grader named Ralph Olsen, probably the biggest kid in school, bigger than Ferraro. He was the catcher on the baseball team. They called him The Backstop, he was so big. What was he doing here? He lived on the other side of town, the older part, called Westridge. Did he hear there was a Jewish kid available for a beating this afternoon and wanted to take a turn?

"I said, let him go," repeated Olsen.

"Go find your own piss-ant " Ferraro answered.

Olsen walked over to Ferraro and me, making sure to bump the shoulders of the other two kids who were starting to look pretty nervous.

I felt Ferraro's fingers loosen up his hold of me and figured there'd be five permanent dents in me. Olsen was about four inches taller than him. And wider, too.

"What's the matter, can't you count?" Ferraro said. "There's three of us."

"Can *you* count? How about to six?" Olsen said."

Like it was on a cue, another clump of cat-tails moved as five more kids walked out and came toward us. I didn't recognize any of them. But I saw how big they were, bigger than the kids who jumped me, like Olsen. I thought maybe they were ringers, from someplace like Hackensack, where everybody was bigger. Or at least tougher. But then I saw their leather-sleeved letter jackets. They were all senior high football players. And they looked like they shouldn't be messed with, if you know what I mean.

Now I recognized one of them. A huge guy with no neck and one big eyebrow. He stared at Ferraro and said, "We've been hearing what you and your punk pals have been doing to Saperstein, and his family. We also heard what happened to Mr. Velardi today."

"So?" said Ferraro, his thick lips no longer forming a grin. I thought they might just be trembling a little.

"So you guys think you're pretty big stuff. Big enough to pick on smaller kids like him."

"He got two of our buddies in hot water with the principal. He's a rat squealer."

"And what are you?" said the one eyebrow guy. "The protector of those stupid jerks that call themselves the Black Cats?"

"Pussies," chimed in one of the other huge guys.

Then Porcupine Head did a dumb thing. He stepped up and said, "Why don't you guys mind your own business. This is between us and him."

Another of the bigger guys said, "Yeah, you're right. It's between you and him. O.K. Which one of you feels big enough to take him?"

Oh, jeeze, these guys are a real big help, I thought.

Porcupine head leered. "I'll take the little kike," he said.

"Good enough," said the eyebrow. "He's yours."

Thanks a lot. With friends like him, who needs enemies?

Porcupine head came up close and gave me a hard push. It knocked me backwards, but I stayed up.

"Wait!" shouted Olsen. "There's just one condition."

Porcupine head look confused. "What are you talking about? What conditions?"

"I forgot to tell you the rule. You can't hit him back."

"How am I going to take him if I can't hit him? You stupid or something?"

A series of whistles and *ooohhs* came from the other five athletes. Olsen stepped up to porcupine head and bumped his chest into him. "Stupid? That what you said?"

"I just asked, how am I supposed to defend myself?"

"Against a smaller kid like him? Guess maybe you can go into a crouch. Or fall down. Just make sure you don't hit him, that's all."

"Forget it. I'm not going to stand here and let a little Jewboy swing at me."

"Yes you are," said Olsen. "Unless you want me. Or one of them," flicking his head back toward his friends. "Take your choice. Him or us."

The kid all of a sudden didn't look so tough. More like worried. He looked at Ferraro and Schacklee like they were supposed to help him. But they didn't seem interested in that. They just stood there.

"O.K., Saperstein," Olsen said. "This is your chance. I want you to think about everything this jerk has said to you, everything his stupid friends have been doing to you. Remember all the times they chased you home. And go get him."

I couldn't believe what was happening. It felt like I was in a movie. Or a dream maybe. Sure, I wanted to kick the crap out of that big fat jerk who was looking like he wanted to be somewhere else. But something held me back.

"But would that be a fair fight? When he can't hit back?" I asked Olsen.

"Yeah, it's fair all right. These jerks have been making your life miserable all year. Your brother told us you go to bed crying over what they do to you. And what have you ever done to them? Nothing except be what you are. That's what makes it a fair fight. Now come on, we're not going to stand here all day."

I stared up at Porcupine Head. Even though he had to be worried, he still had that stupid superior look on his face. But I just couldn't take a punch at him, until he said something that changed everything.

"You and your Jew family started all this trouble."

That was all it took. Like in a fast newsreel, I saw my mother, with a worried look on her face. Then my father, picking me up in the driveway and giving me a hug when I was a little kid. And my brother, teaching me how to throw a curve ball. And this big pig had the balls to even mention my family?

I just put my head down, like some kind of bull or a crazy person, and went at him, swinging both fists like a windmill. I felt one punch sink into a soft stomach. Another one got him on the cheek. My knuckles didn't even hurt. I just kept swinging. Some of the punches missed. But I guess enough of them hit something and sent him moving backward. He stumbled.

"O.K., O.K.!" Porcupine Head shouted.

I stopped and was breathing real hard. I could feel tears running down my cheeks, and I wasn't even ashamed of them. "No, it's not O.K., you fat tub of crap. Don't you ever mention my family again. I'll kill you if you do." I still wanted more of him. So then I did something I didn't even believe I could do. I swung real hard with my right fist, and it went up in the air and landed right on his jaw. I didn't even feel it, at least not until later. It made a smacking sound like a bat hitting a baseball. Then it was in kind of slow motion, when Porcupine Head went back, his eyes all big and wide, and, splat, he landed on the street. I stood over him like it was a prize fight in a ring. I felt like dancing, but I didn't, of course. I just kept staring down at him. I saw a red spot on his chin, smaller than the one on Mr. Velardi's gym shoe, though. He wiped his hand on it, and made it smear. I kept thinking, like a ring announcer, *"That's it. It's all over. A knockout in the first round with a tremendous uppercut that came from nowhere."* I even heard a crowd cheering up in my head somewhere. Then the kid raised his hand, I guess because I looked like I wasn't done. But he was. He didn't say anything. He just kept holding up his hand. I sure wished Joe Louis could have seen it, but hey, you can't have everything.

"Nice job." It was my newest hero, the human backstop, standing next to me and looking down at porcupine head. "You finished?"

"I guess so. Unless he wants to say something about my family again."

"How about it?" Olsen said to him. "Anything more you want to say?"

The kid just shook his head.

"Why don't you go home and maybe put something on your knuckles," Olsen said to me.

I looked down at my knuckles and I saw that almost all of them were bruised, even bleeding a little. But I liked seeing that. And my fists were beginning to hurt bad. I liked that, too.

• • •

A couple of hours later, I was in my room, trying to stick Band Aids on where my knuckles got raw.

"What the hell happened to your hands?"

I looked up and saw my brother standing in the doorway to my room.

"You're supposed to knock," I said and tried to pick up all those torn-open wrappers, and the things you peel off, from my bed.

"Don't tell me you got in a fight."

I didn't answer. Stanley came over and sat down on my bed and started looking at my face.

"Looks like you didn't get hit. That's good," he said. He put his hand on my shoulder, the one that The Dentist nearly punched holes in with his fingers. "Want to tell me about it?"

"Just some kids from the ninth grade. The usual thing."

"They ganged up on you?" He kept looking at my face like he was supposed to find bruises and stuff.

"Actually, I ganged up on them."

He just nodded and smiled. I guess he thought I was trying to be funny, which everybody knows I'm really not.

"Some bigger guys, in letter jackets, were there," I said. "They were on my side. One of them told this kid from the football team, a kid with fat lips and buck teeth, the guy they call The Dentist, to let me go."

"Ferraro," said Stanley. "Figures.".

"And then they made one kid, this one with a real little head on a big body, they made him fight me. Only he wasn't allowed to hit me."

"Was the one who made him fight you named Olsen, by any chance? Big, blond kid?"

"Sounds like him. Nice guy."

"Sleepy Olsen. Yeah. Nice guy. Heck of a hitter. So it was you against a big kid with a little head. Do a good job on him?"

I just shrugged, getting kind of embarrassed.

"Make him go down?"

"I guess. Maybe he tripped, though."

"Why were they after you?"

"You have to promise not tell Mom and Dad."

"Why not?"

"You know how upset they get when that stuff happens at school. Especially Mom. Promise not to tell?" Stanley nodded. "On Grampas"s *tallis*?" He nodded again, but with a sigh. "Yeah, yeah, on his *tallis*."

I wanted to make it official, the promise. So I got out the blue velvet bag that our grandfather's white prayer shawl was kept in and handed it to Stanley. He shook his head and put his hand on the bag and said, "I promise."

I told him the whole story, about what happened in the gym, the knife in Mr. Velardi's foot, being in the principal's office, and then what happened on the way home. At one point, I thought I saw something sparkly coming out of the corner of my brother's eye, but I looked away from it. You don't just ask a guy with the hardest fastball in New Jersey if he was going to cry.

When I was done, Stanley just sat there looking down at his hands, shaking his head. Then he got up and looked at the pictures of my sports heroes on the walls. He went over to the window and stared out of it. I saw his shoulders sort of moving up and down a couple of times. I felt like putting my arms around him and telling him not to worry, everything was O.K., even in front of Joe Louis, Mel Ott and all those other guys. But I didn't. It's not what you do with a big strong brother.

Stanley hung around a while, talking about baseball and other stuff he probably figured would take my mind off what happened at school and on the way home. It didn't really, but I tried to make him think it did. When he finally left to go to his room he punched me on the shoulder and said, "Get some sleep, O.K.?" He said it a lot softer than he usually talked. And he looked sad when he walked out.

CHAPTER
6

After everything that happened at school, and after school, and even after hearing through the wall how my parents were worried about everything that was happening to me, to all of us, I knew it was time. I belonged on that Queen Elizabeth on my way to England, in my uniform. The Giants could go on to win the pennant, maybe even the series, without me in the right field bleachers or at my radio. After all, like everybody says, there was a war on, right? And I was a man, wasn't I? The rabbi said I was as soon as I finished chanting the *haftorah*. Not that I knew why that all of a sudden made me a man, just because I memorized about ten minutes of Hebrew out of the torah and chanted it in my really sucking singing voice. I didn't feel any different that day. There wasn't any new hair all of a sudden on my arms or chest, or down there. My voice still squeaked most of the time. But, hey, if the rabbi says I'm a man, I'm not going to give him an argument or anything.

Anyway, I started doing this thing I always do when there's something big I'm trying to decide, like whether to ask Judy Stofan (she's known as Stof-Butts, because she likes to smoke) if she wanted to meet me at the Little Brown Jug. It's the town teen rec center, and on Friday nights, there's a dance there. But mostly we hang around the room with our hands in our pockets. The girls wait against the wall for kids to get brave enough to ask them to do a fox trot or maybe a lindy.

So what I do to help make up my mind about important things, is I ask my heroes on the wall, in the pictures I cut out from *Sports Illustrated*. This time I wanted to get advice from two of my heroes who know what it's like to be treated bad because of the color of their skin or their religion, Joe Louis, the champ of all time, and one of the first Jewish ball players to make it into the majors, Hank Greenberg, who was called the Hebrew Hammer for the way he could hit, plus Jesse Owens, who won four gold medals and broke one world track record at the 19036 Olympics. With Adolph Hitler sitting in the stands. I don't know if they were chased home from school every day, like me. Maybe they got worse than I get. I wouldn't be surprised.

Anyway, I had one of my talks with them, figuring it might help. I know it's pretty strange, talking to pictures and, worse, hearing them talking back to me. It's kind of a movie I make.

"Mr. Louis, and Mr. Owens, I got to make a decision. Should I go ahead and do this thing I started, with the army uniform and all? I know I want to do it. But now I've got these jitters, and some sore knuckles, too. Maybe it was a stupid idea."

"Hey, kid," said Joe Louis, with his fists clenched in front of him, staring down at me with one of his eyebrows higher, like he always does. "You're not the first person to take a chance and do something you got to do."

"He's right," said Jesse Owens, standing on the Olympic winners platform with those medals around his neck "You think getting chased up a rope by a kid with a knife is the worst thing that could ever happen? No siree. You ought to hear what that Hitler guy said about me all those years. He did all he could to take away these medals that should never go to a black person but belong to Aryan athletes. I was booed and called more names than you could dream of. I still here them sometimes"

"We don't mean to be tough on you, kid," said Joe Louis. "But if you think all I ever hear when I'm standing in the ring at the end of the fight is, 'Way to go Joe,' guess again, my young fan. I hear things I wouldn't repeat, even in the locker room. But my point is, and I think Jessie here would probably agree with me, if you got a plan to do something about what's coming down on you and the rest of the world, if you've got a chance to help make things right, then you best be going about it. Right, Jessie?"

Breaking into a grin and nodding, Jesse Owens said, , "That's right. It's like the man said. Sure, he's in the army now, not in the ring, but I guarantee he even hears stuff there that could make most of us think twice about trying to be champions. Listen to the Brown Bomber kid. Don't throw in the towel. Follow what's in your heart. Know that a lot of people won't like what you're doing. Including your parents."

"*Especially* your parents," Joe Louis said. "What are you, maybe fourteen or fifteen?"

"Thirteen," I said back to the picture.

"Well, now," said the champ. "That's pretty young to be going off and doing what you're thinking about."

Jesse said, "Yeah, but didn't you just go through a ceremony your people do, you know, that says you're a man now?"

"It's called a bar mitzvah."

"O.K. You're a man then. Go do what a man has to do, and your parents will understand."

"That's right," Joe the champ said. "Remember the thing about fear, like what President Roosevelt said. Don't be afraid of it. Face it. And do yourself, and the rest of us, proud."

That did it. It convinced me that these heroes of mine, if they only could have met me for real, in person, they'd say the same things their pictures did. Don't ask me why I know it, I just do. They had a lot of their own bad stuff going on. Probably worse than mine. They understand.

I said, "Thanks. That helps." Then I heard in my head the voice of the President, Mr. Roosevelt, telling everybody the worst thing to be afraid of is being afraid itself, or something like that. And I knew I was doing the right thing, even if my parents would think I should be in an insane asylum for trying a stunt like the one I was going to do. But I still had to do it. Come on, there's a war on, isn't there?

• • •

"You've got to swear to God you'll keep it a secret, for the war effort."

That's what I said to Gordon. I guess I must have been trying to come off like some kind of secret agent.

He laughed at me. "The war effort? You think you're Sergeant York or something?"

"You don't believe me?" I said.

"Oh, sure, I believe you. You're going to Europe to help with the invasion. Bull-pippy."

"Sshh. Don't talk about it," I sort of whispered.

Gordon looked around at the empty locker room in the school basement. "Hey, there's no one here. I guarantee you, the lockers don't have ears."

"You just have to swear to God you won't tell anyone where I'm going."

"First of all," he said, "I don't have the slightest idea where you're going. And second of all, it's pretty funny asking me to swear to God. How can I swear to something I don't believe in? And don't give me that foxhole crap again."

"You have to swear on something," I said.

"How about on my Wendell Cooper autograph?"

I panicked. That was the famous catcher, the only Giant who would never give an autograph, and who threatened to throw us off the subway platform when we chased him down after a game. We thought he meant it, the way he growled instead of talking.

"You didn't tell me you got him. How did you do it?"

He really started laughing now. "I let him throw me off the platform."

"Very funny. Seriously, swear you'll keep the secret."

"O.K., O.K, I'll keep your dumb secret."

I pulled out a stack of envelopes, all addressed to my parents, on V-Mail envelopes.

"I need you to put one in a mailbox every few days until I get home."

Gordon looked at me like I was totally gone crazy. "What are you talking about? They'll have a Teaneck post mark, not France, or England, or wherever you're supposed to be."

"I know. But they'll figure it's just the way the post office works when there's a war on, you know, like that's how they keep where troops are a secret. And I say in all of the letters that I can't tell them where I am, but I'm fine, staying away from bad stuff, and all that."

"Come on, your parents are smarter than that."

"Yeah, maybe they are. But they're patriotic, too. I don't think they'll want to ask a lot of questions or stir up any trouble with the Army."

"Why don't you mail them yourself, from wherever you are?"

"Because I don't want them to know where I really am. It'll be a secret. You know, loose lips."

He looked like he was maybe starting to believe me. "You really think you're going to do this, get on some ship and get into the war someplace in Europe, don't you?"

"Why not?"

"Doesn't it scare the crap out of you, the whole idea?"

"I have nothing to fear except fear itself."

Gordon again rolled his eyes. "That's the corniest thing I've ever heard."

"It wasn't for President Roosevelt."

"Oh, excuse me, Mister President. Don't you get it? You're a thirteen-year-old kid who has some crazy idea that he can do anything."

"He can climb a rope pretty well." That deep voice shook us both up at the same time. We turned and saw Mr. Velardi standing there by the wooden bench between the green metal lockers. He was dressed like he always was, grey sweatshirt, khaki pants and white gym shoes. The right one had a piece of adhesive tape where Schoo's knife went through.

I started to panic when I realized maybe he heard what Gordon and I were talking about. That would be bad, real bad. But he didn't act like he heard.

"He did it in record time, as a matter of fact," he said to Gordon. "For junior *and* senior high." Mr. Velardi had a big envelope in his hand. "I've been looking for you," he said and kind of limped over to me. "Here, this is yours. You earned it."

I took the envelope without even looking at it, but I didn't have the foggiest what was in it.

"Aren't you going to open it?"

I finally looked down at it and saw the name on the label: Baumgartner's *Fine Stationers*. I knew that was Bumpy Baumgartners's father's store. She hated the name, not the last part, the first part, Bumpy. She got it for the bumps she always had on her knees and elbows and all from being a real tom boy, climbing trees and ropes, getting into football games and even a fight once in a while. I always kind of liked her, even if she did act more like a boy than a girl most of the time.   "Aren't you going to open it," Mr. Velardi said again.

So I figured I'd better do that. I pulled out a heavy piece of paper with gold around the edges and the name of the school on the top. Then there was my name, in that funny lettering like something from England.

Down below it said, *40-foot rope climb, 9.3 seconds, record for Teaneck Junior and Senior High Schools, May 1, 1944.*

"We do that whenever a new school record is set. Mr. Baumgartner donates the certificate and we thank him in the Te-Hi-News," said Mr. Velardi.

"Thank you, Mr. Velardi. Thank you a lot. I appreciate it." And I did. I never had anything like that before, except maybe a paper that thanked me for being the camp bugler.

"Keep it in a special place, Saperstein. It's not every day somebody breaks both school records. I tell you, that's a real gift you've got, yes sir, a genuine gift." He looked down at Gordon, who seemed bored by the whole thing. "I heard you mention President Roosevelt."

"We were talking about what a good president he is" Gordon lied.

"He's a great man. Of course, he can't win that war over there by himself. He needs all the help he can get from our boys. But he gives one fine speech when he has to." He looked at what I was still holding underneath the paper he gave me.

"What are those, V-mails?" he said.

My mouth got dry all of a sudden. "Yes."

"Got someone in the family over there?"

"They're for my parents," I said, telling myself I didn't lie, since they actually did have somebody already over there, my two uncles.

"It's a good thing, the way everybody pitches in to the war effort. The only way we're going to beat the Germans and the Japs is with young men going over there from every family, regardless of who they are, whatever religion, you know what I mean?"

"Yes, I know," I said, casting a glance at Gordon, who was biting his lip to keep from laughing.

"Well, don't be hanging around here, if you're done getting dressed. Mr. Bosch wants to come in and mop up."

That was like a signal for Gordon and me to get out of the locker room, which we really wanted to do anyway. We moved as quick as we could without actually running, which might have made Mr. Velardi get suspicious.

When we hit the heavy wooden door with chicken-wired windows, it flew open with a loud thumping sound, and we almost fell out on the black-top playground. Gordon bent over like he was going to split a gut, he was laughing so hard. I started laughing, too, but not like I was splitting a gut. I was still pretty nervous.

"The only way we're going to beat the Germans and Japs is with everybody joining in, even us," said Gordon, spit dribbling out of his mouth, he was laughing so hard. "He thinks he's going to get a brotherhood award for giving you a certificate and telling you that even you can do your part." Then, "Hey, did you see the hole in his gym shoe?" Gordon asked. "He's probably going to wear it like that the rest of the year. Maybe he thinks someone will get Mr. Baumgartner to make him a certificate. *For courage beyond the call of duty, for being a dart board for Donnie Schoo's knife. this certificate of honor is awarded Mr. Velardi, who now holds the all-time Teaneck High School record for having really crappy luck.*

CHAPTER

7

To my mother, my father and my brother,

There comes a time in every man's life (and I feel I am a man — didn't the Rabbi say I was?) when he has to do what is right. I have decided what is right for me, when I think about all that has happened to us lately. There's a war on. Everybody tells us that, every day of our lives — the butcher, when we ask for steak, the gas station man when we try to fill up the car, even Mr. Solomon at the candy store when we ask for a Hershey Bar. That's why Mom saves tin cans and bacon fat. I think I know why tin cans are needed, but I've never figured out why bacon fat is something they need to fight the Germans with. Anyway, there definitely is a war on, a terrible war. Dad, I know how sad you are that you can't go and fight the Germans, but it's not your fault you're too old to join or be drafted. You're a very good air raid warden, doing your part to make sure people obey those blackouts. You're also a very good Coast Guard Auxiliary officer, and when you go out on Charlie Moore's fishing boat on weekends, you spend more time looking for German submarines than you do fishing for flounder. And you also have won six Army-Navy E-Flags for your contribution to the war effort making insignias for the troops over there. So please don't feel you're not doing your part. I'm proud of what you do. The trouble is, there's nothing I can do here at home to help win the war. Oh sure, I buy war stamps ever week, and I've got a bunch of bonds already. But that's not enough. I believe that if the Rabbi is right, and I am a man, I have to do my part. I don't have children or a wife to support. I don't even have a girlfriend who will miss me. So it just makes a lot of sense for me to go and do my part. Now you may wonder why I think I have a part to do. Why should a thirteen year-old kid think he should go and do something about Adolf Hitler and all the terrible things he's doing? As I tried to explain to everybody not long ago, I think a lot of this must be my fault, but I know no one agrees with me. I just don't think it's very fair for all those people who aren't Jewish to fight our battles for us. Why does Mr. and Mrs. Flannagan's son have to go over there and fight? They're not talking about burning and gassing Irish people. Or maybe they are, and we just haven't heard about it, or Herbie Schoo doesn't want to tell us. I remember that time we all were out for a ride in Ridgewood, looking for a house to buy, and we saw that sign that said Welcome to Ridgewood, a Christian Community. *Dad, you said it was how they let us know that they don't want "our kind" in their town. Well, isn't that the same thing Hitler is telling us, that he doesn't want "our kind" in his town, or actually in his country or the whole world? But he's not just telling us we can't buy a house over there. He's telling us he wants to kill us instead, or at least that's what Herbie and those other kids say. You know something? I believe it. So, that's something I have to try and do something about. Now I don't want you to worry about me, even though I know you will. I'm really O.K. By the time you read this letter, I'll be reporting for duty in the United States Army. I can't tell you where I'm going, because, well actually, it's a secret. The truth is, I don't know where I'll be. But I'll be with a lot of people who'll take care of me. And I really don't want anyone getting anybody in the Army in trouble for letting me join up. They don't take kids my age, honest to God. I have to do a little fudging to get in. It's my fault, not anybody's in the recruiting office or any other place. I'll send you letters, I promise, but I won't be able to tell you where I am. It's like going to camp a little early this year, but maybe the food will be better (just kidding). I love you all and I will miss you all, even my big brother. Please root for the Giants to win the pennant while I'm gone. And remember, we have nothing to fear but fear itself. (I didn't make that up, but it's a good thing to keep in mind).*

Your loving son and brother and, I hope, devoted soldier

I left the letter on my bed, which I knew my mother would see first thing in the morning, when she always checks to see if I made it. I took one last look around my room, at my heroes on the walls, and threw a snappy salute at Joe Louis and Mel Ott like I was in the army, which I know is kind of dumb. Then I gave a big va-fangoo with my arm to Wendell Cooper, who never did get a chance to throw me on the subway tracks. He'd probably like the idea of me going someplace dangerous.

I took a deep breath and went to the door out to the hall. But I stopped when I saw on my desk the most valuable possession I ever had, my baseball with all the autographs of the Giants, except one, of course. I decided it should go where I go, even though I knew a soldier is only supposed to take essential stuff into action, but wasn't that ball essential? So I stuffed it in my knapsack and tiptoed out of the room.

The only thing I heard in the hall was my father's snoring. The sound all of a sudden made me real sad, when I thought about when I'd ever hear it again. I felt like I was going to cry, which isn't a good thing for a soldier to do, even an imitation one. I took a real deep breath, and sneaked downstairs. I made sure not to step on the two stairs that always creaked.

So there I was at five-thirty in the morning, standing on the sidewalk in front of my house, which was really quiet. So was every other house on the street. I couldn't hear any snoring out there. I looked at the flag with the two blue stars for my uncles and wondered if there'd ever be one there for me. I felt this strange kind of lump just under my throat that I managed to push down. I turned back for one last look at home, and was glad no lights were on. But then I saw, or thought I saw, something in the window of my brother's room. It looked like the white curtain was pulled back by a hand. I couldn't see anything else. Then the curtain went back again, and the hand was gone.

I waited a few seconds to make sure the coast was clear, and started out down the street, with a helmet on my head, a knapsack on my back and combat boots on my feet.

I wasn't very far from home when a milk truck slowed down and stopped at the corner of Cedar Lane and Prince Street. The guy driving it leaned out and took a good look at me. I really hoped he wasn't our milkman.

"Everything O.K., soldier?" he yelled out to me, smiling and friendly.

I nodded and made my voice as deep as I could. "Fine, thanks." *Jesus, I sound awful. Like a midget* I thought.

"Guess it's none of my business asking why you're out here alone," the driver said. "I'm sure whatever it is, you're doing your job, and God bless you for that, soldier."

I just waved and kept walking, trying to look as though I was doing my job, like he said, and he revved up his truck and kept on driving. *He called me soldier,* I told myself, and I liked the sound of it. I also liked the sound of milk bottles clinking together when he drove away, but it also made me a little sad, I guess.

By the time I reached Route Four, which is the way to the George Washington Bridge and the city, I saw the first light coming up in the sky. There are no sidewalks along the highway, just a skinny little path through the grass, probably made by Boy Scouts hiking up to the Palisade Cliffs, which are neat to climb down and back up, as long as you're careful for copperhead snakes that are supposed to be all over the place, even though I never actually saw any. I always walked real carefully, though, just in case, like I guess you're supposed to do when you're crossing a mine field over in France or someplace else in the war.

When I went under the bridge that crossed Route 4 next to Teaneck High, I started singing the alma mater to myself, I guess as sort of an official goodbye for awhile.

On a hill she stands majestic, noble to our view. Glory, honor, praise, allegiance, these to her are due. Friendships made within her classrooms, lasting fine and true. Sing her praises, lift our voices to the sky. Hail to thee our alma mater, hail to Teaneck High.

Hail, I guess, to the good things that happened there. And try and forget the bad ones. You're in the Army now. Sort of.

• • •

By the time I reached the George Washington Bridge, I started feeling hungry for one of the four Baby Ruths I packed to eat. I stopped to open one and caught my first look at the Hudson River going all the way down to the end of Manhattan, and I could make out the dark shapes that were ships along the docks, waiting to go out to sea. I knew one of them was the Queen Elizabeth, but couldn't tell which one. I looked over the railing that came up to my chin, and down at the water, two hundred feet below me. The candy bar wasn't exactly a breakfast, but it tasted pretty good. When I was finished, I dropped the red, white and blue wrapper over the rail and watched it just float back and forth, like it was in no hurry, on the way down to the river. A seagull swooped down and made a pass at the wrapper, maybe thinking it was a smaller bird, and then flew away. I wondered how long it would take me to hit the water. A lot less time than the paper wrapper, I was sure. I once heard that you can count one-one-thousand for every sixty feet you drop, which would mean something like a three-and-a-half-second plunge. Would a seagull check me out on the way? I once heard that a person would be unconscious before he hits the water, so at least you really wouldn't feel anything like the world's biggest belly flop.

I started walking again toward the New York side. Actually it was more like marching. Horns honked at me, and I started to worry about someone asking a cop what a short soldier in a helmet and stuff was doing on the bridge, but nothing happened. I started singing *Over There* to myself, keeping time with my boots hitting the cement. *The Yanks are coming, the drums drum drumming....*

Pretty soon I went past the tower on the other end of the bridge, and found a narrow sidewalk that went down a long ramp to the West Side Highway. I really started feeling better about everything because every step was getting me closer to the ship I knew was waiting there. But I did feel kind of sad, too, thinking about my parents, who must have read my letter already. I know my mother would be crying, and my father would be trying to calm her down. I didn't like thinking about it, how it would worry them pretty awful. I figured my father would try and tell my mother not to worry, that it was just a nutty scheme their son had dreamed up and he'd probably be home by supper time. And when I didn't show up then, or tomorrow, or the next day and the next, they'd realize I really was going to do what I said. I wanted to make them proud of me. And I hope when they figured it all out, they wouldn't be too mad at me.

Step it up a little, I told himself. I was getting pretty hot from the walking and pushed the helmet back up from my eyes and wiped some sweat away. Then I opened my second Baby Ruth.

And we won't be back 'til it's over, over there!

CHAPTER
8

There it was, at 63rd Street, underneath the West Side Highway, the big, beautiful Queen Elizabeth, looking just like the pictures I studied, except for one thing. Gray paint. But that was O.K. I guess it's harder for the U-boats to see it that way.

Everything else there was painted dark green, even the headlights on a couple of hundred trucks and jeeps lined up and waiting. There were maybe a few thousand soldiers, all in green, too, getting out of the trucks and standing in a long line along Pier 43. I looked up at the huge smoke stacks on the ship and saw grey smoke coming out of them, so I guessed they were getting ready to shove off pretty soon.

A bunch of MPs were holding clipboards and checking things and people. I could smell the oil again that I remembered from the army and navy store. Must have been the trucks, the ship and all the guns around. There was a lot of noise, too, people shouting orders out to other people, engines revving, brakes screeching, horns honking. Guess that's what happens when there's a war on. I also saw this flock of seagulls that were squawking and fighting their own war over a bunch of garbage on the pier.

I saw in a newsreel at the movies that the ships that were going over to Europe were made to carry 1,700 passengers, and now they were going to be taking 15,000 soldiers. I looked up at the Queen Elizabeth again and tried to figure out how they were going to squeeze that many people in. And right away I figured there was going to be no such thing as privacy. Everybody was probably going to have to sleep together and do everything else that way, too. I wondered about taking showers with men older than me and that made me pretty nervous, because, well, I'm still growing, and don't even have hair down there. It also meant ten days of so without doing what I did every night in my bed. That'd be an all-time record, I figured. I wondered if guys who are twenty still do it every night.

"Hey, what is that, a Boy Scout?" I turned around fast to see three soldiers, all of them with cigarettes hanging from their mouths and looking and laughing at me.

"Yeah, you," one of them said. "Either you're a scout, or they lowered the minimum age in this man's Army."

Would this be it? Would my secret mission be over before it ever started?

"What do you mean?" I said, trying to sound as old as I could. And I was afraid they might notice my woman's jacket buttoned the wrong way. Next they maybe would pull off my helmet and see the newspaper rolled up in it, and the peach fuzz on my cheeks and the zits on my chin. And my goose would be totally cooked.

"It's O.K., kid," one of the other soldiers said, with a thick Brooklyn accent. "Hey, if you're big enough to fit in a uniform, you can get in this mess like the rest of us. Ain't that right?" he asked of his two buddies. They just shrugged, like maybe they didn't care that much.

"How old are you, anyways?" the Brooklyn guy asked me.

"Thirteen." Why didn't I lie and say eighteen? I'll tell you why. Because they'd know I was full of it.

"Sorry, kid, that ain't gonna work for ya, saying you're under age. Neither will telling 'em you got flat feet, you're blind in both eyes or you don't have no pecker. Everything's been tried already, every excuse in the book, to get out at the last minute. They just wave you on with the rest of us and off you all go. Nice try."

"What's your unit?" one of the other guys, a corporal, asked.

"Rangers," I said. It wasn't totally a lie. I was a squad leader in the Camp Chickawaw Rangers Platoon during color war.

"Holy shit, they're taking squirts like that into the Rangers now?" one of the others said. "That's robbin' the goddamn cradle for a job that gets your ass shot off in the first wave. They oughta be ashamed."

"Yeah, well, good luck kid," said the third guy, who was getting kind of friendly now. "Just watch your ass over there."

"Want a smoke?" the first one said, holding out a pack of Camels.

I shook my head. "Thanks. Don't smoke."

"Well, you better start, kid. You gotta have somethin' to keep your nerves from explodin' all over the place."

"Yeah, and to keep from pukin' your guts out on the way over," said the Brooklyn guy.

"See you later," I said, and started to walk away like I had to be somewhere. Then I heard one of the three guys get on somebody else.

"Well, I'll be a monkey's goddamn uncle. Hey, whaddy doin' here, deliverin' Chinese for dinner?"

I saw a soldier, taller than me, who stopped walking and just stared at the guy who said that. He had yellowish skin and black hair.

"Whose army you lookin' for?" one of the three guys said, sounding pretty mean. "The Japs are shippin' out from Tokyo, not New York." That got a laugh from the guy's pals. And it made me feel bad for the short soldier.

Then I heard an older voice, one that sounded important, from behind me.

"Any problem, son?" I saw a man with grey hair, wearing captain's bars on his jacket and he was talking to the guy they were laughing at.

"No, sir, no problem," he said, looking pretty upset.

"What's your unit?"

"Ranger Battalion One."

"Well, now, I wonder if any of these dog-faces understand what it takes to make it in that outfit? I hear the average Ranger can take down three men with his bare hands, in fact, has to, before he can graduate." He looked real hard at the three hecklers, who all of a sudden got quiet and uncomfortable.

"Well, better keep moving, son. Your unit's about ready to board."

"Thank you, sir," the soldier said. I noticed he did actually look either Chinese or Japanese. I don't know how to tell the difference, and it doesn't matter if he's wearing an American uniform.

"Good luck, private. We're all going to need it," the officer said.

I started walking toward the ship, figuring I probably should try to get on it before anyone else asks a lot of questions about how old I really am and stuff like that.

The Asian private caught up and started walking with me.

"Looking for the Rangers?" he asked me.

"I guess, yeah." I figured I might as well try the Rangers, even though there was no way I could take down three guys like the officer said.

"I lost track of the unit," the soldier said. "I was looking for a place to mail a letter. Guess they're up ahead, getting ready to board. I don't remember you."

"I'm new," said Saperstein.

"I heard they sent in a new squad. Did those guys give you a hard time, too?"

"Those three? Oh, they were just making some cracks about how small I am."

"Well, I'm not much bigger than you. But that's not what they were thinking about with me. They don't like what I look like, or what they think I am."

"I know what that feels like."

"How would you? You're not Chinese."

"No, but a lot of people don't like what I look like, or what I am, either."

The soldier studied Saperstein, then shrugged. "I don't know, you don't look any different than everybody else around here. A little smaller, maybe, that's all."

"Thank you."

"For what?"

"For telling me I'm not different from them."

"Hey, that's no compliment. Guys like those three, you don't want to be anything like them. They're just jerks who don't know any better. They're going to be fighting the same war we are, and they'll find out in a hurry what really counts. When someone's shooting at you on the beach, and you've got nowhere to crawl to or hide, you're going to be awfully happy to see somebody next to you, and it won't mean anything what he looks like, except for one thing: the color of his uniform. And you know something else, when I get hit, my blood's going to be the same color as yours, and the same as theirs. What's your specialty anyway?"

I thought about that and wondered what I should say. I mean it's not like I was a sharpshooter or anything.

"Ropes, I guess."

"You mean climbing up 'em?" I nodded. "Same here. Where did you learn how to climb?"

"Teaneck Junior High."

"No, seriously, where did you train?"

"It's true. I picked it up in school." I didn't bother telling him about going fast enough to stay ahead of the kid who wanted to cut my penis off.

"Did you take advanced in basic? Advanced in basic. That's like jumbo shrimp," he said and laughed. "That's funny."

I wasn't sure why it was, but I laughed a little anyway.

"Maybe I'll see you later, aboard ship," the Chinese soldier said. "But I may not find you, since you people all look alike."

I had a feeling I was going to like this guy. Guess we had something in common, being different from other people. Only it was probably worse for him. At least people couldn't look at me and figure right off the bat I was different, until they found out my name, or asked me what religion I am. And those are two things I didn't try and exactly advertise.

"Come on, soldier, we don't have all day. Get in line."

It scared the pants off me, that barking voice behind me. I looked back and saw a big soldier wearing an MP arm band, staring at me. He jerked his head at this line of troops that must have been a few blocks long, going up to the gangway of what I knew for sure was the Queen Elizabeth.

Even though he shook me up, it felt good being called *soldier*, the way he did. I said, "Sorry, sir," and saluted him.

"Jesus Christ, didn't they tell you in basic you don't salute corporals?" he growled at me.

"Yeah, I was just kidding," was all I could think to say.

"Now they send us comedians. What the hell is next? You don't even look old enough to wipe your own ass," the corporal said.

I had the feeling this might be the end of my big trip before it started. The corporal stared at me like my social studies teacher, who really didn't like me very much, as if he just caught someone who didn't belong there, a spy maybe. He blew hard on his whistle. Was he calling for help? Why would he need it?

"Move that goddamn truck, soldier. Now!"

Another close call, which I thanked God for letting me out of again. The MP wasn't whistling for help with me. He was just trying to get the driver of a canvas-covered personnel carrier, which was blocking traffic, to move out of the way. The driver, a frustrated private, started arguing with the corporal, who pulled out a small notebook and started writing.

"You want an argument, soldier?" he said to the driver. "Fine, you can have one with the Port Captain, who'll be happy to listen to your story — before he busts your ass down to something lower than you already are. Now, are you gonna move it, or are you gonna lose it?"

I began thinking I was in a war movie, or at least a newsreel, which made me straighten up a little, as the line started moving faster and closer to the Queen. Finally, after maybe half-an-hour or so, I reached the bottom of the gangway. I couldn't believe it. I was actually going to get aboard, unless, of course, somebody else decides I didn't belong there. But it didn't happen. When my boots hit the wood of the gangway, one of them got stuck on this cleat thing and I fell smack into this big guy in front of me.

"Watch where the hell you're going, buddy," the guy said to me.

"Sorry," I said. "I tripped."

"That's obvious. Hope you don't do that on a beach over there. You might trip over something else. Like a land mine. Know what I mean?"

"I'll be careful. Promise."

"Promise? What are you a little kid or something?" The soldier turned around and tried to see under my helmet, which was even lower down on my face after I bumped into the guy.

"That's what it looks like to me. A kid. Christ, they're taking everything these days."

I finally reached the top without tripping again. It felt like I was going into a dark hole, sort of into the guts of a giant whale, like Jonah. I couldn't see anything except the guy in front of me and another soldier standing there with another clip board, waving his hand at all of us.

"Come on keep it moving. This ship isn't waiting for anybody. Let's go. Get aboard and find your unit, and assemble there, on the double."

There was no way I could follow that order on the double or anyway else, since I didn't have a unit, unless there was one for stowaways. So I figured I'd just roam around and try to blend in with fifteen thousands guys.

I ended up at the front of the ship, on a deck where they kept the humongous anchors. There were two soldiers who looked almost as young as me, leaning over the railing and looking down at the dark green water. I squeezed in between them figuring I wouldn't stand out.

"Forty-fahv feet," one of them said, in this thick southern accent.

"Sheeeet. At least sixty," the other one said, with the same kind of accent. Then he made this disgusting noise and let loose a big gob of spit. The two of them watched the spit fall down to the water and started counting.

The spitter said, "There you go. Sixty feet, like I said.

"Nah, with this wind, spit ain't accurate. Need somethin' heavier."

"Like a body," said the other guy. He looked over at me. "How much you weigh?"

Oh, my God, they both sound just like Wendell Cooper, the catcher who wanted to throw me off the platform. Only now it's into the water, instead of in front of a train.

I acted like I didn't hear the stuff about how much I weighed, and moved away like I had someplace to go, which I didn't. I could feel my heart beating real fast. Actually, I could even hear it inside my helmet. When I was walking away the two southern guys started laughing and hooting like they were real funny. I heard one of them say, "Sheeet, he looks like he's 'bout to piss his pants." And that's when I knew it was time to find another place to try and act like I belonged on the ship. I saw a door open and went through it. Now there was soft red carpet on the floor, instead of the wood and steel outside. I could smell food cooking, too.

"Hey, soldier, whatcha doin' up here?" It was someone else with a southern accent. But it was different from the guys on deck. I turned around and saw why. It was a tall black man in a white jacket, carrying a tray with a silver coffee pot and two cups on saucers.

"Me?" I asked.

"Well, I don't see no other soldier anywhere, do you?"

"I guess not."

"This is officer country."

"They have their own country?" I knew right away that was a stupid thing to say. And I guess the man with the tray thought so, too.

"That's a bad attitude to start this trip off with. You best not let anyone with brass on their collar hear you talk like that."

"I didn't mean it to sound like that. I never heard of officer country, that's all."

"Never been on a ship before, huh?" I shook my head.

"Guess that's an honest enough mistake, then. Come on, I'll show you how to get to where you belong."

I got behind him and walked along this hallway that was lined with closed doors and looked like it was a couple of miles long.

"Where you from?" the black man asked.

"New Jersey. How about you?"

"*What* about me?"

"Where are you from?"

"Just about everywhere. Chicago, St. Louis, Memphis."

"You like being a waiter on a ship?" All of a sudden he stopped walking and all the coffee cups on his tray hit each other.

"You best be careful about that kind of wise-cracking. I've whomped bigger men than you for mouthin' off to me. Understand?"

"I'm sorry. But I didn't mouth off."

"You didn't, huh? I get this shit all the time. Mostly from crackers from down south, though, not from New Jersey. I got seven years in this man's Navy. Just because they don't see fit to send us off to radio school, or turn us into bos'n mates and make stewards out of us instead. Don't mean we're any less Navy people. They put us on these ships to be with the brass that's goin' over to England. Guess they figure the English Navy guys don't know how to serve meals to American officers. But don't let this white jacket fool you. Fact is, seeing as how there ain't no stripes on your arm, I outrank you. I'm a Petty officer, third class."

All of a sudden I felt like I was about six inches shorter than when I got on the ship. I wished I could keep on shrinking until I just disappeared. *What a total, stupid jerk. Couldn't you have figured out that the ship was run by military people, and wouldn't have civilian waiters for God's sake?*

"I'm really, really sorry," I said. "I didn't know, sir."

"And I ain't no sir. Well, it don't matter a whole lot, I guess. You really thought I was some kind of civilian?" I nodded. "Actually, it would be a pretty good job to have, if there wasn't no war on, and they were taking rich people over to England like they used to. Of course, then they wouldn't be assigning people like me to do what I'm doing. They'd put those white English guys back on the job."

"That wouldn't be fair."

"That's the truth, all right. But that wouldn't stop 'em. Never has. Fair's not a word they pay much attention to."

"I know what you mean."

"How *would* you?"

I looked into his dark eyes. They looked angry. I thought about telling him how I was chased up a rope with a knife and about the Black Cat Gang. But I didn't think that was such a good idea.

"I guess I really wouldn't know," I said.

He started walking again, and I followed him, a couple steps behind. We came to a shiny varnished mahogany door with no window in it. The black man stopped and nodded at it.

"That'll take you down where you belong."

I had no idea where that was, except it was someplace outside of officer's country.

"Thanks," I said.

"Yeah, don't mention it. And try and keep your ass out of here. You don't want to mess with those people."

"I will. And, I'm sorry for, well, if I insulted you."

"You probably didn't mean to. What's your name, anyway?"

"Saperstein."

The man thought about something. For the first time there was a smile on his dark, shiny face.

"That tells me something, I guess. Maybe you do understand."

• • •

A loud, long blast of a giant horn shook the whole ship and all the people on it, including me. I actually felt the horn blast going through my body, down my legs to the bottom of my feet. I guess that was the United States Army's and the Navy's way of telling us we were on our way. Or, actually, underway, which is what you say when you're on a ship.

I was standing out on the main deck on the side away from the dock, where it wasn't as crowded with people waving to anybody left down there. It was just a few minutes before six, and the evening rush hour was on. Two red ferry boats, filled with cars and passengers looked like they were racing with each other across the Hudson to New Jersey. The boats had big gold letters that said Erie and Lackawanna Railroad. My father rides the ferries a lot when he leaves the car home to save gas for the war effort. I had a feeling he wasn't on a ferry or a train that day but probably at home trying to figure out if I really meant what I said in my letter and where I really was. I took some deep breaths and told myself I was doing the right thing.

I leaned over the rail more and saw two tug boats up against the ship, pushing it out, so we could turn and start down the river. I couldn't figure out how two little boats like that, with a bunch of seaweed stuff on the front and rubber tires around the side, could push the giant Queen Elizabeth anywhere, but I figured they knew what they were doing.

Pretty soon I could see the Statue of Liberty. When we got close, I heard a huge cheer go up all over the ship. A couple of guys next to me were yelling things like, "Wish us luck, lady," to the big green statue. One of them looked at me and pointed at it, and I saluted the Statue, and then gave it a big wave. I guess the other guys approved of what I did, and they saluted and waved, too.

I went to the other side of the ship and saw we were going past what I knew was Ellis Island, the place where my mother and father, and their parents and my uncles and aunts, all took their first steps onto America. My father liked to tell me stories of how all those thousands of people, who were waiting to get into New York from Russia, from Poland, from Italy and Germany, mostly couldn't speak any English. They would get confused when the guards would ask them questions, like what their names were. A lot of them thought they were getting asked what their jobs were. Next thing they knew, they had new names, like Silversmith or Butcher, stuff like that. I don't know if it was true, but I do know people with both those names, and I'm pretty sure their parents came through Ellis Island.

I also remember something my father said whenever he talked about seeing the Statue of Liberty for the first time: "I knew I would never see such a beautiful sight again." Then he would stop and go over to my mother and kiss her on the cheek. "Until I met your mother, of course." He liked saying that, and did it a lot. I think my mother liked it a lot too, because she would always give him one of those fake little "oh go on" nudges.

A whistle blew again on the big speakers. Then a voice came on.

"This is the Captain speaking. We are now underway and the watch has been set. I want to remind all hands, officers and personnel in transit, that we are operating under war conditions, and will remain that way until our arrival. I don't need to tell you that the enemy has U-boats plying the North Atlantic, looking for vessels like ours. We will be escorted the entire way by four destroyers, which will join us as soon as we leave the harbor. Still, we must assume that we are at all times vulnerable to attack. The ship will be in total blackout at night, and the smoking lamp will be out at all times on deck after sunset. It is imperative that procedures are followed to the letter, and that everyone aboard this vessel remains alert. If anything the least bit out of the ordinary is observed, it is to be reported to the officer of the deck, or a master-at-arms, immediately."

Now that worried me, not so much the warnings about U-boat attacks, or the extinguished smoking lamp, but the order to report anything out of the ordinary. Which is what I definitely was. Would I get reported when someone saw how my jacket buttoned the wrong way? Would it be the too-big helmet or the stuff I put in it to make it less too-big? Or would it just be my changing voice? I saw myself in the brig, all alone. There'd be a court martial. A plea for mercy. *Is there a mandatory death penalty for stowing away aboard a transport ship during time of war? How do they do it, the death penalty? A firing squad? No, the ship's too crowded and somebody could get hurt. A hanging? I don't think there's a yard arm on this kind of ship. And keel-hauling would definitely be out of the question.*

The next announcement I heard was about food. And that was a relief, seeing how I hadn't eaten anything all day except a couple of Baby Ruths.

"Now hear this. First mess call for enlisted personnel in transit. Form lines on the o-seven deck, aft, port side. First call is for all personnel with service numbers beginning with an odd numeral."

I looked at my mail-order, fake dog tag and sure enough, it began with the number seven. But what if no numbers started that way? Back to the brig again, I guess.

"Eaten yet?" I looked up from my tag and saw the Asian Ranger I met before.

"No, have you?" I said, pretty happy to see a friendly face again.

"I tried. But when I saw what they were serving, I decided to wait."

"For what?"

"Another ship maybe. One with a better menu."

"They have menus?"

"No, but you get a choice, out of which big kettle you want your slop from."

He took me down a hallway and then a bunch of stairs all jammed with soldiers going up and down, bumping into each other and once in a while swearing, mostly about what they ate. One guy said "My dog wouldn't eat that shit. And he's one hungry som-a-bitch. Ate a whole live chicken once." I looked at the Asian guy and he just laughed, like it's what GIs do, complain about stuff, specially the food they get to eat. We used to do that at camp all the time, too.

We ended up in a huge room that didn't look much like a mess hall where fifteen-thousand soldiers eat. It must have been a dining room for the rich people who used to be on board. But there weren't any tables and chairs or fancy dishes. Just a whole lot of GIs holding metal trays with some kind of glop on them and looking for someplace to sit down, like on the floor.

"Grab yourself a tray," my new friend said. I did, and also the only silverware that was there, a big soup spoon. "Here's where you get to make your choice."

He pointed to two big kettles that looked like the ones in jungle movies where the natives cook people. The stuff inside them smelled strange, kind of like wet clay that I used to make ash trays out of in arts and crafts on rainy days. It was the same color, too, gray.

A soldier with a bunch of the grey stuff saw me and said, "Those Limeys that cook here call this crap stew."

"And what might you bloody Yanks call it?" It was definitely the voice of an Englishman, a big Englishman, in a dirty apron, standing over one of the kettles. He had this huge wooden thing in his hand that I guess he stirred the stew with. It looked like a canoe paddle and was a couple feet long. He hit it a couple of times with his other hand, staring at the guy who didn't like his cooking very much.

"Who you callin' a bloody Yank?" the guy with the tray said.

"The whole bloody lot of you," the big man answered.

"Yeah, well, I hear that bloody means the same thing as *fucking*. So you're calling us fucking Yanks."

"No, I'm calling you bloody damn Yanks. I don't know anything about your sexual activities, and I can't say I'd want to."

The soldier stepped up to the kettle and stared back at the Englishman. Then he turned his tray upside down and let the grey glop slide off back down where it came from. He slammed the tray against the kettle a couple of times and threw it on the floor.

"There's your shit-stew back, Limey," he said.

Now there was real fire in the Englishman's eyes. He came around the kettle and dropped the paddle on the floor. Then he grabbed the soldier in a bear hug and just lifted him right off the floor with his enormous arms. He carried him like a bag of groceries over to another big kettle, and lifted him up in the air.

"What the hell are you doing?" the soldier said, in a real panic all of a sudden.

"I'm letting you have a taste of our other offering. Perhaps you'll find it more to your liking."

The soldier kicked his feet in the air, and the Englishman swung him higher than the top of the kettle, which had more grey glop in it than the other one. And he plunked him down inside it. The soldier landed with a sick sound, a heavy *thwunk,* like a rock hitting a bunch of mud.

"For chrissake, will somebody get me the hell out of here before I get cooked in this shit!" the guy shouted.

Finally, two other soldiers, looking pretty scared, like they might be next, grabbed the guy's hands. They tugged and pulled until they could get him up over the top of the kettle and watched him slip down to the floor. When he finally got up, looking like a clay soldier now instead of a real one, he just stared at the big Englishman, who had his arms crossed.

"Is that batch any more to your liking?"

"I'll get your Limey ass for this," the soldier said.

"I don't think so, mate. Her Majesty's Maritime Service doesn't take kindly to buggering of its personnel." Then the Englishman slapped his hands against each other up and down and got back behind the first kettle.

"O.K., chaps," he said, "Step up and help yourself to the HMS Queen Elizabeth's prize stew, made from a centuries-old recipe."

"Yeah, that's the problem. It tastes like it was made a couple centuries ago," said a big, older GI with sergeant's stripes on his jacket.

I figured there'd be another dumping, but nothing happened. The Englishman laughed. "That's right, sergeant, it's the aging that makes it so very delicious."

Then the Englishmen looked down like he was going to go after me next, maybe because I was so small. But no, instead he said, "Let's go then, it's not going to come to you."

Thwunnck again. This time it was a large gob of stew landing on my tray. I almost dropped it, it came down so hard.

"Don't be dropping Her Majesty's fine cuisine on the deck, now," the big man said.

"Thank you, sir," I said.

"*Sir?* Well, that's the first time I've been called that, by a Yank, or anyone else for that matter. Here now, that deserves another helping. Come on."

I didn't really want one, but I didn't want to get the guy mad again, either. So I stepped up to him and held out my tray, feeling like little

Oliver Twist in the orphanage, only I really didn't want "more, sir." But I got it anyway.

"It's not as bad as it looks — or smells," the Asian soldier said when I kept staring down at my two helpings. "Try it."

And I did. And it wasn't.

CHAPTER

9

It was just after eight on my first night at sea. I was standing out on the deck, where everything was pitch dark, with the lights that have to be out in wartime. All I could see was a lot of stars in the sky and white foam down in the water alongside the ship. It was pretty peaceful after all that stuff going on at supper time. The Asian soldier was standing next to me. We mostly just looked down at the water going by, not saying much.

"Thinking about home?" he asked me.

"Yeah. I'm wondering what my family's doing now."

Actually, I knew pretty well what they'd be doing. It was time for supper, but I don't think there was any food on the table. I could see my mother and father just sitting there, shaking their heads, like they finally believed I really did go and do this crazy thing with the Army. I almost could hear them, and see them.

"I just can't believe it. I can't believe it," my mother would say, holding a lace hanky that was soaking wet from her tears.

My father would be holding the letter I left in his hands, looking like he read it so many times he had it memorized. He would read it one more time, just shaking his head all the time. My brother would sit there at the table, too, but this time he wouldn't be making any jokes about me or anything else.

Now I could see someone else at the table, a guy from the Army, a captain or major maybe, with a bunch of ribbons on his uniform.

He'd be talking now.

"I wish I could tell you more than I know at this point. All I do know is your son wasn't inducted into the Army today."

"Are you sure they'd tell you if he was?" my mother would ask.

The officer would get kind of irritated at that, like he was an important guy and would know all the inside stuff. Then he'd say, "Yes, ma'm, I'm quite sure. I contacted every office in my jurisdiction today, and the answer was the same in every case. No one by the name of Saperstein has enlisted in recent months, nor has anyone by that name been processed today."

"What if he used a false name?" my brother would ask, which is just like him.

"He couldn't have, unless, of course, he had forged papers — birth certificate and such — from another person. I seriously doubt someone his age could have accomplished that."

"He's very bright, my son. Maybe he could have done that," my mother would say, like I could hear her, which made me feel pretty good.

"Of course, Ma'm. That's why we have to be careful. We have to stop people from getting into the armed forces without being eligible."

"I know that," my brother would interrupt. "I read the papers and listen to the radio. And I think it's funny that you think people are dying to sign up. They do that after they get in, the dying."

And that would be where my father would put a stop to things. "That's enough," he would say to my brother, like he really, really meant it. And then he'd say to the officer, "I'm sorry. Our son sometimes thinks he's Myron Cohen."

"Who's that, sir?"

End of story.

. . .

"So, what do I call you?" the soldier who was still standing next to me asked.

"Saperstein."

"O.K. I'm Kaufman"

Kaufman? I looked at him wondering if I heard right.

"Yeah, I know, everyone finds it pretty funny. My parents are both dead. I was adopted when I was three, by a family in New York."

"Named Kaufman?"

"That's right. I bet you'd never figure me for Jewish. Those guys back at the docks missed a real opportunity. They thought they were just picking on a Chinaman. If they only knew, they could have had a bonus, a two-for-one. You know, a guy who does laundry and goes out for Chinese food on Sunday, too."

"That's what my family does."

"Laundry?"

"Chinese food on Sunday."

"I'll bet they call it *going for Chinks*."

"Yeah, they do. But they don't mean any harm."

"Of course not. I'll bet some of their best friends are Chinks."

"No. I don't think they know any."

"Well, if they did, they'd find out we're not very noisy in restaurants, but we do tend to stick together. And we're really good with money."

I started liking this guy, this Chinese-Jewish soldier, figuring we really did have stuff in common, the way a lot of people didn't like either one of us even before they knew us.

"Do you like being Jewish?" I asked him.

"I guess it's O.K. It got pretty funny, though, when I was bar-mitzvahed. I swear, the rabbi would always look at me like he expected me to start chanting in Chinese. And it's really funny the way people at the synagogue would always talk to me real slow, pronouncing every word like they didn't think I understood them."

"But you don't even have an accent or anything." I tried to imagine him chanting his *haftorah* in Chinese. Pretty strange.

"Tell me, Saperstein, why did you do it?"

"Do what?"

"This. You know, sneaking aboard the ship, into the army."

Oh my God, he figured it out. Maybe he's really an agent, an FBI guy or something, and he's been tailing me. He's not really Jewish or even Chinese. Could be Japanese, one of those double agents that the Army got to find people who sneak aboard ships. Should I jump? Sure, go ahead. A lot of good your whale badge from Camp Chickasaw is going to do you out here. All you can swim is a mile, and that was in a lake, with a counselor in a rowboat next to you.

"You look like you're going to throw up. Or jump over, or something," Kaufman said.

"Why do you think I sneaked aboard?" I finally asked.

"I don't know, just a feeling. I especially get it when your voice cracks. What are you, thirteen, maybe fourteen?"

I didn't know what my next move should be, or even if there was a move that would do any good or keep me out of trouble. I just kept looking down at the water, which looked very cold and very deep.

"Hey, relax. I'm not going to turn you in," Kaufman said. "Look, if you want to get into this war, that's your business. I just don't get it. Why would you want to go when you don't have to?"

"Did you have to go?"

"Well, I would have had to, eventually. I figured if I signed up, though, I could get what I wanted. The Rangers. Otherwise, if I waited for the draft to get me, who knows where they would have put me. Maybe in the kitchen, with the way I look and all."

"With a name like Kaufman?"

"That's right. Maybe they would have made me a shop keeper. Or something with money. Anyway, don't get any ideas like going over the side."

"What makes you think I'd do that?"

"The way you were eyeballing the water over the rail. I have a feeling. But let me tell you, Saperstein, that water's colder than a witches left tit. You wouldn't last more than a few minutes."

"You're not going to tell anyone?"

"Who would I tell? And why? They probably wouldn't even care. It's not like you've broken some secret code or something. Or you're a spy for the Germans. You're a kid with some crazy reason or other for wanting to go where you don't have to."

"But I do have to."

"What is it, problems at home? Can't get along with your parents or something?"

I didn't have an answer for him.

"You're too young to have girl-friend problems, or at least the kind that would make you run away and join the Foreign Legion. So, really, how old are you anyway?

"Almost fourteen."

"Almost fourteen. Well, hell's bells, I'm almost fifty, if you figure that nineteen is close to it. And what is it that makes you think you have to do this thing?"

I figured I should at least try and explain why I did what I did, at least to Kaufman, who I had a feeling I could trust. So I just started to tell him everything that happened. He didn't say anything, and just kept nodding and looking at the water, too. I told him about the rock through our window, the crap that kept happening at school, my record-breaking rope climb, even the story that didn't have anything to do with what I finally did, the one about my ass nearly getting thrown off a subway platform.

When I finally finished, all Kaufman said was, "You think he really would have thrown you on the tracks?"

I thought that was pretty funny. After all the stuff the Black Cats did to me and to my family, the rock through the window, the fire, the stuff that made me feel the war was my fault, all he mentioned was the thing outside the Polo Grounds. Maybe Kaufman just liked baseball.

"O.K., tell me this," Kaufman said. "When you get over there, do you think you're going to want to kill people?"

I couldn't think of an answer for that one. The truth was, I never really thought about actually pulling a trigger of a gun, which would send a bullet smashing into a human body and killing it. To me, doing my part was something else. I wasn't sure what it would be yet, maybe something like climbing up ropes to get to the top of something, or carrying stretchers that went into those green trucks with big red crosses painted on them. I don't really like guns much, except those 22's we shot paper targets with in camp. I liked the smell of gun powder, especially on the shooting range that was made out of old wood, which smelled good, too. But using a gun to actually kill somebody, that's not what I wanted to be doing.

"Well," Kaufman said. "I'm waiting for an answer. Do you want to kill people?"

"I just want to help end the war."

"And the way that happens is, you kill people, more of them than can kill of us. It's really pretty simple. Whoever has the most people standing when it's over, that's who wins. Right?"

"I guess so." But I didn't really guess so. "I feel like I want to be David, going up against Goliath," I said

"So, you think you can beat the Germans with a slingshot?" Kaufman asked.

"Maybe not a slingshot. Maybe truth."

"And how does that work? You go and tell them to stop killing and gassing people long enough to hear the truth about what they're doing? Besides, maybe they believe *they're* David and we're Goliath. We're a bigger country than Germany is, aren't we?"

I hadn't thought about that, probably because I was always the one being chased. To me, Hitler was the bully, like Herbie Schoo with a knife, chasing me up a rope. And just guns weren't going to stop him. It would have to be truth, too. *Praise the Lord and pass the ammunition, and we'll all be free*. I liked the song enough, but I didn't think you just shoot all the bad guys in the world. There are too many of them.

"Anyway, you don't have to worry about being turned in, as long as you don't go and do something dumb," Kaufman said.

"Like what?"

"Well, I think you ought to keep your theory about warfare to yourself. You start talking about David and Goliath, or about Hitler being like a guy chasing you with a knife, you're going to get the kind of attention you don't want. Just follow the basic rule of Army survival: don't ask questions, don't give any information that isn't requested, and don't volunteer for anything. And you won't have anything to worry about. Well, except for U-Boats that might torpedo the crap out of us and send us to the bottom."

"I don't worry too much about U-boats."

"And why not? Haven't you heard how many ships they've sunk?"

"Yeah. But they don't always just sink ships."

"What do you think they're doing out here? Fishing?"

"Kind of. Sometimes they have to get things they need, for their spies."

And that was when I told the story about my father's friend Otto and the German submarine that captured his fishing boat that was out having a nice sunny day catching porgies in Peconic Bay. It was the first time I told it to anyone, because my father said it was a secret, with the war on and everything, especially the part where they took everybody's American money and driver's licenses. But I figured it was O.K. to tell Kaufman, seeing how he's in the army. The whole time I was telling it to him, he just stared at me like I was maybe crazy, or just a liar.

Then he finally said, "Maybe they're planning to go get you and hold you hostage because you know what they were doing, you think?"

That made me suck in a big breath and start worrying about a U-boat showing up in the middle of the ocean and looking for me. But that was pretty dumb. How would they know I was on the Queen Elizabeth anyway?

Then Kaufman started laughing out loud and shaking his head. "Relax, Sappy. I'm just pulling your leg. Don't worry, those guys have more to worry about than finding a Jewish kid from New Jersey. I don't think old Schickelgruber is sending them out to find you."

"Yeah, I guess not," I said, but the idea still gave me the creeps.

"Anyway, where are you bunking," Kaufman asked.

"I don't know yet. I haven't found a place."

"It might be a good idea to get started on that. Want to see where I'm holed up?"

"Sure. Do you think there's any room there?"

"The way they pack 'em in, my guess is they can always squeeze in one more. Come on. You like swimming pools?"

"Yeah, I do. They have one on the ship?"

"Three of them."

"And you sleep next to one of them?"

"Not exactly next to one. I'll show you."

I had to move pretty quick to keep up with Kaufman. He just stepped through hatch openings and down stairways like he did it all the time. We went down four floors (decks, he reminded me) and then down a long hallway (passageway, he reminded me again) to the back of the ship (stern), then back up two decks. Kaufman said it was because we had to go around a restricted area.

"Officer country?" I asked.

"Yeah. You know about that? Not bad."

We came to two heavy, wood doors, with small round windows you could see lights through. Kaufman pulled one of the doors open and bowed to me.

"Welcome to the pool, Private Saperstein. But please, no diving."

When we got inside, all I could see were people, a lot of people, it looked like, in the bottom of the pool, and no water. There were things that looked like beds, sort of, real close together and piled four high, with maybe a foot and a half between them. I watched a soldier, a heavy guy, trying to squeeze in one of the beds on the third row up, and it didn't look like he was going to make it, until two other guys pushed him in and everybody got a big laugh. Poor guy, I felt sorry for him, especially when one of the guys who pushed him yelled out, "Looks like he's in there until we get to Europe."

"It's not much, but we call it home," Kaufman said. "Want to see if they have any accommodations for you?"

I looked down at all the soldiers in the pool, maybe a couple of hundred of them, all sweaty, in their undershirts, smoking cigarettes, complaining about stuff, laughing sometimes, but looking like they were ready to get into the war and do something about it. I remembered what Kaufman said about who wins the war: *Whoever has the most people standing when it's over, that's who wins.* How many of these troops, all sweaty, smoking and laughing, will be standing when it's over? It made me sad to think that some of them wouldn't be going back on another ship.

Then I heard a loud tapping sound. I looked across at the other side of the pool and saw a soldier sitting behind a big metal can and tapping on it with drum sticks. Then another guy, with no shirt on, got up close to the drummer and started playing a harmonica. I knew the tune. It was *Ain't She Sweet.* Then some other soldiers started to sing it. S*ee her comin' down the street. Oh I ask you very confidentially, ain't she sweet.* Something about the song, and the way those sweating guys had a good time with it, made me finally think that things maybe were going to work out, and I wasn't going to get caught and in all kinds of trouble. I only wished my family knew I was O.K. and could pretty soon stop worrying about me.

When the song finally ended a long time later, everybody, and I mean everybody, started clapping and whistling down in the pool. The harmonica player and the drummer bowed, and so did the singers. Maybe they weren't Les Brown and His Band of Renown, but they sounded good enough to me to be on stage at the Paramount in New York.

"See, we even have live entertainment," Kaufman said. He put his fingers in his mouth and let out this huge whistle, and a bunch of other guys did the same thing.

"Come on," said Kaufman, "Want to meet our drummer?"

"Hey, Charlie, I got someone here who needs a place to sleep," Kaufman said. The drummer smiled and nodded, and wiped his sweaty forehead with the hand he was holding his drum sticks with. He looked at me, as if he was wondering what a kid was doing on the ship, but then he smiled and stuck out his other hand. I shook it, and it was soaking wet, like the rest of him.

"Charlie Hensel," he said.

"Saperstein. Glad to meet you."

Charlie looked at Kaufman. "They're taking them younger and younger, aren't they? Where you from, Saperstein?"

"New Jersey."

"I've been there, when I stayed in New York for a summer. All I remember is those smelly pig farms. They're something awful."

"Yeah, I know what you mean." I was really trying to make my voice sound deeper, I wasn't sure it was working.

"I hear there are some nice parts of New Jersey, though. The seashore. Live near it?"

"No. I live near the George Washington Bridge."

"Hey, I walked across it once. You ever do that?" Charlie said.

"Yeah, I have," I said. But I didn't say I just did it that morning.

Kaufman said, "Somebody screwed up and didn't give him a bunk assignment. Got any ideas where he can sleep?"

"Doesn't surprise me, the screw up, with half of the east coast jammed in. There's so much confusion, somebody who isn't even in the army could probably just walk on board and never get noticed."

"I suppose so," said Kaufman, giving me a quick look and making his eyebrows go up. "But who'd want to come with us if he didn't have to?"

"You're right," Charlie said. "This isn't exactly a Caribbean cruise now, is it? What's your outfit, anyway?" he asked me.

"He's a Ranger, too," Kaufman said before I had a chance to admit I didn't have an outfit.

"Well, you're in for some fun over there," Charlie said. "I'm Air Corps. Mostly work on planes, trying to keep them in the air. I won't be climbing up any cliffs like you guys. But, we all have our jobs to get done."

"How come they didn't make you a musician?" Kaufman asked him.

"I guess they didn't hear from my agent in time. Anyway, I made this gig for myself. You play an instrument?" he asked me.

"The trumpet. I was a camp bugler."

"No kidding," said Charlie. "Which camp? Dix?"

"Chickawaw. It's in Maine. A summer camp."

"Oh, well, that's O.K. Did you bring your horn with you?"

"No. There was no room." *That's all you would have needed, walking down Route Four at five in the morning carrying a trumpet, too.*

"Maybe you'd like to sit in, if we could rustle up a horn for you."

Kaufman said, "And where are you going to find a horn?"

"The same place I'm going to get some real drums. I made friends with one of the British crew people. He's some sort of master-at-arms. Wears a badge. Anyway, we got to talking about music, and he started reminiscing about the band that used to play in on the ship before they converted it to carry us. Seems the band left the ship, but their instruments didn't. There's a little room way down on the seven deck, a storage locker, actually. That's where the instruments are. He told me for sure there are drums. And I'm willing to bet there's a horn in there, too."

"How are you going to get him to let you in, and get the instruments?"

"I've already taken care of that. My new friend happens to love American big-band jazz. Ever hear any of the Stan Kenton *Artistry* series?" he asked us.

That was like asking me if I ever heard of Mel Ott or Hank Greenberg. I love Stan Kenton's music. especially the Artistry albums.

"He's one of my favorites," I said. Kaufman shrugged like he never heard of Kenton.

"Well, our master-at-arms is now the proud owner of two complete *Artistry* albums, and I've got a key to the instrument locker," Charlie said, holding up a heavy brass key with a crown and the letters HMS Q.E. stamped on it.

"Pretty smooth, Charlie," said Kaufman. "What do you say, Saperstein, ready to go blow your horn with this guy?"

"Besides the bugle calls, I mostly know some modern jazz, and a little Dixieland."

"Hey, I groove on Dixie," Charlie said. "Can you do the *Saints?*" I nodded. "*Lullaby of Birdland?*" I nodded again. "And how about *Boogie Woogie Bugler Boy?*" That got a really big nod from me. It was the number I played on the last day of camp, over the P.A. system, instead of reveille. It got a cheer from every cabin, and a little chewing out from the head counselor, who really liked reveille a lot more.

"That's enough for me. You've got a medley already," Charlie said, with a great big smile.

"Meet me back here tomorrow after supper, around seven? I'll have a horn for you, drums for me, and maybe a sax for the guy on harmonica."

"He'll be here," Kaufman said. "He just has to get over his first-timer jitters. Hasn't been in uniform very long, have you kid?"

"See you then?" Charlie asked me.

"Sure. I'll be here."

"Good enough. Now I'm going to get in the shower line. With any luck, I ought to be getting wet by midnight. Eight-to-the-bar," he said, the way real musicians talk.

Right, eight-to-the-bar," I said back, which kind of made me feel like a musician more than a kid hiding on a ship, for a minute anyway.

"Come on, let's see if we can find you a place to sleep," said Kaufman.

He took me down a ladder to the bottom of the pool. We had to step over duffle bags, clothes and a whole lot of people just standing around or lying in bunks with their feet hanging out. And it smelled like the sweat in gym at school. Kaufman stopped and pointed to an empty bunk on the bottom row in a corner. It was just a few inches up from the floor. There was this thin mattress folded in half on it.

"At least you don't have to do any climbing to get in it," Kaufman said.

"Just a lot of bending and squatting." He pulled the mattress open, and I saw why the bunk was empty. There was this big brown stain all over it. "You probably don't want to find out what it is. Just turn it upside down."

I pictured my bed at home, big enough for a couple of people, all clean, the way my mother always kept it, smelling like ironed sheets and Rinso, never sweat and urine.

"It's O.K., kid," Kaufman said. "I'll see if I can find you another mattress." He poked me on the shoulder, like he knew what I was thinking.

That was some night, the first one on the mighty Queen Elizabeth. When you're jammed in between the tile floor of a swimming pool, a big fat guy with the lump of his butt about an inch from your nose, a smelly, snoring guy who talked in his sleep in a southern accent, right next to you, you don't exactly sleep. You just try to lie still, and don't turn over. It'd be impossible, with the big butt on top of you and the snore-talker next to you. Kaufman never did get back with another mattress, so I tried to breathe through my mouth the whole night. I also figured out the swimming pool must have been right over the engines, because I didn't just hear them all night, I felt them, too, like being in a big Mix Master or something. I tried to make the time pass by practicing the keying on an imaginary trumpet for *Boogie Woogie Bugler Boy.*

Finally, when it felt like my first night at sea was actually a month, this blast came from somewhere. It was a bugle, real scratchy, like a record, playing reveille. And all the smelly, sweaty people started moving, and complaining and swearing and all, trying to wiggle out of their bunks.

"Was that you snoring all night?" this big, real hairy guy next to me said.

"No, not me."

"Yeah? How do you know you didn't snore when you were sleeping?"

"Because I wasn't sleeping. I couldn't."

"That's what they all say: *'I didn't sleep a wink,'*" he said, trying to sound girly, "when they're really sawing wood for most of the damn night. That what you do?"

"No. I swear, I didn't sleep enough to even begin snoring."

"Yeah, bull-shit."

"And what the hell you think you were doin', lard-ass?" It was the voice of another big man, but with not as much hair as the guy in the bunk on top of me.

"What, you tellin' me I was snoring? You're full of crap."

I figured I was going to be in the middle of another fight, like when the guy who got thrown in the kettle of gray slop, but it would take all those guys so long to squeeze out of their bunks, I could be gone before anything started. So I slid out off the disgusting mattress, grabbed my shoes and clothes, put them on and headed up the ladder and out of the pool.

I nearly bumped into Charlie the drummer at the top.

"Hey, Saperstein, where you going in such a hurry?".

"It was getting kind of strange down there," I said.

He had this big grin on his face. "Got something to show you. I was busy last night, after you left." He got up off a big wooden crate he was sitting on and opened the top. Inside was an open black leather case with blue velvet lining. And sitting there was a trumpet, so shiny it looked like nobody ever used it.

Charlie looked real proud of himself. "What do you think?" he asked.

"Wow, it's beautiful. Never seen one that nice."

"Think you can do it some justice?"

"I don't know. I wouldn't want to mess up on it."

"Why don't we see what you can do?"

I couldn't do that at first, pick it up. What if I got it smudged with all the dirt I picked up down in the pool. But Charlie just nodded at me, until I did pick it up. I looked at the bell part and saw my face perfect, like in a mirror. There were these words engraved on it in swirly letters: *HMS Queen Elizabeth*.

"Where should I go to play it?"

"Nowhere. Give it a try right here. Maybe you can get some of those guys in a better mood."

I thought about all of them in bad moods trying to get out of their bunks, and figured it might not be such a good idea to play a strange a trumpet for them. It could come out like a bunch of squeaks for all I knew.

"Go ahead. Don't be nervous," Charlie said. "Try a few bars of *Bugler Boy.*"

I just kept staring at myself in the bell.

"You *can* play it, can't you?"

I guess I had to do it, seeing how I told him I could. It was a challenge, but nothing like being dared to climb up a rope at school. The trumpet felt good. I wrapped my left hand around the three valves and put the middle three fingers of the right hand on the white caps on top. I worked the keys up and down, and smelled the oil that kept them sliding nice and smooth. Next I wet my lips and put the silver mouthpiece against them and could taste the metal, like always. I squinted my eyes almost shut and blew a first, long note. It came out a perfect *G,* and sounded soft and round. Then I took a deeper breath and out came another note, a shorter one. All of a sudden I was playing *Bugler Boy,* kind of quiet at first, and then a little louder. The notes just started coming out like I wanted them to. Charlie had this big grin, and his head started going up and down with the beat. All of a sudden, it started feeling real good being there on the ship, with a couple of new friends, Charlie and Kaufman, and I didn't care about the crappy mattress, about no sleep, about the grumpy guys next to me. I was a soldier and, on top of that, a kid who could blow a horn.

Some of the troops that were sitting around the edge of the pool, trying to get away from the stink and all, were watching me when I played. A few of them were nudging each other and pointing at me. Some of them even began clapping with the music. Then two of them started jitterbugging together, which really looked strange, in their khaki undershirts and baggy drawers. Nobody cared about two guys dancing. I guess when it's in the middle of the ocean and there's a war on, everything's O.K. It almost felt like being back at the Little Brown Jug on Friday night, but not quite, actually.

As I got close to the end of the song, I saw Charlie moving his hand in a circle, which I guess meant I should keep playing, from the top. So I played what I figured was a bridge and went back to the beginning, and everybody started clapping again. Charlie ducked away for a minute and then came back. He was pulling a big snare drum on a shiny silver stand. He sat down on the wooden crate again and started playing with me. He was good, Charlie was, real good.

At the end of the second chorus, he yelled to me, "I'll take it."

I hit a wrap-up and stopped, and watched Charlie. He went into this amazing drum solo and it got the crowd, which was getting bigger all the time, stomping and clapping with the beat. They yelled out stuff, too, like "Go, man, go," and, "Hit it, Charlie."

Then it was over, even though I didn't want it to be. All the guys didn't either. Charlie came over and pointed at me, and yelled out, "Private Saperstein, straight from Jersey, on the horn!" And the crowd gave me a hand, a lot of whistles, too. It felt just like the time I threw out a guy at home from center field in a game-ending double play against Camp Kohut. I got carried off the field that time on the whole team's shoulders. That wasn't going to happen here on the ship, but that was O.K. Then I did what any musician should do. I nodded a little and then pointed to Charlie. He beat out a roll on the drum and stood up and nodded, too

"Kid," Charlie said to me later, "that was just about the finest rendition of that tune I've heard. Where did you learn to blow like that? They teach that kind of playing at some kid's camp?"

"Actually, I did take some private lessons." It wasn't my favorite thing to do. My teacher, Mr. Klein, had the worst breath I ever smelled and he loved John Phillips Sousa and hated jazz. I guess maybe the jam sessions in the basement with Gordon on clarinet and another kid, Hiram, on drums helped.

All of a sudden I felt a big heavy hand grabbing my shoulder. I turned around and saw the face of the big guy in the next bunk. He was real close, and his breath smelled like Mr. Klein's.

"Hey, kid, that horn sounds a lot better than your snoring."

"That wasn't me," I said.

"Whaddya mean it wasn't you? I seen you there playin.'"

"I mean it wasn't me snoring."

"Don't matter if you do or you don't. You play one mean horn. And I got a chance to boogey. It took me back to Brighton Beach. I won a contest there, at the casino, dancin' to that same number. You know Brighton?"

I nodded that I did. My grandparents actually lived there. When I looked at the big guy's face, I couldn't believe what I saw. Tears. I mean it. He was crying. He wiped his nose with this huge hand that seemed too big for a guy who can cry.

"I'm glad you liked it. And I really enjoyed your dancing, a lot, I swear."

"Yeah, well, thanks. And don't worry if you make some noise at night, it's O.K. Just try keepin' it down to a dull roar. Maybe play a lullaby or somethin'?"

He held out that hairy hand and I grabbed it to shake, which was a mistake. It was like I put in a vise in shop class, it was so tight. I couldn't help making this noise that wasn't a word or anything.

"What'd ya say?" asked the man.

"Nothing. Just thanks."

"Don't mention it. What's you name, anyways?"

"Saperstein."

"I should of figured. Only a Hebe or a Shine can blow a horn like that."

Charlie chimed in. "Come on, give the kid a break. Don't be calling him names."

"Who's calling names? I'm payin' him a compliment. Hebes and shines have natural rhythm, don't you know that? You never saw Jolson in *The Jazz Singer?* He's a Hebe, and he puts black on his face to act like a shine at the same time. You didn't know that?"

"Well, I can't say I ever came across that kind of information," Charlie said.

"You're pretty good yourself on the drum," the big man said.

"Thanks. And I'm not even a Hebe or a shine."

The guy stared at Charlie, like he wasn't sure if he was being made fun of. I guess he didn't think he was, because he kind of smiled, with just half of his mouth. "Yeah, well, maybe you've got some blood nobody ever told you about."

"I'll check that out, " Charlie said.

"Anyway, my name's Tiny," the guy said to both of us. "You need anything you can't get on this big tub, let me know. I got friends."

"Thanks, Tiny," I said, trying not to laugh at his name. He was about the biggest guy I'd ever seen. He kind of reminded me of Lenny in *Of Mice and Men,* which we had to read in English class.

Kaufman came up to me. "Hey, I heard your performance. Nice job. You made yourself a lot of friends down in the pit. Want to get some breakfast? It should at least be worth seeing what they think we eat in the morning."

"Sure. But I haven't showered yet."

"Don't worry, it's an informal affair. Besides, it would take you a week to get through the shower line. We'd be in England by then. Come on. Want to join us, Charlie?"

"I was hoping for room service, but they must be running late," he said, like he wasn't making a joke, even though he was.

CHAPTER

11

As the big ship steamed on its way to England, I tried pretty hard to stay away from crowds of people, figuring the trumpet playing thing was maybe not such a good idea. What if someone important, like an officer, figured I shouldn't be on the ship? Just as I was heading away from a bunch of guys playing some kind of touch football on the open deck, I heard someone shouting at me.

"Hey, squirt, want to get in the game?"

It was one of the guys who were clapping and dancing when Charlie and I were playing. He was all sweaty and breathing hard and pointed a football at me.

"No, thanks, I have to go somewhere," I said.

"Go somewhere? What, you got some way to get off this tub? If you do, I want to know about it."

"Down below. I have to work on my gear," I really didn't have any idea what gear I had to work on. I hoped nobody was going to ask me.

"You must be in Fitzgerald's platoon. He's a real pain in the ass with his gear inspections. I feel for you, kid."

I also didn't know who Fitzgerald was or what platoon I was supposed to be in. So, I just started walking to a big steel door, I guess I should call it a hatch, and said, "Thanks, anyway,"

"Yeah, well, maybe you don't play football. Probably were in the marching band, right?"

"Yeah, with one of those fruity uniforms," another guy said.

93

"Come on, leave the kid alone," the guy with the ball said. "He's O.K."

They went back to playing ball, and I went down to the lower decks. It did feel kind of good, though, being "O.K." It's better than being a kid who wore a fruity marching band uniform and might get found out.

In the next couple of days I started getting used to life on a ship. One thing that was good was how I didn't get seasick like a lot of the troops did. The waves get pretty big that far out from land, and even though the Queen Elizabeth is a gigantic ship, it rolls and shakes like the fishing boats my father took me on. I guess I had sea legs and a lot of those other guys sounded like they never were on a boat before, except maybe the ferry on the Hudson River. The sea sick thing started making the swimming pool smell even more than from the sweat, because some guys just leaned over the edge of their bunks during the night and heaved before they could wiggle out to go to the bathroom — the head, I should say.

Speaking of the head, I was in there early in the morning the next day to brush my teeth and got into another spot I didn't want to be in. A tough looking guy was using the next sink and shaving. He saw my metal soap dish with a Boy Scout emblem on it. He started grinning at me, and I saw where a bunch of his teeth were missing. I wondered if he got into fights or anything like that.

He said, "Good thing we have a Boy Scout with us. If we have to build a fire, you can probably get one started for us."

I smiled a little and figured that was a dumb thing, leaving my scout stuff out. Then I said all I could think of. "Yeah, like they say, be prepared."

"Like who says?" the guy said. And he was looking scarier and scarier, with white shave cream all over his face and the big grin with black spaces between his teeth.

"That's the motto. Of the Boy Scouts. You know?"

"Yeah, I know. You think I don't know the motto? Like I'm maybe too dumb to know it?"

"I'm sorry if I said something you didn't like," I said, hoping maybe that would help. But I don't think it did.

"What are you, anyway?" the scary soldier said, his eyes getting narrow now. It definitely wasn't looking good.

"What do you mean?" I asked, playing dumb and wanting to definitely get out of the head.

"Are you a dago or something? You're pretty dark, like most *eye-talians.*"

"No, I'm not." *Oh, God, even here, on the way to fighting the war?*

"Yeah, well it won't do any good to try and hide what you are. I think you're a dago. I know one when I see one."

"How can you tell?"

"Black hair, black eyes. And usually a smell. Garlic. Like spaghetti sauce."

"My hair's brown. So are my eyes. Do I smell like garlic?".

He just kept looking at me. "Well, they look black to me, the eyes and the hair."

"It's the light in here. If we went outside, you'd see they're really brown."

"You know, it's not just the Germans we been fighting in this damn war. It's the *eye-talians,* too."

"Yes, I know that. But they already surrendered, the Italians did."

Now he looked confused. "What are you talkin' about? I didn't hear about any dago surrender."

"It's true. They're out of the war. Mussolini's gone."

"When'd that happen?"

"Last month. It was in the papers and Life Magazine. Really, I mean it. Seriously."

"Well, I haven't had time to read no papers or magazines. I've been training, to beat the krauts and the dagos and getting this damn war over with."

"Me, too. Only I just happened to see a paper someone left on a table, that's the only reason I know about it."

"I still think you're *eye-talian* and are trying to hide it."

"I swear to God, I'm not."

"You swear to God a lot. That's not a Christian thing to be doing." He paused. "You *are* a Christian, aren't you?"

O.K., here it comes. It didn't really take long at all to get from a hater of Italians to a Jew-hater. But it never does. It just means jumping from one set of dark eyes to another, as simple as that. The question was, though, what was he going to do about it?

"Well, are you or aren't you?"

"Am I what?" I didn't really think his memory was that short, but it was worth a try.

"A Christian, damn it."

"No, I'm not." I thought of closing my eyes so I couldn't see the knife that I figured was going to be pulled now. It might hurt less if I didn't see it coming.

"So. Maybe you're not a dago after all. They're Christians. So what are you, anyway? Don't tell me you're one of the chosen people?"

Now that's one of the words I really hate, *chosen.* I mean, really, how would you like to walk around waiting for the next time you're chosen. Like you're walking down the sidewalk and a bunch of kids jump out of the bushes and choose you to lose your pants. Or you're in gym, like I was, and you're chosen to climb up a rope fast enough so a guy with a knife can't catch you and re-circumcise you. No, thanks, I'd be a lot happier if I wasn't a chosen one. Whoever started using that word about all of us didn't do us any favor. It actually could have been better if we were the un-chosen, or even better, the ignored. Can you imagine if we were God's ignored people, so everybody would just forget about us and leave us alone? I like that idea actually.

"I guess that's what you are, a chosen one, since you're not answering me," the guy, who I really wished would just start shaving again, said. "I didn't expect to run into one of you people on this ship."

"Aren't we allowed?"

"That's not the question. Fact is, you people don't generally get into the war. You manage to buy your way out of it, don't you?"

I figured I was probably going to get thrown overboard by this Neanderthal standing next to me, so what could I lose by telling him what

I thought of his stupid words. First I tightened up my throat so I might sound older than I really was, not that it would necessarily save my ass, and said, "Look, I don't know where you get your information, but you're totally wrong about buying our way out of the war. That's some crap that bigots and stupid people in general pass around, and it's so far from the truth that it could make anyone with half a brain throw up. In fact, you're making me want to throw up, all over you. I feel like puking my guts out, stuff that would stink so bad you'll smell of it for the rest of the war, no matter where you go. Strange, awful stuff that's only found inside chosen people like me. So, I'm warning you, let me out of here, or I'll let go with everything I've got."

I waited for the crunching sound, of my nose first, or maybe my jaw, or a couple of teeth. Instead, the guy's mouth flew open and nothing came out of it. Then he took a slow step back, making just enough room for me to get past him to the door. But I didn't push the door open to run out. Something made me stop and turn back to look at the guy.

"And something else," I said. "There are a lot of Italian people fighting this war on our side. But stupid people probably don't know that either." That's when I definitely should have gotten my chosen ass out of there. But no, I had to get one more shot in. "Wait, I think I feel it coming. The biggest vomit I've ever had in my whole life, I swear to God."

Do I ever wish I had a Brownie camera with me. Because if I did have one, I would have taken a picture of the guy. He just stood there, looking at me like I was really going to do it, heave my guts across the room and right onto all the white shaving cream that was still on his face, even into his open mouth and through the spaces where there should be teeth. But I didn't have a Brownie, just a big, serious look on my face like I meant what I said. And then I did one last thing. I made this gagging-like sound in my throat, and he must have thought, here it comes, and he grabbed his stuff and went out the back door of the head, in a hurry, actually. I just looked up at all the pipes and stuff in the ceiling, as if someone was up there watching out for me and said, *Thank you dear God. That's what I*

call a save, like in the ninth inning when Johnny Mize steps up to the plate
and knocks the big one out of the park with three men on.

I was moving so fast to get far away from that head and the guy in it,
I didn't notice this big sergeant coming my way. "I've been looking all
over for you, kid."

"You want to see me?"

"No, the CO does."

The commanding officer? He couldn't have already heard I was
threatening to throw up on somebody, no way. Still, it scared the crap out
of me.

"Did I do something wrong?"

"You'll find out. He's waiting for you in the battalion office. On the
o-three deck. Colonel Lindquist."

"He wants to see me now?" I asked him.

"Well, he sure as hell doesn't want to wait until you can work him into
your schedule. Now would be a pretty good time."

I started wondering how long I would last in the sea if I just chucked
it all and went over the rail. "How do I find o-three deck?"

The sergeant looked at me and pointed his finger to a sign on the
ceiling, with a red zero and a one on it. "You're standing on the one-deck.
Then you start counting. Every deck above has a zero in front of it. Think
you can figure out where o-three is?"

"I guess so. Two decks up from here."

I walked toward a ladder going up and he stopped me.

"Hey, kid, he's not so bad, as long as you don't make him feel like
you're second-guessing him. There're only two words he wants to hear:
Yes, sir. Keep that in mind and you'll probably do O.K."

"Yes, sir," I said. Which almost made the sergeant smile. He didn't
have to tell me that he doesn't get called sir.

Now I was walking down the passageway (that's hallway at sea)
on the 0-3 deck. I saw a white cardboard sign taped on a closed door:
SECOND RANGER BATTALION HQ. I stopped and wondered whether

I was supposed to knock on the door or just open it. How do you know on a ship?

"You lost?" It was a voice that sounded familiar. I turned around and there was the tall black man I stupidly thought was a waiter, still carrying a tray with coffee cups and a silver pot.

"Didn't I tell you yesterday about officer country?"

"The battalion commander wants to see me."

He rolled his eyes. "You must be in some kind of deep shit, if the man himself wants you. I'd suggest you knock on that door, in that case, real nice and respectful like. And don't open the door until someone tells you to."

I followed his advice. Nothing happened when I knocked. I knocked again, a little harder. A voice came through the shiny wood door.

"Come in, damnit."

It wasn't what I would call an invitation. Actually it sounded like a dare. I opened the door and peeked inside. There was an old man maybe about my father's age, with a grey crew cut and skin that looked like a catcher's mitt, all tan and leathery, and the kind of eyes that could probably see through me and even the big wood door behind me.

"Don't just stand there, soldier, get in here if you've got some business."

"The sergeant told me you wanted to see me, sir."

"What sergeant? We got a lot of them on board. Be specific, soldier."

"I don't know his name, sir."

"War is won by paying attention to details, soldier, every last one of them."

"Yes, sir," I said, still thinking about what the water would feel like over the rail.

"Sit down, son." All of a sudden his voice was kind of softer, almost like my father's, not like someone's who'd put you in front of a firing squad for not knowing a sergeant's name.

I sat down in a gray steel chair with a green leather seat, like they have in the principal's office at school. It felt like that's where I was. Only instead of school stuff on the walls, there were all kinds of maps with little ships stuck all over them. There was a stack of radios that looked like they were all on, but nothing was coming out of them. The officer's desk was filled with stacks of papers and folders and loose-leaf books. And there was a smell of old burned stuff, which I guess was tobacco. Then I saw why. The CO picked up a pipe and lit it with a Zippo lighter and took a couple of long puffs. He blew out a smoke ring, and it got bigger and floated close to me.

"Tell me son, how did you get on board?"

"Just like everyone else, sir." *This is it. He knows. It's over.*

"Not true, son. The other fifteen-thousand men didn't sneak aboard, now did they?"

"I meant I came aboard on the gangway, sir."

"What's your name, son?"

"Saperstein, sir."

"What is this all about? You want to get into the war, is that it?"

"I want to do my part, sir."

He took another puff from his pipe and blew another ring. Now two of them were floating up to the ceiling like the ones that come out of the Camels sign in Times Square, only smaller, of course.

"But you're too young to be here legally, am I right?"

"I'm not eighteen yet, sir."

"That's obvious, Saperstein. Something tells me you're a pretty long way from eighteen. Maybe fifteen? Fourteen?"

I half-swallowed the word when it came out. "Thirteen."

"Did you say thirteen?"

I tried to sink down into the chair, as if I could go right through it. "Yes, sir."

The CO swung his chair around and looked up at all the maps on the wall and said, "I've got a thirteen-year-old boy on this ship who wants to do his part. We're on our way to the biggest battle of the entire war, with the largest force in history, and I've got a young stowaway to worry

about." He spun back around to look at me. "Now just what do you suggest
I do with you, young man?"

"I don't know sir."

"That doesn't surprise me one bit, that you don't know what I should
do with you."

"I'm sorry, sir." I tried to keep myself from crying, I was so scared.

 "Now don't go teary on me. That's the last thing we need right now.
Understand?"

"Yes, sir." I swallowed hard and took a deep breath.

"I'd like you to tell me what made you pull a stunt like this. I'd really
like to know."

I guess I thought when someone as important, and scary, as him asks
a question like that, I'd better answer it. So, I just started telling him the
stuff that made me decide to do what I did, everything, the Black Cat
Gang and all the rest, even buying the woman's uniform and the helmet
that was too big. I guess I talked pretty fast, because I was out of breath
when I finished. And him, he just sat there and stared at me for a while,
blowing those smoke rings, before he said anything.

"And that's it? That's what made you think you needed to put on a
uniform and get yourself in the middle of the war? A bigoted kid who
chased you up a rope with a knife?"

"Yes, sir, I guess that's it, at least part of it, maybe the biggest part."

"What's interesting is, you don't seem to be bent on revenge. You
want to change what people have been doing to you, and to a lot of other
people in the world. But you don't want to hurt them. Which makes me
wonder what kind of soldier you'd make."

"You mean the part about whoever has the most people standing up
when it's over is the winner?"

"I suppose that's one way of putting it, son. But it's an over-
simplification in today's warfare. Still, basically, that's what it gets down
to. When we get to our mission, do you have any idea how many men are
going into action on one single day?"

"Thousands?"

"More than a hundred thousand. The biggest invasion force ever amassed in the history of modern warfare. And, to use your analogy, we've got to make sure we have more men standing than they do when it's all over. But that means something else. We've got to lose as few as possible. And that's the God-awful thing about what we do. We lose men. Good, young men, who, just a few months ago, were doing very different things. Much more pleasant things, like going to school, taking a vacation with their parents, marrying their girlfriends. Now, they're being asked to do something they never would have dreamed they'd have to do one day: kill people. Worse, they're going to be asked to face the very real possibility that *they're* going to get killed. You see, son, war is a lot more than climbing ropes or proving the enemy wrong. It's a dirty, terrible business of killing. That's why we don't get people your age involved. At least we wait until someone is eighteen, although, so help me God, I don't know who figured out that's an acceptable age to start killing people, or getting killed. A lot of people, and sometimes I include myself, think an eighteen-year-old is still a boy. Guess it's because I've got one that age myself."

"Is he home with his mother?"

"No, son, he's not with his mother. He's somewhere in the Pacific, doing what you want to do. He may not feel guilty about the war, the way you do, but he thinks it's his responsibility to do something about it."

"Maybe he wants to please you, sir."

"You think he can please his father by putting himself in the line of fire?" I couldn't tell if he was angry or sad.

"I don't know, sir. I guess I want to do things that'll please my parents."

"Even though I haven't met your mother and father, something tells me that the only thing that would please them right now is to know that you're all right, that you're going home to be with them, where you belong."

"I belong here, sir."

"Are you ready to start killing if you have to? To maybe save your own life?" he asked.

I had to think about that. I tried to picture holding a gun in my hand, feeling how cold it would be, smelling the oil I remembered from Sam's Eighth Avenue Army and Navy Store. Then I tried to picture a guy maybe four or five years older than me, but still looking like a kid, a scared one, in a grey uniform and a different kind of helmet, the German kind, staring at me. I had my finger on the trigger, but it wouldn't move. Maybe because I didn't want it to.

"I guess I'm not ready," I said "But maybe I'll get ready — to kill people, I don't know, sir."

"I don't think you'll get ready, son, not in time to do anything in the way of killing the enemy on this tour of duty. But I've got an idea. Actually, it's a problem I've got, and possibly an idea of how to solve it."

He got up and started walking back and forth, real straight. "Let's start with the problem. You've managed to do something no one else has done in this war, at least as far as I know, slipping aboard a troop ship headed for war .Let me ask you something, son. Have you noticed that people on this ship aren't talking about where they're going, or what they're going to be doing when they get there?"

"Yes, sir, I guess I have noticed that."

"Don't you think it's strange? After all, soldiers generally talk about one thing when they're shipping off somewhere: Where they're headed, and what to expect. Well, there's a simple reason these men aren't talking about their destination, about their mission. You know why? Because they absolutely don't know. Oh, sure, they know they're going to storm a beach somewhere. Some of them know they're going to have to climb up cliffs on the beach. But what they don't know is where that beach is going to be. Tell me, do you have any idea where these men are headed?"

"The beaches of Normandy? In France? Arromanches?"

The colonel's mouth fell open. He shook his head, waited, and then said, real low, "Where in God's name did you get that kind of information?"

"From my French book."

"What French book?"

"I'm studying French in school. And I was reading about the Normandy region. I figured if the invasion was going to land the army in France, there was only one place where it would really work. The beaches at Normandy."

"Do you realize how many people – people in very high places, generals even – have been wrestling with the problem of where to land an invasion force in Europe this last year? Do you have any idea, son?" I didn't answer him. "These men have studied everything from weather and tide reports to the kind of trees that grow in every part of Europe, even how many goddamn cows there are in each place. Cows, for God's sake. The President of the United States, the Prime Minister of England, of Canada – they've wrestled with the question, too. And you're sitting here, in this little office, all thirteen years of you, and you're telling me you know where the best place is for an invasion to take place to liberate Europe?"

I just shrugged, which was probably the safest thing to do.

"And you're also telling me that you acquired this knowledge, this wisdom, from a textbook, in some junior high school French class? Is that what you're telling me, son?"

I shook my head.

"So, that's not the case? It wasn't in a damn school book?"

"It wasn't a textbook. It was this book I checked out of the library for extra credit, for a report."

"I can't goddamn believe what I'm hearing." He looked at me real hard, with his eyes squinting. "Are you a damn spy, son?"

"No sir, I'm not, I swear to God. Seriously, I mean it."

Then the colonel grinned at me for the first time. "Of course, I'm not saying there's anything to this idea of yours about where the invasion's going to happen. You understand that, don't you?"

"Yes, sir, I understand."

"I'm not confirming anything. Got that?"

"Yes, sir. I've got that."

"Good. Now, let's get back to this idea of yours – that you want to do your part. You see, I have a real problem with this whole business of you being on this ship. And it's not just me. I've talked to some of the people I have to answer to. Generals, in fact, and told them we've got someone on board who slipped through all our security, without being noticed. And you know what they're telling me?"

"No, sir, I don't."

"They're telling me that we can't afford to do anything about getting you back home where you belong. You know why?" I shook my head again. "I'll tell you why. Because if we let it get out that someone got through and onto this ship, as easily as you did, it would create a huge problem for us. The command of the United States Army, along with the Brits and the Canadians, too, can't let the entire world know that getting into the very heart of a top-secret operation is all that easy. Wouldn't you agree, son?"

"Yes, sir, I guess I would agree."

"That's good. I'm not saying that the Army can't admit it when it's made a mistake. In peace time, we probably could. But not when we're at war. Just think what these fifteen-thousand men, who are headed for war, would think of the people who give them orders to storm a beach, or charge a pill box. They might not have the kind of faith in their commanders they need to take orders like that, would they?"

"No, sir, I guess they wouldn't."

"So, where that leaves us, son, is this: You're not going anywhere for now. You're staying on this ship until we get to our destination. We don't have a choice about that, anyway. We can't exactly put you over the side to a waiting cruise ship that's headed in the other direction, can we?"

"No, sir, I'm really sure you can't do that."

"And, once we're in England, we'd still have the same problem, of looking very bad to the entire world. So, here's the way this situation looks to me. As much as I'd like to notify your parents that you're all right, and you'll be headed home soon, I can't do that, either. We're in a state of total radio silence. No messages anywhere. Not even back home. Especially not back home. Understand?"

"Yes, sir, especially no messages back home."

"Son, have you ever heard the song, 'You're in the Army now'"?

Of course I heard it. *You're not behind a plow. You'll never get rich digging a ditch, you're in the army now.* "Yes, sir, I've heard it."

"Well, that's what's happened here. You asked for it, and you're going to get it, at least until we can find something better to do with you. You're in the Army, son, whether you like it or not, whether *I* like it or not. We're stuck with each other."

"I'm really sorry, sir, that I did all this. That I caused so much of a problem."

"Did you really think it wouldn't cause a problem?"

"I didn't think anyone would notice, to tell you the truth, sir."

"Well, that might have been the case if you hadn't played your famous trumpet solo and stayed a little less visible, if you'd maybe stayed somewhere below decks, don't you think?"

"Yes, sir. I see what you mean."

"Well, then, there's really no point in going over what might have been. What we need to focus on now is what's going to be. An invasion is what's going to be. We've already established that. You're in the Army now. We've established that, too. Let's say it's been done through a field induction. Know what that is?"

"No, sir I don't."

"Well, no one else does, either. Because I just came up with the concept. We have something called a field promotion. It happens in time of war. Someone does something in a battle situation, and there's a reason to promote him, to lead a squad, maybe, when the real squad leader's become a casualty. Or, to recognize exemplary performance in the field, with a promotion to sergeant, say, or even a field commission to officer's rank. Now in your case, I'm simply carrying that idea a little further. With a field induction. I'm using my authority, as a line officer, to induct you into the United States Army, with a special, war-time waver of the minimum age. Who knows, we may just be making a little military history here, don't you think, son? The field induction. Do you understand it?"

"Yes, sir, I understand it. Thank you for inducting me."

He sat back down again. "I'm glad we had this little talk, and that we came to this understanding."

I had no idea of what the understanding was, other than that I'd been inducted into the United States Army by someone who had the authority to change the rules. And I didn't know what I was supposed to do next.

"Well, soldier, are you just going to sit there the rest of the day, or are you going to get back to your unit and carry on?"

"The problem is, sir, I don't have a unit to go back to."

"Maybe you do now. How about Company C, First Ranger Battalion?"

"Is it really O.K. for me to do that, to join the company?"

"I'd guess you do, because I just made it O.K. And don't get any funny ideas. Just because you're in the Army doesn't mean you're going anywhere after we land in England. It's just easier to deal with you if you're not a civilian."

I couldn't believe it. Any of it. "Thank you sir," I said, feeling pretty proud all of a sudden, being a Ranger now.

When I left the battalion office, I had to do one thing quick, report to my unit, but I had no idea where it was.

"Excuse me," I said to someone who looked familiar, from the swimming pool.

"What's up kid?"

"I'm looking for the sergeant."

"Well, I'm not looking for him." He turned to a couple of buddies. "Hey, you guys looking for the sergeant by any chance?"

"Hell no."

"No way."

"Sorry, squirt, but you must be the only one who's looking for the sergeant. What do you want him for, anyway?"

"I need to report to him."

"And why's that?"

"I need to tell him I'm in C Company now. This is C Company, isn't it?"

"You're in Company C? " Hey, Jonesy, we taking sawed-off squirts who play the trumpet now? What's the matter, weren't there any women available?"

"Must not have been. No cripples left, either. So I guess they're down to squirts."

I remembered what the CO said, that I was officially in the Army now, but there was no way I was going to tell these jerks how it happened, seeing how it was a secret and all. So I just walked away, looking for the sergeant.

"Why don't you butt-holes lay off the kid?"

It was Kaufman standing there.

"Oh, now we're hearing from Fu Man Jew," said one of the butt-holes, a pretty big guy to be messing with.

But that didn't bother Kaufman. He didn't say a word. He just threw a punch that was so fast the guy couldn't see it coming, and landed on the guy's nose.

"Jesus Christ, my nose," he yelled, holding his hands over his face.

Kaufman stood there, waiting for the guy he hit or anyone else to do something.

"You didn't have to bust his goddamn nose," said one of the other guys. "He was just giving you a hard time," he said, looking worried, probably for his own nose.

"Nobody calls me that anymore," Kaufman said, looking like he was on fire.

"We're supposed to be fighting the goddamn enemy, not each other," said the one with a bloody nose.

"You've got a point there. Maybe you'll keep it in mind the next time you want to hassle Saperstein. Or call anybody names."

"Come on, Schultz," one of the others said. "Let's get out of here. The medics can take a look at your nose." He pushed his buddy to get going and gave Kaufman a bad stare, but it looked like he wasn't going to say anything, to stay on the safe side.

"Wow, that was some punch," I told Kaufman. "You get in a lot of fights?"

"Nah, I try and avoid them, actually. But sometimes you don't have a choice. Those guys have been needling me for a long time now. It was time to teach them a lesson. I don't want to hear any more wisecracks about being Chinese, or being Jewish, or both. Didn't you feel that way after what those kids did to you at school?"

"Yeah, but I'm not much of a fighter. Maybe just once." I saw myself going after that big fat kid, Squirrel Head.

"You know, you can't spend your whole life running from it," Kaufman said. "Even when guys are bigger than you are, you got to find a way to stand up to them, to let them know they're not going to get away with pushing you around."

I thought about telling him what I did to the guy in the head, but I didn't think throwing up on somebody was what he had in mind.

"I guess I have to work on it," I said.

"If you want some help let me know. Meanwhile, I'm betting you don't get pushed around by those jerks anymore."

"That was pretty funny, what one guy said to you, Fu Man Jew," I said.

"You think that's funny?" His eyes got real narrow, and I thought, oh shit. But then he said, "Actually, it is," and he smiled and punched me, not hard, on the shoulder.

I learned something that day on the big ship. A couple of things, I figure. I ended up not feeling so small and not belonging anywhere. Maybe it wasn't such a bad idea, what I was doing.

CHAPTER

12

On the fifth day at sea, just about when I was settled into everything, well as settled in as a thirteen-year-old Ranger can ever be, I heard this big commotion out on deck, with a lot of cheering and stuff. I thought maybe it was the daily touch football game. Or maybe Charlie was playing a drum solo.

When I got out there, I saw everybody pointing out in front of the ship and I heard this one guy shout, "Land! England!"

"Yeah, man, it's bloody old England," another guy shouted in a fake English accent.

"And it's not *foockin'* America, now, is it?" This time the accent was real, I could tell. It was one of the English guys, a really big one, who must have worked down in the kitchen. His shirt and pants were so covered with stains from food , you really couldn't see any white. And he wasn't very friendly.

The first guy, who looked a little worried about the big English guy said, "What's that supposed to mean?"

"You may not like Her Majesty's food, or her vessel, but I'll not have you defaming her land."

"I don't know what the hell you're talking about."

"You're telling me now you didn't refer to the motherland as *bloody?*"

"Well, yeah, I did. Isn't that what you call it?" the soldier said.

"No, that's not what I call it. It's what I call something I'm taking a particular dislike to."

"I thought it meant something like *jolly old England*."

"Nothin' like it at all."

"Hey, I'm sorry, pal. I didn't mean any offense. But I am glad to see your country out there. Can't wait to put my feet down on it."

"Just be careful when you do," said the big Englishman.

"Sure thing, yeah, I'll do that." He obviously didn't want to tangle with a guy with really big arms and all those stains on his clothes.

Then the Englishman noticed me standing there and watching. "And what might you be starin' at with such intensity?" he asked.

"I don't know. I just thought it was interesting how a word means different things to different people."

He looked at me like I was something strange, which I had gotten used to. "You're a bit on the young side for goin' over there, aren't you now?"

"You know how it is. When there's a war on."

"It's true, I guess. They tend to reach down in the barrel, don't they."

I wasn't sure whether it was a statement or a question.

"Well, don't be givin' it a thought. If you're young for this sort of thing now, you won't be for long. What you'll be seein' has a way of agin' a body in no time a-tall. What are they callin' you, anyway?"

"Mostly *squirt*."

"I meant, what's your name?" said the big man.

"Saperstein."

"Saper-shtein?" he repeated, adding his own *h*. "Don't tell me you're one of them."

"Who?"

"The Gerries. That's a Gerry name, isn't it now?"

"No, I'm the farthest thing from German. They'd go crazy, the Germans, if they heard you call me that." He stared at me some more. "I'm Jewish."

"Ah, I see your point. No, they wouldn't be liking that. But *foock* 'em if they wouldn't. I just hope you're settlin' on givin' 'em a good piece of your foot right square in the bum. What they've been doin' to your people, you damn well should."

"Are you going to be in the war?" I asked him.

"They tell me I've been in it for three years, ridin' back an' forth across this bloody ocean. Her Majesty's Maritime Service. But things are lookin' to change now. I put in for one of those little floating coffins that take you blokes into the beach. We just might see each other on one of 'em, don't you know?"

"You want to be on a landing vessel?"

"And why not? At least then, a man gets a chance to see what's tryin' to shoot his ship out from beneath his feet. Out here, you don't see a thing if someone's out to sink you. You just hear a mighty sound like thunder and feel the guts of the vessel gettin' blown wide open, tellin' the sharks dinner's on its way."

"You've been torpedoed?"

"Three times."

"On this ship?"

"No, they haven't been able to catch us yet. I was hit on three different ships. Freighters. They all went to the bottom."

"And you survived? In the water?"

"That I did."

"What about sharks?"

"One of them fancied me." He pulled up a leg of his stained pants and I could see this big red scar that curved across his calf where most of the muscle wasn't there anymore. I counted twelve teeth marks there. It made me kind of sick.

"That's awful," I said.

"Tell me your story, if you have one."

"I guess I don't. At least not like yours. I've only seen a shark once, and it was in a tank, at Coney Island. They have an aquarium there."

"I know. A fine one at that."

"You've been there?"

"Yes, I have. And I've taken myself a ride on the coaster. The parachute jump, too. And those bangers. You call 'em hot dogs. Chap by the name of Nathan makes 'em. Had a few of those, I might add."

I liked this guy. His accent made him seem more Irish than English. I pictured him as a no-monkey-business captain on the high seas, barking orders to everybody, or even a pirate with a peg leg because a shark ate his real one.

"Where's your home?" he asked me.

"Teaneck. That's in New Jersey."

"Not familiar with it. A proper place for a lad to grow up before he goes off to war, is it?"

"Pretty good, actually."

"What of your people? Are they pleased that you'll be doin' your part?"

"I'm not sure they are. They worry a lot about me."

"They never stop doin' that, I hope you know. That's what mums and dads do. Doesn't matter whether it's in New Jersey or old Jersey. Same thing everywhere. They bring us into the world as helpless pups, raise us, teach us right, they hope, and then someone snatches us away from them to go an' do battle somewhere. I'm at least twice your age, and my people still fret. Although, they've become fond of my duty here on the Queen. They think we're too big to be shot out of the water. But they have no way of knowin' how much that bloody bastard Hitler would like to put a few holes in our mid-ships and send us to the bottom."

"We made it this time."

"We're not home yet, even though we can see it," he said. He kept looking at the land in front of us. "Good lookin' sight it will be, going into the harbor. No Statue of Liberty, mind you, but still impressive. You'll see ships like this, lined up at pier side, dozens of 'em, unloading thousands of your mates, ready to give Gerry a mighty run for his money. And it's none too soon. If we don't stop Mr. Hitler, he's going to perfect those rockets of his and level half of England before he's through. We'd appreciate it very much, thank you, if you'd get on with that invasion and bring him to his knees. We're losin' people left an' right in the cities. They spend their nights in subway stations, and then come out in the mornin' to find their homes nothin' more than piles of scattered bricks and smolderin' lumber. A terrible sight it is. Then there are the sights we aren't sure about, but keep hearin'. Those places where they take all the Hebrews, to do them in. It's a ghastly thing."

"I know," I said, getting to feel both scared and sad. He heard about the ovens, just like we did at home.

"Do your mate Grigsby here a little favor, will you?"

"Sure. What can I do?"

"I want you to kill one of those Nazi bastards for me. Just one will do, thank you. And when it's done, I want you to look him in his glassy eyes that won't be seein' anything again, and I want you to say, 'That's for Jenny Grigsby.' Will you do that for me?"

"I don't know if I can."

"And why can't you be doin' that? You're surely goin' to be killin' some Gerries, or you wouldn't be goin' where you're goin'."

"That's just it. I don't think I'll be doing any killing."

"And, pray tell, how are you goin' to be in a war and not do any killin'?"

"It's a pretty complicated story."

"I imagine it is. Well, that's all right, then. I'll be findin' me someone else to do me the favor, someone who figures that if he's goin' to war he should be plannin' on doin' some killin'."

"I hope you're not mad or anything."

"So now you think I'm daft, do you?"

"I mean, I hope you're not, you know, angry."

"If I was, you'd have the privilege of bein' the first to know of it."

"Who's Jenny Grigsby?" I asked him.

"She *was* me mum, God rest her soul."

"Oh, I'm sorry," I said. "Something happened to her in the war?"

"Yes, somethin' indeed happened to her in the war. Death happened to her."

"How?"

"That's somethin' I'd prefer not to be talkin' about, to you or to anyone, for that matter."

I thought about all the air raids in England, about the people living in subway tunnels, and the piles of bricks and burning lumber he mentioned. I wondered if Jenny Grigsby ended up under all that stuff.

"I'm very sorry for whatever happened to your mother."

"Well, don't be. It's not your fault, this war we're in, now is it?"

I didn't answer him. How could I? What would he think if I told him how I believed the Black Cat guys who told me the whole war, and Hitler, was my fault. Some things you have to keep secret, and not just when there's a war on.

CHAPTER
13

The big ship didn't reach the dock until after it was dark, which is different from what I expected. I guess I thought there'd be a big crowd of people watching us leaning over the rail and waving and stuff. But there was no one there, except some dock workers tying ropes and Army officers in green jeeps talking to each other and pointing. When I asked Kaufman about it, he told me they waited until it was dark because they didn't want the whole world to know that a huge bunch of fighting men from the U.S. were getting off a ship in Southampton to do something really big over in France. Made sense.

I was ready to get off and onto some solid ground long before we started moving down the gangway. I found the Ranger company the colonel assigned me to and got in this long line that went all the way down one side of the main deck to the other side, and back again. The English crew people were getting ready to get down on the dock too. Maybe they got a day off or something.

"Mind your p's and q's, now Saperstein, and keep your powder dry." I knew who said that before I saw him, Grigsby. He didn't have the white cook's uniform on with all the food gunk. Instead he was wearing a clean green uniform with some badges sewn on it. One was a parachute.

"Keep his powder dry?" Grigsby said to a guy in line, nodding toward me.

"Powder? does this kid wear makeup, for cryin' out loud?"

"You'd be wise to button your lip there, Yank," Grigsby said to the soldier, who looked like he didn't want any argument with the bigger Englishman.

"Hey, Saperstein, you know that guy?" It was Kaufman, who was standing a little behind me.

"Yeah. He's one of the cooks."

"The hell you say. He's a British commando. Those guys are born mean. They can kill a man with two fingers, like that." He jabbed two at my throat.

"Why would he tell me he's a cook?"

"I don't know. Security, I guess. But I'd stay away from a guy like that."

"The Germans killed his mother. He can really kill you like that, with his fingers?"

Kaufman nodded. "He can snap your neck and paralyze you, too, from behind. It's creepy what those guys can do. Just be glad he's on our side, and try to avoid him."

"Don't forget my message to Gerry," the Englishman called back to me.

"What message?" Kaufman asked. "And who's Gerry?"

"The Germans. That's what the English call them. He wants me to shoot one of them for him, and give the guy a message."

"He wants you to give a dead guy a message? See, what did I tell you? They're crazy. It must be something they do to them in training. So, you think you're going to kill a German?"

"No, I really don't. But if I see one who's been shot, I'll give him the message."

"Do yourself a favor, Sappy, if you do that. Make sure a medic sees you talking to a dead guy. You might get sent home early for being, you know —" He twirled his finger around his ear.

I finally got to the place on the deck where the gangway went down to the dock. An Army captain was standing there under a red light that made him look pretty scary. He didn't smile, but just looked at everybody going past him and said stuff to them when they went by.

"Good luck, men. Go get 'em, soldiers. Give 'em hell." And like that.

It was finally my turn to get on the gangway. I grabbed the steel railing. It was wet and cold. I could smell garbage and gasoline from down on the dock, the same smells from back in New York. My boots were slipping on the gangway, which was wet, too. I was real careful. All I needed was to fall down and they'd know I was no Ranger. They don't do that.

When I got close to the bottom, I heard people giving orders.

"Come on, look alive. Six more to this truck, that's all. You, next truck. Come on, keep moving. We don't have all night."

Pretty soon I was on the concrete dock. I started to shiver and could see people's breath. Everybody seemed to be pretty happy about getting off the ship and away from the food and sleeping in a swimming pool. It was finally my turn to lift myself up into this big truck with a canvas top on the back, and a lot of guys crowded together, sitting down. I put my palms on the steel edge of the truck floor. Problem was I was kind of short to pull myself up and spin around like everyone else. I tried anyway, but I didn't make it and slipped back down and landed on the pier on my back. It hurt pretty bad, and I had the wind knocked out of me, so I was gasping to breathe. Maybe this was it for me.

Then I felt hands under my armpits, and figured it was one of those tough looking guys yelling at everybody.

"Guess you misjudged it." It was Kaufman. "You O.K.?"

A soldier with an MP arm band came over. "What's the problem here? Come on soldier, get up and in the truck. Don't hold up the parade."

"He slipped," said Kaufman.

"Yeah, well there's no room for slipping. This is the real thing. Go on, get in."

I closed my eyes and pictured being back in the gym and Herbie Schoo with a knife telling me he was going to cut my pecker off if I didn't get up the rope in hurry. I guess that did it. Somehow I did this thing that was like squeezing everything in my whole body into my arms. It was as if they were someone else's, now, really weird. And they pulled me up until

I could get my feet on the edge of the truck floor. I got up, real shaky, and sort of fell down onto a bench. Then a lot of guys started clapping for me, like I was back on the ship playing the trumpet. I'm not sure I liked that part, because I was feeling pretty stupid. Kaufman was standing down on the ground and he didn't clap. He just raised his fingers in a v-for-victory sign, like Winston Churchill, and hopped up on the truck like it was no big deal. Maybe it was *his* arms that I had for a couple of seconds, I wondered.

"It's O.K. kid. You're a Ranger now." I thought it was Kaufman who said it, but it wasn't. Instead it was this tough-looking guy, maybe twenty or so. He reached over and knocked his fist on my helmet.

"Yeah, kid. Maybe we'll make you an official mascot." It was another guy I didn't know.   "He doesn't have to be a mascot. He can hold his own," Kaufman said.

The truck started moving and the engine was so loud everybody had to shout. And you couldn't see much because they pulled a curtain-like thing down over the back.

"Anybody know where the hell we're going?" somebody yelled out.

"Yeah. They're taking us on a tour of the Royal Palace, didn't you know?"

"That's in London, dummy. Geeze, didn't you go to school or nothin?"

"This is Southampton, isn't it?"

"It ain't Lionel Hampton."

"Gimme a break with those rotten jokes, will you?"

"Whaddya want from me? I'm a born comic."

"Yeah, well somebody ought to give you the hook. You're not making it."

"O.K., listen up." It sounded like an older guy. "When we get to camp, pick any tent that's open. No briefing tonight. Reveille's at o-five-hundred. You'll get briefed then."

"Hey, Sarge, where we going?"

"That's for the Army to know and for you not to find out yet."

"Is the Queen gonna greet us?"

"Yeah, she's gonna serve tea and crumpets."

"O.K.," said the sergeant. "That brings something up you all should pay attention to. We're guests in this country, although not for long. While we're here, we're expected to show respect for the way they do things. That includes the Royal Family. Don't be making jokes about them. The people don't take kindly to that at all. They're very loyal to their queen. Some of our guys have been known to get their lights punched out for making wisecracks about her."

I guess everybody in the truck figured they should do that, show respect, or maybe about getting their lights punched out, because it got quiet in there.

Maybe a half-hour or so later the truck slowed down and then stopped. I heard the driver yell out the window, "Got thirty for Bravo."

"How do you want your eggs?" I couldn't believe they were going to serve us eggs that time of night.

"Over easy," the driver said back.

"O.K. Second left, then first right."

Duh, it dawned on me. It was the password, to make sure we weren't a bunch of Germans in American uniforms on an American truck trying to get in someplace secret, as if that could happen. But I guess you have to be really careful. It made me think of a war movie they showed at the Teaneck Theater one Saturday afternoon. There were these soldiers in their fox holes looking out into the night, being real quiet, and then a twig or something broke. One soldier asked who was out there. The answer was something like Corporal Smith. Then our guy looked suspicious at his buddies and asked, "How many homers did Di Maggio hit in forty-three?" The guy in the dark said, "Two hundred," and our guy said, "Oh yeah? Take this you heinie bum," his machine gun went off and then everything was quiet. "If you're still alive out there," the guy with the gun said, "tell your fuehrer to get you spies subscriptions to the Sporting News before he sends you out to infiltrate us." That line got all the kids in the theater clapping and cheering.

I was a lot better getting off the truck than on it. I just jumped and didn't even fall when I landed. I followed everybody else, including Kaufman, into this big square tent. There were all these wooden cots lined up. You could actually sit up on these, not like on the ship. I picked an empty one near the front, figuring I could get out in a hurry if I had to, like if I had to go to the bathroom or something during the night. I plunked down my knapsack on a green blanket that covered the skinny mattress and felt I might get a pretty good night's sleep there. Even the mattress was clean, no ugly stains.

Kaufman saw me and came over and threw his stuff down on the cot next to me.

"Do you know where we are?" I asked him.

"I'm guessing we're about twenty miles out of Southampton, judging from how long it took us to get here. Probably just outside that small town back there. Actually, I think we're in a cow pasture."

"How can you tell?"

"Didn't you get a whiff of the cow shit on the way in?"

"Oh, I thought that was something else."

"Like what?"

"A lot of these guys are always farting. From the food on the ship, I guess."

"Wow, you *are* a city boy. Can't tell the smell of cow shit from a fart. You need to get out in the country some time."

A sergeant, not one from the ship, came into tent and said, "As soon as you get settled in it'd be a good idea to get some sleep, because you're not going to be doing much of that after tonight. Reveille's in four and-a-half hours. Chow's at 0-four-thirty, and muster's at five-hundred hours." I still had to count on my fingers what military time was. But the morning was easy. It was later, when it got into thirteen hundred or twenty-two hundred that it got confusing.

"Jesus Christ, four hours of sleep?" said Kaufman. "Big sports, these guys are."

"This ain't the Ritz Hotel or nothing," said a guy in the cot next to me.

"No shit," said Kauman, and then he rolled over.

I settled in for my first night in Europe. I pulled the blanket up close around my neck and tucked my chin in it because it was cold in the tent. The wool blanket felt just like the one at camp, and smelled like it, too, like moth balls. That made me think about the nights there, in a cabin instead of a big tent, with eight kids in it instead of a hundred or so.

Pretty soon I was asleep and having this dream that I have a lot, about my first dance of the summer at Chickawaw. It was with Camp Waseatta, a girl's camp a few miles away. That's where I met Marcia Feinberg, the same age as me, and real pretty. It took me a while to get up the nerve to ask her to dance. Actually, I didn't do the asking. She did. I guess she noticed me staring at her legs, which were real brown and long, and her short shorts showed them off real well. She wore a white blouse that was kind of tight over her breasts. She walked over to me and said, "Are you going to ask me to dance, or just stand there staring at me?"

That threw me for a loop. "I wasn't staring," I said. Which was a big lie, because I couldn't take my eyes off her.

"Well?" she said.

"Well what?" That was brilliant of me, wasn't it.

"Do you want to dance with me?"

"Yes. Definitely. I'd really like to dance with you, seriously, I mean it."

And that's what we did. The music was slow, which was nice. I held her as close as I dared, considering if I got too close, well, you know what happens when you're up against a girl with great legs and a tight blouse. She must have noticed that I was trying to keep from bumping into her with, well, down there. I didn't want to poke her, God no, I didn't.

But she stopped all of a sudden, and I didn't, and ran right into her. She looked at me with a big grin and said, "Well, now, it feels like you're glad to see me, as they say."

I kind of thought she did the sudden stop thing on purpose. A couple of my cabin mates thought so too when I told them about it afterwards, and how she didn't try to pull back. I did, though, actually, but she held on to me too tight for me to move away, so I just kept dancing that way. And it was the greatest thing I ever felt, if you can imagine. We danced for three songs that way. Finally my counselor, Ray Finotti, came over and whispered to me, "What's the matter, Saperstein, are you stuck?" And he grinned and walked away.

Well, there I was, back again at camp, in my dream, dancing with Marcia, not in a cot with a hundred guys around me.

I felt something on my arm, a shove.

"Hey, Saperstein, what are you moaning about?" It was Kaufman, shoving me.

"Nothing," I said.

"That's hard to believe. You better let go of that before someone sees you."

He was looking at me, below the waste, and I realized I was holding my penis, which was very hard, making a lump in the blanket. I was too embarrassed to say anything, but just moved my hand up to my stomach like I was just scratching it.

"It's O.K. There are probably a whole bunch of guys doing the same thing, but not next to me. You woke me up."

"Sorry," I said and turned over on my stomach, hoping that would make things go down.

• • •

I got back to sleep again, and the next thing I knew I was having another dream. I was in camp again, and not at a dance, and I was playing reveille on my bugle to get everybody up. It was strange, like it was really happening. That's because it was, and I wasn't dreaming. Somebody was playing reveille. Actually it was a record. I could tell by the scratchy sound coming over some speakers into the tent, waking everybody up. Guys were complaining it was the middle of the night, yelling things like "shut the hell up" and "shove that horn up your ass," sort of like what I used to hear at camp, but a little nastier.

Then there was another scratchy record playing mess call, which I used to do, too.

"Let's see if what they feed us is any better than the crap on the ship," somebody yelled out.

Actually, it was pretty good, the breakfast we got in a long mess tent. You went through the chow line with metal trays and first somebody plopped down scrambled eggs, which tasted powdery, but pretty good. Next came ham slices, and then some white stuff that looked like cereal, but wasn't really. I found out what it was when a guy with a southern accent at the next table said, "Man, these grits are the real thing. Haven't had 'em in a coon's age."

"Careful about that *coon* talk," said a soldier sitting across from him, sort of pointing his head at two Negro cooks in white uniforms working in the chow line.

"Oh, yeah, forgot about that. Just habit," said the southerner. "Besides I mean raccoons, not, you know, colored guys."

After breakfast, there wasn't much to do except wait for the muster we heard about, but it never really happened. Kaufman said that's mostly what you do in the Army. Hurry up and wait for something. Some guys read paperback books, and others tried to go back to sleep again. I laid on my cot and tossed my autographed baseball ball up in the air and caught it, over and over.

The tent was pretty quiet, until a guy stuck his head inside the flap and yelled, "I know you guys can't climb ropes worth a crap, but any chance you now how to jump 'em?"

"What are you, some infantry pansy wanting to play jump rope?" some guy yelled.

"Get oudda here," another one shouted.

"I'm not kidding," the guy at the flap said. "There's a bunch of English kids, little girls, out on the road who want to learn American jump rope games. They're cute as hell. Hey, it's better than sitting on your butts all day."

There was a whole lot of groaning and wisecracks about little English girls. Then a few Rangers got up and one of them said, "Nothing much else to do around here," and headed for the door. Then a few more got up, too, and did the same thing. Kaufman looked at me, like he was asking me a question. I shrugged my shoulders and we both started walking out.

One of the Rangers in front of us said, "Hey, I bet the squirt knows all the routines."

"I told you, get off his back. He's a good kid," another one said.

"I was only kiddin'. Relax. Hey, squirt," he called out, "You comin'?"

I guess if I had to be called something, squirt wasn't the worst thing I could think of, and they said it like they maybe wanted me to stick around. I liked that.

When we came to the gate we went through the night before, there was an MP standing there watching us. "Where do you think you're going?" he said.

"Just outside the gate," the soldier who came and got us said. "To help those kids over there." He pointed to a group of a dozen-or-so girls, who seemed about eight or nine years old. They stood waiting against a stone wall in front of an old house. One of the girls held a long rope that looked like a clothesline. They watched the soldiers and the MP, who turned to study the girls, and then back to the men.

"Aren't they a little on the young side for you guys?" the MP said.

"Hey, get your mind out of the gutter. I've got a kid that age," the guy who brought us over said.

"O.K., O.K., go on out. But don't go any further away. Camp orders. You have to stay in sight of the gate."

"Thanks," the soldier said. "By the way, do you know *strawberry shortcake?*"

"Go have your tea party with the girls, wise guy."

I could hardly believe my eyes when I saw these soldiers walking over to jump rope. Here were grown men, fighting men, who were itching to kill as many bad guys as they could, and maybe even get killed themselves, spending their last free time skipping rope with young English girls. I asked Kaufman why they would do it.

"It's the boredom, mixed in with the terror. Everybody knows what we're going to do in a couple of days. You get a choice. Either keep getting scared about what might happen, or tell yourself you're so bored with all the waiting that you need something to break the monotony. And can you think of a better, more stupid thing to do than jump rope? Besides, think about this. What's the whole world asking us to do?"

"Fight?"

"Not just fight. Maybe die fighting. Maybe take a bullet in the gut that'll rip you wide open, and you lay there staring at all that slimy stuff you're trying to hold in with your hands. Or seeing a helmet in the sand next to you — with a head in it, your buddy's head."

That was enough to make me feel like I was going to heave. But I fought it down.

"And what are these kids asking us to do? Jump rope with them. So, how would you rather spend this boring time? Thinking about what could happen to us, or playing a dumb game with some cute kids who probably don't get to have much fun anymore?"

I got the point. Then I saw this girl, maybe two or three years younger than me. She walked over. She had on a heavy wool coat that looked too big for her and worn out around the cuffs, like it once belonged to a big sister, knee socks and brown leather shoes with buckles. Her hair was long and brown, with a straight part down one side. Her cheeks were red, probably from the cold air, or maybe because she was embarrassed. But it was her eyes that got me. They were this bright, sort of purple' color. Now she reminded me of Elizabeth Taylor in "National Velvet." She came pretty close and stopped, looking at me with those great eyes.

"Would you help us with our jumping?" she asked me. She had that neat English accent, just like Elizabeth Taylor, and all of a sudden I stopped thinking about what Kaufman said, the getting killed and all. It felt like I was someplace safe, like home.

"I haven't really jumped rope," I said, which was a little fib, since I did it a couple of times with my two girl cousins from the Bronx, but I didn't want the guys I was with to know it. I had enough problems already, if you know what I mean.

"One of the other Yanks says you're good with ropes," she said and pointed to Kaufman. He just had this big grin on his face.

"What kind of help do you want?"

"We need people to hold and turn the ropes for us. And we also want to do some of the jumps we've seen in American cinema."

Cinema. I knew the word, but I never used it. I pictured myself back in Teaneck, asking some of the kids if they wanted to go to the *cinema*.

"Do you know Double Dutch?" the girl asked.

"Actually, yes, I, uh, do know it." I didn't tell her my cousins taught me it.

"It is American, isn't it?"

"I guess. I don't know why they call it Dutch, like Dutch treat. That's what we call it when people go out somewhere and they pay for themselves."

"That's funny," she said, with a little giggle.

"We also say we're in Dutch when we get in trouble, in hot water."

"That's funny, as well." she said.

I didn't know what else I should be talking about. I only knew I wanted to keep talking, even though she was younger than me. And I didn't have any, well, wrong ideas about her. She's just a nice girl, the kind you respect.

"Hey, Saperstein, you gonna stand there all day flirting, or help these kids out?" one of the soldiers yelled out to me.

"I'm not flirting. I'm just trying to explain stuff."

"Yeah, sure," he said. "Hey, young lady, watch this guy. He's a slick operator."

She looked at me and smiled. "Are you? A slick operator?"

"No, really, I'm not, seriously."

"I'm sure you're not. You seem like a nice American soldier."

"Thank you."

She turned around and skipped over to the other girls who were waiting and whispering to each other. She said something to them and they all laughed. I didn't know what she said, but I just hoped it wasn't about flirting and being a slick operator. Then she came back to me and said, "We would like very much to learn Double Dutch from you. But we hope it won't get you into Dutch, or hot water."

I have to admit that I liked this girl, but I knew nothing could ever happen with her. I mean, how could I possibly marry an eleven-year-old? We could be friends, though, which I was hoping might happen before we left for France.

"We're ready. Shall we begin?" she said.

"Sure. You need two ropes."

"We have them. By the way, I don't know your name."

"Saperstein."

"Is it Mister Saperstein?"

"Just Saperstein is O.K."

"I'm Veronica. And just Veronica is all right as well," she said. Then she turned to her friends, who were watching us."Come, two lines now, for Double Dutch."

The other girls giggled and eagerly lined up. Veronica approached the group of waiting soldiers.

"Could we possibly have four twirlers?" she asked them. Nobody said anything. They all just looked at each other, like when a sergeant asks for volunteers to go on a dangerous mission. Finally, Kaufman walked over and picked up one end of a rope.

Then I did the same thing.

"O.K., guys," Kaufman said. "Don't be bashful. We need two more. I promise I won't tell anyone back at camp." He thought a moment. "Actually, I *will* tell 'em you skipped rope if you don't twirl it."

That was all it took to get two more guys to come over.

"I think we're ready," Veronica said.

All of a sudden I felt like I was in charge of something, which I wasn't really used to. I tried to sound like a drill sergeant, which is a big laugh, and started giving orders to soldiers.

"O.K. It's really easy. You get one rope going first. Then, everyone in the first line takes a turn in and out. Next, the second rope, that's you two guys. The ropes are supposed to just miss each other. And the rest of the jumpers go in and out. It sounds hard, but once you get the rhythm, you'll see, it works."

"Shall we begin?" said Veronica, who signaled Kaufman and me to start the first rope going. She jumped in, and got into the rhythm like a pro. On each jump, her coat flew open, and I saw more of her legs, even above the tops of her knee socks, when her plaid skirt rode up. I tried not to think of how pretty she was, which wasn't easy.

Veronica signaled a second girl, who replaced her, and then the third and the fourth.

"Now the other rope," I called out. The two twirlers overlapped their rope with the first one, and now we had two of them going. Veronica jumped in, all smiles, and did the double jump like there was nothing to it. The others did the same thing, laughing and hollering like it was something they weren't used to doing, which they probably weren't, with the war and all the air raids.

"How about Double Dutch with pepper now?" I shouted.

"With pepper? What's that, Saperstein?" Veronica said

"Faster, that's what."

"All right, then. Let's do pepper. How fast must we go?"

"As fast as we can twirl, and as fast as you can jump."

The four of us twirled as fast as we could. You could feel the wind from the flying ropes that made this slapping sound when they hit the cobblestones, and the leather shoes hitting, too. We twirled even faster until one of the girls got tripped and all the others fell into her and went down in a pile like a bunch of dominoes. They just stayed there on the ground, giggling and pointing at each other. And for a second, I thought maybe I'd like to move back there, to England, when the war was over and maybe wait until Veronica was old enough to get married and we could have kids and all that. But it was just for a second.

"So," Veronica said, all out of breath and laughing. "That was Double Dutch, with pepper, was it?"

"Are you all right?" I held out my hand to help her up. She grabbed it with hers, which was real warm and a little wet. She stood up and brushed dust from her coat.

"Yes, I'm fine. It was great fun. Thank you."

I looked around at the pile of giggling girls on the ground and at the Rangers who were watching and looking pretty happy about it all. I couldn't help thinking that the world is on fire with this awful, crazy war, people killing and getting killed, and everyone who came over on that ship is going to be in the middle of it pretty soon, and we're playing jump rope with little girls. Maybe it was a strange thing to do. But I actually couldn't think of anything that would make more sense than what we just did.

"We better get back," one of the soldiers, a corporal, said. "We're not supposed to be out here in the first place."

Every single guy was looking pretty happy, winking at the girls, and the girls were looking up at them like they were heroes. A private reached into his field jacket and pulled out two Hershey Bars. He asked if anyone else had any bars. Then another guy pulled one out, and another held up two bars. I didn't have any Hersheys, but I did have two Baby Ruths I was saving. I was going to save them for an emergency, and I figured this was one, for some kids who probably hadn't had any candy since the bombs started dropping. I swear the girls' eyes were about to pop out of their heads when they saw the treats. One of the girls stopped and just stared at the candy bars, maybe afraid of them.

Then Kauman said, "It's O.K., ladies. We have so many Hershey Bars and Baby Ruths, we couldn't possibly take them all with us. And if we tried to eat them all before we left, we'd get sick."

It was Veronica who finally stepped forward. She looked curiously at the Baby Ruths in my hand.

"What is a Baby Ruth?" she said.

"It's peanuts and caramel, wrapped in a delicious coating of sweet milk chocolate." I guess I sounded like a radio commercial.

Veronica reached out and took one. She looked at the wrapper, and other girls looked at her. "Yes, that's exactly what it says. Peanuts and caramel, wrapped in a delicious coating of sweet milk chocolate. Thank you, Saperstein."

"I hope you enjoy it," I said.

That was all it took for the rest of the rope jumpers to stop being so shy, and they took the candy the we were holding out. They all did this funny thing, I guess they call it a curtsy. And then the corporal said we had to go, even though we really didn't want to yet.

".Where do you live in America?" Veronica asked me.

"A place called Teaneck. It's in New Jersey."

"Actually, I've heard of New Jersey. But not Teaneck."

"It's not very big. I was born in a place called Jersey City."

"Not *New* Jersey City?" she asked.

"No. But now that you mention it, it would make sense, being in New Jersey."

Then, out of the blue, she said, "I thought perhaps you might like to come for supper this evening."

Now I really didn't know what to say. The idea of a real supper, cooked in a pot instead of a big tub sounded pretty great. So did having it with a family.

"I don't know if I can do that. They might not let me come out of the camp. Or, if I did come out, maybe I couldn't get back in."

"It sounds quite confusing to me," she said, chuckling.

"I know. It is."

"I could ask my mum if it would be all right to have a guest, just in case you could come. Would you want to wait while I do that?

"Thank you very much, but I think I should get back into camp. It's really nice of you to ask."

"Well, maybe if I see you again tomorrow, you could find a way to get out." She paused. "And back in."

"O.K., then. Well, it was fun, showing you Double Dutch."

"Yes! With pepper, too. Thank you."

I saw the other girls looking at me pretty close and trying to hear what Veronica and I were saying. I guess they thought we were flirting after all, but I hoped they realized I was too old for that, or she was too young. Or both.

"Good-bye, then," I said.

"Good-bye. And thank you again for the Baby Ruth."

When I went through the camp gate, I stopped and saw Veronica watching me and waving. It felt good. But a little sad, too. I waved back at her and walked through all the tents, there must have been a hundred. And I told myself there'd be plenty of time to talk to girls after the war. Still, thinking about a home-cooked meal, cooked by someone's *mum,* gave me that funny feeling in my chest, the good-bye feeling I used to call it when my parents went home after visiting day at camp. I figured maybe the next day I'd get a chance to go to Veronica's house, and I even started practicing to myself saying stuff like, "How do you do, sir? Nice to meet you, ma'm. This is a nice house." But what if it had been hit by bombs, like what was happening in London, and there was no roof?

Actually, I never had the chance to meet Veronica's parents and see what shape their house was in. Kaufman told me all of us who went out the gate were in some kind of trouble, and we had to watch our step and not try it again, because we were going to pull out for somewhere, maybe in the middle of the night. So I just stayed on my cot and tossed my ball like I did at home all the time. When I watched it go up and back to me enough times, I usually fell asleep. And that's what happened there in the tent.

Then all of a sudden I was sitting in the left-field stands at the Polo Grounds, watching my Giants play the evil Dodgers. Wendell Cooper stood up from his crouch behind home plate, called time out, and trotted over to where I was sitting, in the first row, so it had to be a dream, because I never got to sit in the first row, except on my birthday last year when my father took me to the game. Cooper stood there, looking even bigger than he really was, in his mask, shin guards and chest protector. Nobody could figure out why he came over and was looking at me.

He yelled up at me. "Hey, kid, got somethin' to write with?"

"Sure," I yelled back. "I have this swell Paper Mate pen that writes upside down and under water."

"Will it write on cowhide?"

"I don't know. They never said."

"Well, lemme have it, and I'll see."

I kind of froze. Not that I didn't want to give him my Paper Mate. I just kept remembering what he said he wanted to do to me on the subway platform.

"Go on, kid, give him the pen," yelled a guy behind me.

Another one yelled, "He won't steal it from you. He's got plenty-a-pens."

I leaned over the wall and dropped the pen to Cooper. He caught it in his big catcher's mitt. Then he reached in his back pocket and pulled out a shiny new baseball. He wrote something on it, then tossed it up to me. Thank God I caught it. Who knows what would've happened if I dropped it. I tried to stop my hand from shaking so I could read what he wrote. When I did, I saw what it was: *To a fearless Giant fan and good friend, Wendell Cooper.*

"Well, kid, now you've got the whole roster. And you don't have to chase me down any train platforms any more. O.K.?" he shouted up to me.

"Yes, sir, Mr. Cooper. Thanks a million."

"Call me Wendell, O.K.?"

I couldn't do that. Not just because he was older, but because he was a New York Giant. Then he trotted away, back to home plate, 365 feet away. The fans in the left field stands started clapping. It was for him, but I thought maybe it was just a little for me, too. People started stomping their feet on the metal floor of the stands, and it just kept getting louder and louder.

All of a sudden I woke up and saw where the metal banging was really coming from, not in the Polo Grounds, but from a big garbage can at the front of the tent. A sergeant was standing over it and banging it over and over.

"Rise and shine, up and at 'em. It's time to make some history," the sergeant said and he kept on banging the can.

"Jesus Christ. Do you have to bust our eardrums?" a sleepy Ranger groaned.

"What time is it?" another one said.

"Three-thirty," said the sergeant.

"In the afternoon?"

"Three-thirty on the morning of June 5, 1944." The way the sergeant said the date, he made it sound special.

"Let's go. Mess hall closes in a half-hour. Get a move on, unless you want to move out on an empty stomach," the sergeant barked at us.

"Hey, Saperstein," Kaufman yelled over to me. "This is it. Hear what he said? Make some history."

Actually, I was wishing I could have stayed in that dream a little longer. It seemed pretty real. I could even smell the spilled beer and the hot-dog mustard, even the leather of the baseball my new imaginary friend signed. All I could smell now was the oily canvas of the tent and what it's like when a bunch of men who didn't shower are waking up. I rubbed my eyes and when I looked up the big sergeant was standing right over me, holding a stack of white papers.

"Here kid. A personal letter from the boss." He handed me one of the papers, and moved along the other cots.

It was a mimeographed letter he gave me. I had to squint to make it out under the weak light bulb hanging down on a wire.

Soldiers, Sailors and Airmen of the Allied Expeditionary Force, it said at the top.

A chill raced through my whole body. The familiar tingling moved up my legs, and I realized that I was one of that group, part of something called the Allied Expeditionary Force.

You are about to embark upon the Great Crusade, toward which you have striven these many months.

The eyes of the world are upon you. The hopes and prayers of liberty loving people everywhere march with you.

Your task will not be an easy one. Your enemy is well trained, well equipped and battle-hardened. He will fight savagely.

But this is the year 1944!...The tide has turned! The free men of the world are marching together to Victory!

I have full confidence in your courage, devotion to duty and skill in battle. We will accept nothing less than full victory!

Good luck! And let us all beseech the blessing of Almighty God upon this great and noble undertaking.

General Dwight David Eisenhower

I read the letter again, and paid attention to every word, especially at the end...*beseech the blessing of Almighty God*...so I decided to do some beseeching.

"Please, God, bless all of us. If you agree that it *is* a great and noble undertaking, like the General says, please don't let me mess any of it up. It's more important than anything, even the pennant and the world series. Thank you."

CHAPTER

14

As we were all getting ready for the big move out I looked around the tent and felt I stood out like a sore thumb. Everybody else had all kinds of stuff to pack — carbines, M1 rifles, bayonets, ammunition belts, knives and even .45 automatic pistols. All I had was my knapsack and helmet, which I guess nobody noticed, because they were too busy getting ready for where we were going next. Nobody was laughing or kidding around anymore. You could feel how everything got real serious all of a sudden. It felt like time for war.

"Maybe you could be a medic," Kaufman, said to me. He was the only one who noticed I didn't have any equipment. "All you'd need is an arm band with a red cross and some bandages."

The colonel, the one who made me a soldier, came up to me and said, "We need to talk, son."

"Yes, sir?" My voice was weak and shaky and I wondered what sort of trouble I was in now.

"The kid's in for it now," a private who was watching said. Another guy shook his head, like he felt sorry for me.

"Let's step outside," the colonel said and started walking to the open flap. I followed him but didn't say anything.

When we got outside I noticed the colonel had his helmet on now and there was this big pistol, with a pearl handle, hanging on his belt. He definitely looked ready for battle.

"Young man, we still haven't settled this matter of what to do with you."

"Yes, sir," I said. I felt my legs getting numb, and started to shake a little.

I've discussed your situation — *our* situation — with staff, and even with the high command."

I tried to figure out how high the command actually went. I thought about the letter from General Eisenhower. Did someone actually tell him about me? Did he get really mad when he heard? *I sent that letter to soldiers, sailors and airmen — not to some goddamn thirteen-year-old kid. .*

The colonel said, "We can't be sending messages anywhere about you and giving away our position. And there's still that problem of how it would look to the nation, which expects us to be performing with nothing less than perfection now. We can hardly admit that we allowed a child to infiltrate the most secretive mission of the entire war, can we?"

"No, sir, I guess we — I mean, you — can't."

"Well, then, do you have any bright ideas about what we should do with you?"

"Make me a medic?"

"Son, do you have any idea what sort of job a medic is going to have in this operation?" I didn't answer him. "I didn't think so. He's unarmed, but he goes into the thick of battle. He's going to have to dodge everything from machine-gun fire to exploding mortars and land mines. He has to evacuate the wounded — after he makes sure they're not dead. He has to stop bleeding and administer morphine. Do you think those are things you can do?"

"I think I can probably dodge the bullets and help evacuate people."

"Maybe you can, son. But do you think for one moment that I'm going to let you go into the heat of battle? I may be a hard-ass old soldier who can't afford to go soft, but I'll be goddamned if I'm going to let a boy put himself in that kind of harm's way."

"Could I stay with the Rangers?"

"You think that's any safer than being a medic? Let me tell you something about that. These Rangers have been training for more than a year for this operation. They've learned to swim with eighty pounds of gear on their backs, to sneak up on pill boxes and lob grenades in them, hand-to-hand combat, climbing hundred-foot cliffs."

"I can do that," I said. "Climbing cliffs."

"What makes you think you can?"

I told him about what happened in gym class, and how I got the award for breaking the school record for rope climbing. He just shook his head.

"Climbing up a muddy cliff, with no rope to hang on to isn't the same as doing it in gym class."

"There was a guy with a knife threatening to cut off my — ." I didn't finish.

The colonel stared at me. "And how do you plan to dodge the enfilading?"

"I don't know what that is, sir."

"Doesn't surprise me. It's not something they teach in junior high school. Enfilading is raking an area with machine gun fire, constant sweeping, in this case, of the beaches. It's something the Germans are good at. They don't have to aim at anyone, just keep pouring enough machine-gun fire out, and they create a shower of lead that's brutal to get through. The only thing that can stop it is infiltration of their emplacements, knocking them out. But the trick is getting through and up to them. No, son, I don't think that's a job for a thirteen-year-old. Here's what I'm thinking we should do with you. I heard that you made friends with some children outside the gate yesterday. Helped them jump rope, I understand."

That really bothered me a lot, that he found that out. I figured the army has eyes everywhere, like the saying goes. But I didn't like the picture of me playing with girls while everybody else in camp was getting ready to go into battle.

"I was just trying to help them sir — the girls."

"That's fine. And well you should help them. Anyway, I have a feeling you might be able to stay with one of those girls' families. Maybe they can take care of you until this operation is complete, and we can break radio silence to get you sent home."

"But I'm not ready to go home yet, sir."

"You may not be, son, but I'm sure your parents are ready to have you back. Shouldn't you be thinking about them?"

"Yes, sir, I should be thinking about them, and I do, all the time. But I still have to do what I think is the right thing."

"And when you're eighteen, you can do just that. I hope to God, though, we won't still be in a war. But if we are, you'll be free to do your part. In the meanwhile, I think we ought to see about some arrangements for you to stay in a home here. Think about it, you'll be getting decent food, a warm bed and some kids your own age to talk to."

"No, they're younger sir." The colonel looked at me funny. "Those girls. They're only about eleven, maybe twelve at the most."

"I see, yes, they're younger. Well, maybe they have older brothers and sisters. That would help, wouldn't it?"

"Actually, sir, it wouldn't matter. I don't think I should be in somebody's home, when everybody else is going on the crusade."

"Crusade?"

"That's what General Eisenhower called it. In his letter to us."

"I see. I had forgotten that. But, rules are rules. You broke one of them, you know, actually a few of them. And I can't just let you go on breaking any more."

"Yes, sir. I understand. But could I at least stay here in the camp, instead of in a home?"

"That would be possible, except for one thing. In a few hours, there won't be any camp. The army is going to tear everything down and leave the land the way it was in the first place, a cow pasture. Now, if you want to sleep outside with the cows, that's your business. I wouldn't recommend it, though."

The colonel looked at his watch. "I'm afraid I don't have any more time to spend dealing with this problem. If we weren't under orders to depart immediately, I'd help you find a place to stay. But I can't do that. I'm going to have to trust you to do the right thing on your own. My advice to you is, when the sun comes up, go find some of those kids you met yesterday, and see what kind of arrangements you can make to stay with someone. When we've accomplished our mission, I'll make sure someone gets back here to get you on your way home."

The colonel held out his hand. "Son, I admire the courage you showed to get over here, although I have to say I don't approve of how you did it. Truth is, I have to disapprove. It's my responsibility. Besides, I'm a father, I told you that. But, I've got to go now. Good luck, young man. And please, be careful, will you?"

"Yes, sir. I will. Thank you."

I snapped to attention and gave the colonel my best salute, even though I smacked my forehead so hard you could hear it. For the first time, he actually smiled.

"That's a fine salute, son. You've got the makings of a good soldier." And he turned around and walked away, over to the end of the camp where truck motors were starting up and people were shouting orders.

About an hour later, I was standing alone outside the big tent, which was quiet and empty now. I was wearing my helmet and my knapsack was on my back, ready to go somewhere. Everything was happening so fast to make the place a cow pasture again. A lot of the tents were already collapsed in piles on the ground. Most of the trucks were gone, and the ones that were still there were getting loaded up with men and their stuff.

All of a sudden I felt alone out there. It was the first time since I walked up the gangway of the ship that I wasn't surrounded by people, sometimes maybe too many people, but now I kind of missed them. I really missed my family, too. Still, I wasn't ready to go back. I hadn't done anything yet that I could say was doing my part. Playing the trumpet with Charlie? Teaching Double Dutch to some girls? That's not exactly being a soldier. What was I supposed to do, listen to the colonel and stay with a family there until I could get sent home? Or listen to something my rabbi said to me at the end of my Bar Mitzvah, in front of everyone sitting there and grinning at me: *"Follow your heart, always, even if your head tells you otherwise."*

But then I remembered what my mother said to me more times than once: *"Listen to what your father and I tell you. We know what's good for you."*

And the rabbi once said in Hebrew school, "*Always respect your parents' wishes, no matter what.*" I guess that's what my father meant when he said to a friend who isn't Jewish, "Judaism is an on-the-other-hand religion."

How about this one from my mother: *"If your friends are going to jump off a cliff and kill themselves, are you going to follow them?"* Would she say the same thing about climbing up a cliff instead of jumping off one?

Anyway, it was like one big on-the-other-hand and I didn't know what I should do. But then I heard a voice that I knew coming from a truck that was driving by.

"Hey, Saperstein, let's go!" It was Kaufman standing and waving on the back of the truck filled with guys. It was moving slow, headed for the camp gate. "Come on. Get your butt in here."

I started trotting to the truck. My helmet was bumping down on my nose, and the knapsack was flapping against my shoulders. Maybe that was what made a couple of guys inside laugh.

"I'm not supposed to go," I shouted.

"What are you talking about? This is your unit."

I wasn't going to tell Kaufman about what the colonel said and the problem I was having about whether to follow his orders or not. Besides, how could I do that running behind a moving truck? Anyway, I had to make a quick decision, to either try and get up on a truck again or just stay there in the cow pasture. I made a quick decision and said, "Wait up, I'm coming."

Kaufman sat on the back edge of the floor and kept one hand on a bench. He reached out his other hand and I tried to reach it.

"You gotta go faster," he said.

I did the best I could, thinking I was trying to stretch a single into a double, but not with a slide or anything. I pushed one hand up with all my might, hoping my arm would suddenly get longer.

"That's it, I've got you. Just swing yourself up," Kaufman said.

I took a deep breath and jumped up, kicking my feet like crazy, as if that would get me in the truck. It didn't. The truck started going faster and I was about to drop back into the dirt, or maybe cow crap. But then a couple of Rangers inside started yelling at me, with stuff like, "Go squirt" and "You can do it kid."

Then Kaufman screamed, "Pull, goddamnit, pull, Saperstein." And I guess I did, because all of a sudden I was laying on top of Kaufman.

"O.K., O.K., get off me," he said.

"Hey, kid," one guy yelled, "You gonna kiss him?"

Kaufman pushed me off him and I managed to stand up. But then I fell back down when the truck all of a sudden started going a lot faster through the gate of the camp. I just sat on the floor a while and saw a lot of guys smiling and nodding at me. I broke one more rule, getting into the truck, but tried not to think what the colonel would do or say when he found out. I kind of hoped he would smile again and say something like, "I knew you'd do that, son." Fat chance.

The driver slowed down again and made a turn. We were back in town again. I looked out the canvas flap and saw the same girls from the day before. They were waving at us. Then I saw Veronica, holding a rolled up rope. I didn't think she saw me, and figured that was probably O.K., since I couldn't very well jump back off the truck, now could I?

But she did see me. And she ran after the truck and yelled out, "Saperstein! Mum said she would like to have you for dinner. Can you come?"

"Not tonight," I yelled back, and the truck started moving faster again, pulling farther away from her, and she started getting smaller. "When I get back."

She shook her head, like she didn't know what I said. She still looked like Elizabeth Taylor, and I didn't know what I looked like to her. Probably just a strange kid who can't even climb into a truck by himself. But then she did something that almost made me jump off. She put her hand on her mouth and blew me a kiss, which is something I knew I'd never forget. And I didn't. That's no bull.

"Anybody know where we're going?" a guy up front said.

"Hell, I don't even know where we've been," somebody else said.

"Doesn't matter. Whatever this place is, we won't be coming back, that's for sure."

"I don't know. The kid might be. He seems kind of sweet on that young number with the blue eyes."

"I think we're going to Portsmouth," someone else said.

"That's in New Hampshire, for God's sake."

"No it's not." This guy had a southern accent. "It's in Virginia. Don't you know your geography?"

"Hey, genius, Portsmouth was in England first. Whaddya, retarded or somethin'?" It was obviously a New Yorker. He sounded like the big guy who made the Fu Man Jew crack at Kaufman. Which could mean trouble again, being in the same truck and all.

"Yeah, well what's in Portsmouth, anyway?" the southerner said.

"More ships and landing craft than you ever seen down wherever you're from, cracker. Betcha that's where they're gonna load us up."

It was strange, the way Kaufman just sat there on the bench next to me and said nothing. He acted like he didn't hear any of the stuff that was being said. I wondered if he was mad at me, the way he just kept staring at the green canvas that fell down over the back of the truck, almost like he could see through it. I tried staring at it, too, not that I could see through it like him.

Finally I looked at him and said, "Thanks I couldn't have made it if you didn't pull me in."

It was like Kaufman didn't hear me, or that I wasn't even there. Maybe he got tired of helping me. I tried again.

"I really mean it. Thanks," I said.

It seemed like a long time, maybe five minutes, at least, before he said anything.

"Did you say something?"

"A while ago, yeah," I said.

"What was it?"

"I just said thanks for helping me."

"Sure. You're welcome." And then he got quiet again, just staring at the canvas.

Pretty soon I could hear things going on outside, like other trucks, horns honking and whistles. We were getting closer and closer to the noise, and pretty soon it was real loud, people shouting at each other, and more whistles and more trucks driving around, too, the way things sounded back in New York on the dock. Our truck stopped short and a guy opened the flap so we could see outside.

It was something like I never saw before. I couldn't tell how many trucks were lined up, hundreds it looked like. But that wasn't all. There were tanks, too, as far as you could see. And a lot more people than the fifteen thousand who were on the ship. What it looked like to me was every American serving in the army was all of a sudden right there in one place at one time.

When I looked past all the trucks and tanks, I saw something that made me wonder if we were back where we got off the ship again, in Southampton. There was grey as far as you could see, the ground and the sky, like you couldn't tell where one ended and the other started. It was cold and windy, not like it's supposed to be in June. I could see docks, too, that must have gone on for miles, but they looked different from the ones we came off the ship on, so I figured it wasn't the same place. Then I saw rows and rows of landing boats, LCAs, tied up and looking like they were ready to go someplace. It was pretty clear that I was right, what I told the colonel on the ship, that the big invasion was going to be in Normandy, across the gray water, which I remembered from my books was the English Channel.

I realized what General Eisenhower said when he talked about *this great and noble undertaking*. It was looking greater than anything I'd ever seen, enormous, big enough to win a war, I was thinking.

Kaufman was standing next to me, looking over everything, too.

"Hey, Sappy, did you ever see so many people and so much stuff?"

"No. It's amazing. I wonder how long it's going to take to get all these guys on all those boats."

"You'll be surprised. They've been planning this thing for God knows how long. They must have it down to a science. You'll probably be bouncing on those waves out there by tonight."

"What the hell are you doing here?" It was the booming voice of the sergeant from the tent.

"I came in the truck, with everybody else."

"In *my* truck?"

It wasn't really his truck, it belonged to the U.S. Army, I felt like saying, but didn't. I'm not that crazy.

"You know you're going to be in some pretty deep shit with the colonel. Didn't he tell you to stay back there at that town?"

"I guess he did."

"You guess he did? What the hell kind of an answer is that?"

Some Rangers were watching what was going on and shaking their heads, as if they weren't too crazy about the sergeant picking on me.

"So you just took it on yourself to get in the truck and come along for the ride. Don't you know that disobeying a direct order in time of war is serious stuff, kid?"

"Yes, sir."

"And knock off the *sir* crap. Save it for the goddamn officers."

"Yes, uh, sergeant."

He turned around to the guys standing behind him. "What do you think I should do with this kid. Leave him here?"

Most of the guys shook their heads. One of them said, "He got this far. And he might come in handy. We figure he's kind of a good luck charm.

And we heard this story that he's a champion rope climber. Maybe he should just stay with us."

"You know he stowed away, don't you?" the sergeant said.

"Come on, sarge, I figure anybody who wants to get himself in the middle of this crap we're headed fore oughta be able to have his way." It was Tiny, the big New Yorker. The others were nodding.

The sergeant was looking frustrated. He just shook his head for a while and looked down at the muddy ground. Then he said to me, "If you stay, it's your own doing. I'm not telling you to go with us. When my back is turned, if you end up sneaking aboard the same boat we're on, it'll be too late for me to do anything about it, except toss you over the side in the middle of the English Channel. Got that?"

"Yes, sergeant, I've got it." I was pretty sure he wouldn't toss me over the side in the middle of the ocean. I couldn't help smiling about that.

"Something funny?" he snapped at me.

"No, sergeant."

"Listen up," he said in the kind of loud voice sergeants always have in the movies. "You're going to be looking for boat number 367, an LCA. Find where it's docked, and stay close to it."

"What's LCA stand for?" Tiny asked.

"Landing Craft, Assault," said Kaufman.

"Hey, finally it's legal. I'm gonna commit an assault, and can't get arrested for it," the big New Yorker said.

"No, but you might get your head shot off, instead," someone next to him said.

I tried to picture Tiny walking around without a head. At least he wouldn't be so loud. But that's not what I wanted to happen, really, it wasn't.

Kaufman said, "Come on Sappy, let's see if we can find boat three-sixty-seven."

So that's what we did, walking through all these men trying to kill time waiting to do what they were supposed to do next. It was just like a war movie, only with real people, mostly bored and trying anything to make the time go by and maybe even forget about what it was going to be like once the shooting started. We walked past guys playing cards, poker, I guess, only not with money. They were using wooden matches instead, some of them even were playing with bullets to bet with. I don't know what they're supposed to do with bullets they win. Every now and then we saw a guy with a guitar singing with his buddies. I wondered what he thought he was supposed to do with the guitar when it was time to go. You don't just take a big guitar when you invade a beach or climb some cliffs.

Kaufman pointed to all the landing boats. "They're not all LCAs. There's LCTs, for tanks, LCIs, for infantry, LCVPs for vehicles and personnel They oughta have LCDSs."

"For what?" I asked him.

"Landing craft for dickhead sergeants, don't you think?"

"I guess." I noticed a row of different looking boats, almost like they didn't belong there with all the other ones. They looked more like the fishing boats we went out on at home. "What are those?" I asked Kaufman.

"Higgins boats. Made out of wood, and named for the guy who invented them. They can take about thirty men and drive right up on the sand, unload, and then back themselves out to go get another load. And look at that monster, over there," he said, pointing to a really big truck, or maybe a boat, covered by green canvas. "It's a D-D. Stands for duplex drive. It's actually a Sherman tank that's been fitted with a propeller, so it can unload from a landing craft, in the water, and go up to the beach like a boat. When it lands on the beach, the big canvas bag over it drops, and then it's a tank again."

"You mean the tank can actually float?"

"They sure as hell hope it can. They use a whole bunch of inflatable tubes to keep it up in the water. It's like a tank with water wings. But if they hit some sharp stuff on the way in, they could be in real trouble."

"There it is, LCA three-sixty-seven," I said, reading off the white numbers on the side.

"Yeah, it sure is. Ugly looking thing, isn't it? Like a big steel box. Looks like the Brits are running these boats, too. Hope they don't feed us again. Doesn't much matter, though. With that flat bottom, nobody's going to be interested in eating anything, once we get out there."

"Do you ever get seasick?" I asked him.

"Not usually. But you never know with that kind of boat. And that kind of water."

I saw what he meant about the water. It was crashing against rocks and slamming onto the beach. Farther out, you could see huge swells that could probably toss any of those boats around like little tin cans.

"Well, looks like we've got all day now to sit around and wait," Kaufman said. "You play cards?"

"Just Go Fish. and War."

"Do yourself a favor. Don't tell any of these guys that."

I saw a crowd of soldiers standing around a guy who wasn't in uniform and using a movie camera on wooden legs. He was taking pictures of a soldier who was talking to the camera. Over his head was a microphone on a long pole that somebody else was holding.

"Are they making a movie?" I asked Kaufman.

"Those are newsreel guys. You know, Movietone. Why, you want to be in it?"

"No. Really not." I didn't need anything else that would spill the beans about me."Just wondering."

"Well, you may not have a choice." He pointed at the camera. The guy using it was turned around and pointed right at the two of us. "Wave," Kaufman said, with this big smile and then a salute, too.

I didn't do anything and watched the camera guy turn the long lens, and made it get even longer, and aimed right at us.

"Good close-up. Thanks!" he shouted. Kaufman waved at him. And, of course, all I could think about was who might see it, the close-up. Then I really got nervous when the guy with the microphone came over, with a pad and a pen.

"What's your name, soldier?" he asked me.

"I can't tell you that."

The man looked kind of annoyed. "And why not?"

"Security."

"No one else here seems to be concerned about security. I've got everyone else's name I asked for," he said and looked at Kaufman. "How about your name?"

"Kaufman."

"Is that supposed to be joke?" the man with the pad and pen said, looking confused, and maybe more annoyed, too. "If it is, I don't find it funny."

"Why not?" said Kaufman.

"Because I'm Jewish."

"So am I," said Kaufman, and he walked away to watch some card players.

The guy shook his head and walked back to the cameraman. I could hear him say, "You see everything in a war. Even Japs with Jewish names." I don't think Kaufman heard it, which was a good thing.

Kaufman called over to me. "Come on, I'll teach you how to play something a little more interesting than Go Fish."

I followed him and we came to a group of four soldiers sitting in a circle on olive-green metal boxes and playing cards. In the middle of them there was this wooden crate with stenciling on it that said *GRENADES, PHOSPHOROUS. HANDLE WITH EXTREME CAUTION, HIGHLY FLAMMABLE*.

"Looking for another hand?" Kaufman asked the guys.

Without looking up, one of the men who had some cards in his left hand and a cigarette hanging from his lips, just nodded. Another man pointed to a metal box that didn't have anybody on it. Kaufman sat down and I stood behind him. For the first time, one of the men looked up from his cards and at Kaufman's face. His eyes got big and he nudged the man next to him, who also looked surprised.

"What are you doing here?" the first guy asked.

"The same thing you are," Kaufman said.

Now the other two men were studying Kaufman. One of them shook his head, the other grinned and said, "Hey, give the guy a break. You never heard of the Nisei, the Japanese guys on our side?"

"I'm not one of them," said Kaufman. "I'm Chinese."

"Hey, don't get so all sensitive. It's just that you looked like, you know, one of them," said the guy who saw him first. "I can't tell the difference."

"It's very easy," said Kaufman.

"Yeah? How's that?"

"Japanese can't play poker worth a damn. But Chinese, they can clean out a game in four hands. Really ruthless."

One of the players said, "Oh what the hell, I'll take my chances. It's only money anyway."

The others nodded like they agreed. One of them threw down two ten-cards and two sevens on the crate. Nobody said anything and just watched him rake in a pile of wooden matches.

"Fifty cents a match," one of the players said. He picked up a tin can from between his legs and said, "How many?"

"Twenty bucks," Kaufman said. He fished into his field jacket pocket and pulled out two ten-dollar bills. The guy with the can took the money and counted out the matches but kept staring at Kaufman, suspicious like.

"Five-card draw, deuces wild, jacks to open," the guy playing dealer said and he dropped down four piles of cards.

It ended up that Kaufman was off on how long it would take to clean everybody out. It wasn't four hands. But he did it in six. When he scooped up all the rest of their matches, one player slammed down his cards on the crate, and some of the matches flew off and down into the sand. He stood up and stared at Kaufman.

"I don't know what the hell kind of thing you've got going for you," he said. "Maybe it's just some kind of Chinaman's luck — but I'm not interested in this game any more."

"Seems to me you don't have any choice. You're cleaned out, aren't you?" said Kaufman.

The guy was really fuming. He said, "You lookin' for trouble?"

"No," Kaufman said. He stayed pretty calm. "I think we'll find enough of that tomorrow morning."

"Come on, Hanson, relax. He's just a damn good poker player," one of the other guys said.

"Yeah, well, he can be good with somebody else's dough," the loser said and walked away.

"Don't take it personally," one of the others said to Kaufman. "He's a hot head."

"Sorry, but I tend to take it personally when people say things about the color of my skin, mainly because my skin *is* kind of a personal thing."

"We're all in the same boat, know what I mean?" said another man, jerking his head toward the row of landing boats. "We've got just about every kind here. Even got two coloreds in my platoon. And they're damn good soldiers."

"Well, that's real white of you," Kaufman said. He didn't get an answer to that. And we both walked away.

"How much did you win?" I asked Kaufman.

"Looks like ninety-seven bucks. Not bad for ten minutes work. That's five-hundred-and-eighty-two dollars an hour, when you think of it. Beats a private's pay, doesn't it?"

CHAPTER

15

"How about a letter-writing kit, soldier? Compliments of the Red Cross."

I turned around and saw this woman in a green uniform that looked suspiciously like mine, with the buttons on the left side, which I hoped she didn't notice.

"Thank you. I'd appreciate that," I said.

She kind of turned her head sideways and studied me. "My, they're taking you boys so young," she said and handed me this packet. I kept wondering if anyone was ever not going to say something about how young I was, besides me.

"You might want to pass the time getting a few V-mails off to your family. And your girlfriend. You have one, don't you?"

"No, not right now," was all I could think of saying.

"I'm sorry. I didn't mean to embarrass you. It's O.K., not having one. Much better for a young, handsome man like you to play the field."

If only she knew how much I'd rather have a girlfriend than *playing the field.* "Thank you for the writing kit," I said.

"Well, it's not a lot. Just V-mail forms and a pen. I also have razors, if you need one." She looked at me closer, but didn't say anything about me not needing a razor.

"Well, if you have an extra one, that would be nice, thank you," I said.

She reached in a green canvas shoulder bag and got out a white cardboard box and handed it to me.

"So, where are you from soldier?" That helped, the soldier thing.

"Teaneck, New Jersey."

"Oh, I know Teaneck. I'm from New York. Washington Heights. I used to hike over the George Washington Bridge with a scout group. Never made it to Teaneck, though."

"And I've hiked across the other way, to Washington Heights."

"Small world," she said. "You must have enlisted right out of high school."

I wasn't about to tell her I hadn't even started high school yet. "No, I didn't finish." That wasn't really a lie, since I hadn't even started.

"Well then, I certainly hope you'll go back after the war and get your diploma. That way you'll be able to go to college, too."

"Yes, ma'm, I definitely plan to finish school."

"And I wish you'd stop calling me *ma'm*. It makes feel older than I really am, which is something I don't particularly need."

"O.K"

She started to laugh, but then she stopped, and so did I and everybody else out there when there was this huge explosion that made the ground shake and stuff rattle. I saw this thick white smoke coming up from the docks. A lot of people were running to get to it, but more were running away from it.

"My God, what was that?" the woman said.

"Something blew up."

"Medics! We need medics!" somebody shouted.

The Red Cross lady started running toward the smoke cloud. I followed her. There were orange flames I could see now, and it looked like they were coming from about where I watched Kaufman playing cards.

When I got to where the flames and smoke were I saw the most awful sight. A man was on fire. He was screaming for help and running around like that would put out the fire. There was a big crowd watching and yelling for help, but nobody seemed to be able to do something. I couldn't just stand there and watch this poor guy get burned to death. In a kind of flash, I remembered something from a movie, where this soldier got hit by a flame thrower and was doing the same kind of screaming. Somebody wrapped a blanket around him and got him down on the ground to put out the fire. Like it was some kind of message to me, I saw blankets that the card players were sitting on before. So I just grabbed one of them and ran to the poor guy.

I yelled at him to stop. But he couldn't. He kept running around. I could smell his skin burning, which was the most god-awful thing. Then I did it. I just closed my eyes and threw myself at him with the blanket wide open. Lucky thing I didn't miss. When I hit him, we both went down to the ground. Then I rolled over and over with him. I thought I was going to catch fire, which would have made everything worse. My skin would be stinking, too. I don't know how, but the rolling and the blanket made the fire go out. There was just smoke now. But I kept holding the poor guy to make sure he wasn't burning any more. I felt like I was on fire, but it was just the heat from him. He was shaking something awful and making these moaning sounds.

"You can get off him, soldier. The fire's out."

I looked up and was able to see through the smoke two guys standing over us. They both had Red Cross arm bands and had to be medics. One of them dropped a big metal box on the ground and dug out stuff like a hypodermic and scissors. First he started cutting away the poor guy's uniform. The other medic shoved the hypodermic needle into the guy's thigh. That did something to him to make him stop shivering so much and even the moaning.

I heard a siren and it kept getting closer. Everybody moved back when a green ambulance got there and stopped. Two more medics jumped out and ran around the back to open the ambulance doors. One of them carried a rolled-up canvas stretcher. When they got to where we were on the ground, one of them asked, "Vitals?"

The medic who gave the shot had a stethoscope in his ears and was holding the bottom part on the guy's chest. "He's got a pulse, but barely. He's in shock."

"Let's get him out of here," one of the others said. And that's what they did, real fast. It took them just a few seconds to get the guy on the stretcher, stick the end of a plastic tube in the guy's wrist and load him into the ambulance. And then they just beat it out of there, with the siren going like crazy. One of them stayed back where I was still on the ground.

"Come on. Let's get you checked out," he said, looking at me.

"It's O.K. I'm fine"

"You just threw yourself all over a guy who was burning up with phosphorous, and you're O.K.? Come on, don't be a hero."

The medic kneeled down and opened my field jacket. I was hoping he didn't notice how it buttoned. He grabbed my mail-order dog tag and dropped it like a hot potato.

"Christ, it's like a hot poker," he said, blowing on his fingers. He used the end of his stethoscope to shove the dog tag off me. Then he whistled at something. "You've got a perfect outline of an army dog tag burned into your chest. Like a tattoo."

I shook my head when I heard that. He probably didn't know that tattoos on Jewish guys are a sin. Maybe it would be gone by the time I got home. He dug in the metal box again and got out a tube of some stuff. He squeezed a big glop of it on me and covered my tattoo with with gauze and tape.

"Don't take it off, or it could get infected," he said.

"How could I? Isn't it burned into me?"

He shook his head. "I meant the gauze." Then he laughed to himself, probably picturing me trying to get the "tattoo" off. Which made me kind of laugh, too.

"Thanks for everything," I said.

"You're lucky as hell," the medic said. "Phosphorus is awful stuff. Sticks to your clothes and keeps burning until it melts the skin off you."

"It was phosphorus? What made it to go off?"

"I guess there was a crate filled with incendiary grenades. Some jerk who was playing cards or something must have lit a cigarette next to the box. Stuff caught fire, then the box did, too. And pretty soon — pow!

"That's awful. You think the burned guy's going to be all right?"

"Hard to say. But if he does make it, he can thank you for doing what you did. You probably saved his life. And now you're a hero."

"Not really. I just happened to see him on fire, and found a blanket."

"Well, you sure as hell have someone, or something, watching over you."

I know I should probably felt pretty good about everything. But actually, it made me kind of sad when I realized I saw the kind of terrible things that can happen in a war, even before I got in one. I remembered seeing Guadalcanal Diary, where Japanese soldiers ran out of caves after they were attacked with phosphorous grenades. They were screaming and on fire like that guy who just got burned. But nobody was there to throw blankets around them, and they died. This was an accident, though. And they can happen anywhere, not just in a war. Like my mother said, more than once, *You never know, you can be walking down the street and something terrible can fall on your head and kill you.* She wasn't thinking about phosphorous grenades, I'm sure.

I sat down on a stack of boxes, after I made sure they didn't have anything that could explode in them. Some soldiers came up to me to find out if I was O.K. One of them said, "What the hell would make you do something like that? You wanna get killed before the shooting even starts?" I couldn't think of an answer, so I didn't give him one.

The medic who took care of me said, "I'm supposed to file a report, and give you a follow-up tomorrow. But since you're pulling out tonight, that's obviously not going to happen. So you just keep an eye on the burn. If it starts to throb, like maybe an infection, find yourself a medic and have him take a look at it, O.K.?"

"Sure. Thanks. I'll be all right, though. "

"See you around. And good luck where you're going."

I saw the Red Cross worker who gave me the writing kit and razor just before the accident.

"You O.K., Teaneck?"

"I'm fine. My uniform just got a little scorched, that's all."

"It could have been a lot worse. Where did you learn that trick, with the blanket?"

"In a first-aid class I took once. It was in junior high."

"You remembered it well, after all the years."

I started to wonder if I should just get it over with and call everybody together and say something like: *Some of you may be wondering why I look so young compared to everyone else here. The truth of the matter is, I'm only thirteen, I sneaked into the army, I even had to buy my own uniform — a woman's uniform — and helmet, and if my parents knew I was here, they'd split a gut.*

No, that's not what I was going to do. But I did think about it. I figured sooner or later people would stop asking about it anyway.

• • •

This booming voice got everybody paying attention. Card players stopped playing. Nappers stopped napping. And I stopped tossing my baseball in the air.

"In fifteen minutes, religious services will be held for all personnel in the following places: For protestants, in the large warehouse, marked Charlie-eleven, adjacent to the freight pier. For Roman Catholics, in the large storage building, marked Dog-one-o-one. For Jewish men, in the small mess tent. All personnel are urged by the chaplains to attend services of their choice, the last opportunity to do so before operations commence."

It figured. We get the small tent. Since I didn't know how many of us there were, it couldn't have been unfair. But maybe a small building would have been nice.

I have to say it bothered me, the part about *the last opportunity before operations commence.* I got to thinking about things I saw in movies, like last rites, when a priest stood next to James Cagney who was sitting in the electric chair.

It was a good thing Kaufman came up to me, with that smile he always had. "You going to religious services?" he asked.

"You going to the small mess tent?"

"I guess so."

"You *could* go to the big warehouse and act like a Protestant."

"Why would I do that?"

"Just to see what it feels like not to be a minority."

"I don't think I could do that. Can't change anything now."

I remembered something my mother said about that: *Don't forget that you can never fool anyone into thinking you're something else. They see right through it. You are what you are born to be, and no matter how hard you try, you can't get away with pretending you're not. Negroes can't change the color of their skin, and they shouldn't. They should be proud of what they are. So should you.*

"O.K., let's go be what we are," Kaufman said, as if he knew what I was remembering.

The tent actually wasn't as small as I expected. It had regular mess tables and benches. At the front there was this wooden stand that officers used for briefings. Somebody draped a white satin cloth over the top. It was the only thing that made it look like a religious service was going to be there. I looked around at the soldiers sitting on the benches, maybe about forty. I knew it was a lot less than there'd be in the Protestant and Catholic tents.

"At least we have a minyan," Kaufman said. That means ten men, which you have to have for a service, or it doesn't count, I guess.

"Probably some were too busy to come."

"Right. Like the card games weren't over," Kaufman said.

Everybody there sat quietly, the way you're supposed to in a synagogue, even if it's made out of canvas and is small. Their heads were all covered, mostly by helmets, and some by skull caps they must have brought with them. Kaufman and I sat down at an empty table. Pretty soon an officer walked in and looked around. He wasn't too happy with the size of the group, and shook his head about it. He went to the front and put a black prayer book on the white cloth. Then he opened a blue velvet bag and took out a yarmulke and a prayer shawl that he wrapped around his shoulders. Now he looked like a rabbi, except for the khaki shirt and pants. That's when I fished in my knapsack for my own velvet bag and took out the shawl I brought with me.

"I'm impressed," Kaufman whispered. "I never would have thought to bring mine with me."

"You have one?"

"Sure. And it's even got Hebrew letters on it, like yours, not Chinese. What do you think of that?" I was thinking he shouldn't keep making such a big thing about being Chinese. But I guess he had a reason.

The officer at the front looked around and started talking.

"Welcome to our special service. I'm Captain Holtzman. Although I'm not officially a chaplain, I'm a lay rabbi in civilian life. Each of you is about to embark on a journey that will surely have enormous historic impact. But it's also a journey that poses risks — grave risks — to every one of us. We are going into battle in just a matter of hours. I don't have to tell you why we are joining the battle. Every American has a vital stake in the outcome of this war. Every Jewish American has a very specific stake. Our enemy has chosen us for some of the most horrific and inhumane treatment ever visited on a people. Innocent civilians — women and children — have been singled out and murdered for one reason: they are Jews. As you can see, we are but a small number of the total force that will be launching this invasion. But we are here today. We will be there tomorrow, and every day beyond when we are needed. Now, let us pray to our God, to grant us safe conduct through this strife, to keep us from harm's way, to give us the strength to prevail, to grant eternal peace to those who will become our fallen comrades."

I shuddered when I thought about fallen comrades and looked around the tent at all the real serious faces. I couldn't help wondering which ones might become casualties. I started praying for them to myself and the captain started the service.

"Hear oh Israel, the Lord our God, the Lord is one."

And I said to myself, *Please hear us, especially now, dear God. Protect us. Help us to achieve what we have to achieve. Let us all get back home safe and sound, in time for the World Series, which, as you know, begins in late September."*

"What did you think of the service?" Kaufman asked me on the way out of the tent.

"It was nice."

"That's what we always say about any service, it was nice," said Kaufman. "I notice he didn't do the kaddish. Guess it wouldn't be such a good idea, saying prayers for the dead, tonight. Know what I mean?"

"Yeah, I do. How many do you think will be — you know?"

"Hard to say. I read in a book by some English general that when an army plans a ground campaign, like an invasion, it figures on twenty per cent casualties."

"That's a lot," I said, and did some quick math in my head. I saw forty soldiers who were at the service, and then I saw eight wooden coffins next to thirty-two soldiers still alive. Twenty per cent dead. One out of five.

"Yeah. Anything's a lot," Kaufman said, "when they're people you're with. Or when one of them could be you or me." He was looking down at the ground. "You worried?"

"Sure. Who wouldn't be. It's hard to believe that people are going to be shooting at us, trying to get their twenty per cent."

"Well, it's like I said back on the ship. Whoever has the most guys standing when it's over wins it. That's going to be us. Maybe we have only eight hundred left out of every thousand we start with. But maybe they have only seven hundred, or five hundred."

It sounded a lot like a game, or an elimination tournament like the intramural basketball league at school. But the losers don't end up in coffins. The next day, they're back in class.

"You still planning to go in with us?" Kaufman asked.

"Sure. Why?"

"You don't have to, you know. You wouldn't exactly be deserting. A lot of guys would give their left nut to be in your shoes. You can just walk up to the first officer you see and tell him your stowaway story. And your age. You'd be out of here, you know it."

"I couldn't do that."

"Why not? You've already done some hero stuff, with that guy who was on fire. Isn't that enough?"

"It's not that I want to be a hero," I said "I just want to do my part."

"You've got to let go of that guilt crap," said Kaufman. "It's not like we made the damn war happen, you and me."

"It's not?"

"You're not serious, are you?" He stared at me."Jesus, you *are* serious. How the hell do you come up with the idea that we caused this thing. I can see you being self-conscious, with those jerks chasing you home all the time and telling you there's something wrong with you because of what you were born as. And maybe even you begin to believe that some of us bring a problem or two down on ourselves, like sticking together. But, hell, why do we keep to ourselves? Because those other bastards want us to. Otherwise they wouldn't be keeping us out of their clubs, their medical schools, their banks. You tell people enough times to stay away from you, they're eventually going to keep to themselves. Maybe that's wrong. But it's not something to feel guilty about. Or start a goddamn war over."

Medical schools. I thought about what my father said about them: *Either get better grades than the all the other kids, and get in on the quota for us, or don't even think about being a doctor. And don't get the idea that you're going to go to work every day at a bank on Wall Street in a Brooks Brothers suit. They won't hire you in a bank, either. You'll even get funny looks buying the suit. Want to play golf? Better do it on a public course, unless, of course, you can afford to join one of our own clubs, but that makes us like them, doesn't it?*

Then there was the Pete Lawson incident. Pete, a friend of mine since fifth grade, was always telling me about the great seventh- and eighth-grade girls he was meeting at Miss Blair's dance class. It was every Wednesday evening at the local country club. Girls had to wear white gloves and boys had to wear jackets and ties. One day Pete told me about a big dance coming up. Members of the class were allowed to bring a guest. "You can meet some really neat girls," he said. "Some of them smoke and take the white gloves off after the dance and mess around. Want to go?"

Girls that smoked and messed around? Who wouldn't want to go. I planned for it the next two weeks, shining my shoes, asking my mother to buy me a new white shirt and tie, even practicing the fox trot with a diagram from an Arthur Murray Learn To Dance ad from the Saturday Evening Post.

The day before the dance, Pete called me over in the school hallway. He said his mother told him I couldn't go to the dance. The country club didn't allow Jewish people, and on top of that, Miss Phelps's class didn't either. Pete forgot to tell his mother his guest was me. I tried to look like it didn't bother me a lot, but it felt like someone punched me so hard in the stomach I might never breathe again. I managed to, though, and said, "Well, I guess that's the rule. O.K." And I walked away doing everything I couldn't keep from sobbing in front of anybody. Things were bad enough without that.

"All personnel, this is code red. Report to embarkation positions immediately. Code red. All personnel report on the double. Code red." It was the public address system again, and it sounded a lot more serious than religious services.

"Does code red mean what it sounds like?" I asked Kaufman.

"If you're thinking that we're moving out, you're right."

I felt a familiar tingling run up my legs and into my stomach. I even felt a little dizzy. It wasn't that I didn't know this was going to happen, that we were going to get on another boat and this time go into a huge battle. Still, it's different when it actually happens. It isn't something you think about and dream about any more. Now you can smell it and taste it, and, honestly, get scared shitless about it.

The announcement was a like a gun going off to start a race. Everybody was moving double-time, picking up rifles and all their gear and heading toward the boats. The sun was going down over the water, even though you could barely see it through the clouds. It was kind of eerie and dark. The code red must have shook up all the birds, and there were a lot of them, taking off and heading over the water, shrieking like they knew something big was up.

Then there was more noise in the sky, a lot louder than any birds. It got louder and louder, and we all knew what it was, airplanes coming over, looking like they were chasing all the birds out over the water. They flew low enough that you could see what was painted on them, American flags, English ones, too. They were all painted that same darkish green like everything else in the war seemed to be. There were bombers, and fighters and what Kaufman told me were paratroop transports, lots of those, hundreds of them. I never saw anything like it, and probably wouldn't again either. It was like every plane that was ever built was flying over us and headed to the same place we were. You could feel the noise coming up from the ground into your feet and up your body.

"This is it," Kaufman shouted. "You wanted a war? Well, you got it. Come on."

CHAPTER

16

"What do you mean you don't have a rifle?" Kaufman said when we were walking to our boat.

"I never got one."

"You're going into battle with the Rangers, and you don't have a rifle? What are you expecting to fight with, a broom, your bare hands, what?"

"I guess I'm not expecting to fight."

Kaufman stopped and looked at me like I was crazy. "Then, what, may I be so bold as to ask, are you planning to do in this invasion? They don't use bugler boys, you know. This is war, Saperstein, nothing less. People out there are going to try and kill us. We'd better be ready to kill them first."

"I don't have to kill anybody to help."

"So what are you going to do, talk them into surrendering? Play music to them?"

"I'll find something."

He shook his head and started to walk again. "This is really one for Ripley's Believe It Or Not: Boy Goes To War Without Gun. Serenades Enemy Into Submission."

"I can help the medics. I can climb ropes," I said, like I was applying for a job.

"And you can get your ass shot off in the process. Jesus, Sappy, I don't think you understand what it's going to be like on that beach. No one really does. But I do know that it's not going to be a picnic on a blanket."

"It's O.K. I'll be able to take care of myself. Nothing's going to happen to me, honest."

"And how do you know that?"

"If I tell you, you have to promise to keep it between us. Nobody would understand it."

"You have some kind of secret weapon or something?"

"Promise?"

"O.K. O.K., I promise. So what's the big secret?"

"I talk to people in my room at night, all the time."

"Really. And who are these people and how do they get in your room."

"They're on my wall."

He just shook his head and kept walking. I tried to keep up with him.

"You think maybe you've got a screw loose?" He twirled his finger on the side of his head. "People are hanging on your wall?"

"Not the real people. Pictures of them. Like Johnny Mize, Mel Ott, Joe Louis."

"Tell me, do the pictures talk back to you?"

"No, not the pictures. But the people in them, I can close my eyes and actually hear them when I ask them questions. Everything I did to get here, I asked them about. I told them at night what the kids at school did to me, and what my parents were so scared of, like the Black Cat Gang. And ever single one of them told me this was something I had to do, if I wanted anything to change."

Kaufman stopped again, when we were real close to the boat. "If I didn't know better, I'd believe that you get your advice from those guys on your walls. But the problem is, I do know better. This isn't a game in the Polo Grounds. It's a goddamn war. A bloody, vicious war. And a whole lot of the people all around us here are going to be dead by tomorrow night. I like you, Saperstein, and I don't want you to be one of them. In fact, I'm thinking the best thing I can do is go to the first officer I see and tell him the whole story, so they'll get your ass out of here before it's too late."

We just stared at each other for a pretty long time. I thought I saw a tear under one of his eyes, but he wiped it away and looked up in the sky, like it was raining, but it wasn't. Finally, I said, "Please, Kaufman, please don't do that. I came all this way to do something I have to do. If I don't do it, everything those kids did to me, all the things they said, every day, the stuff that hurt my parents so bad, those people will win. And my family and me will lose. Please. Don't stop me. If I do this, maybe some day I'll be allowed to be a doctor or a banker. And my parents will understand and be proud."

Now there was a tear, actually a couple, on my face, and I looked up to the sky, too. That made Kaufman smile, finally. He got close to me, put down his gun and grabbed my shoulder. And he said, "I think I should punch that big Jewish nose of yours so hard it'll break and bleed like hell, and a medic will have to come and take you away somewhere, so you can't get on that boat. That's what I feel like doing." He shook my shoulders when he said it.

"Are you going to?"

He pulled one hand away and made a fist and held it back, like he was aiming. He just stared at me some more.

"Shit, no, I'm not." And he dropped his fist. "I think I'm as fucking crazy as you now. Come on, let's get on that goddamn boat."

"O.K.," I said.

"But would you do one thing for me?"

"Yeah, definitely."

"When we get on our way, would you talk to all those guys on your wall and see what they can do to keep us from getting shot to pieces? And keep talking to them the whole time? Will you do that?"

"I promise."

• • •

I saw the sergeant again, this time dressed totally for battle. The chords in his neck stuck out when he shouted orders to the troops, but nobody seemed like they could hear him. He used his hands instead, pointing to LCA 367, waving the everybody toward it. Then he moved his hand up and down, I guess to tell everybody to climb down into the boat.

It must have taken almost an hour for all the planes to fly over. And it was non-stop. The bombers just kept coming, and so did the fighters and jump planes, even gliders being towed by transports. I couldn't help wondering if there were any American planes left in the Pacific, but I was sure somebody took care of that. After a while the smell of gasoline was so strong, you thought you were swimming in it. And the smoke from the exhausts, that was pretty heavy, too. War smells, I guess, and it probably has to. Even after the planes were gone, my ears were still ringing from all the noise of engines. I could still hear them in my head. And then I heard a woman's voice. It wasn't the letter-writing lady.

"Cigarettes here. Get your cigarettes before you board." She sounded happy, like the cigarette girl I saw in the Copacabana when my parents took us all there for dinner. Only this lady didn't have a short skirt and black net stockings on. She had the same green uniform everybody in the world seemed to be wearing. The soldiers made a circle around her.

"Camels, Luckies, Chesterfield, Kools. One carton per man. Here you go, soldier, enjoy the smokes."

"Hey, Sappy, let's get our cigarettes," Kaufman said.

"Go ahead. I don't smoke."

"You may not now. But I have a feeling you will before long."

"I don't think so."

"Even if you don't, you ought to take your carton It could come in handy where we're going."

"What do you mean?"

"Cigarettes are better than money. You can get things for them."

"Like what?"

He raised his eyebrows and grinned. "Favors. You know."

I still didn't get it.

"From the ladies, for Pete's sake. Don't you know what I'm talking about?"

It dawned on me what he meant. I guessed it did the same thing to the lady with the cigarettes.

"Better listen to your buddy," she said to me, and she raised her eyebrows too. "You just never know, and it's best to be prepared."

I held out my hand to her.

"What do you want?" she asked.

"Cigarettes."

"I know. Which brand? Camels —"

"Sure."

" — or Luckies, Chesterfield, Kools?"

"He'll take Camels," Kaufman said. He took a carton of them and got behind me. He opened my knapsack and put the cigarettes in it, and slapped me on the back, like you do to a horse. "There, for God's sake. You've got two hundred smokes. My brand, in case you can't find anything to exchange them for, O.K.?"

"What's going on over there?" I said. There was a soldier in a white chef's uniform handing something out.

"Chow. They're giving us rations for the trip tonight and for morning. Canned stuff. Powdered and dried crap. Awful-tasting, but that won't matter."

"Why not?"

"From what I hear about these flat-bottom boats, everybody gets so seasick they can't eat anything. And if they do, they heave it all up. Keeps the fish fed."

"So you're not going to take any rations?"

"Sure I am. If I don't eat 'em, I'll save 'em. They could come in handy, too, like the cigarettes." I got this picture in my head of a movie, where a sexy French woman was walking down the street at night, on wet cobblestones. They're always wet in movies. She came up behind me and opened my knapsack, and pulled out a pack of Camels and a can of rations. Then she motioned with her finger for me to follow her.

"That's really true, that you can trade cigarettes and even food with women?"

"Anything's possible. I'm not saying it's right. It really isn't. But it's a fact of life."

"I'd just give it away — the cigarettes, the rations, if someone really needs it. I don't think I'd want to ask for anything back."

"Suit yourself. But don't forget, there's a war on."

We reached the head of the line where the cook was real bored by what he was doing.

"One dinner, one breakfast. Keep moving," he said, like he really didn't care about the stuff he was giving out or whether anybody was going to eat it.

Some of the guys were making jokes. "If I'd known about the dog food, I would've brought my Irish setter with me." "Have you eaten any of this? I doubt it. You're still standing." I guess they thought they were funny, but nobody else seemed to.

I took the two meals from the cook He was tall and skinny, and he looked like he did this job for a long time. When he looked at me, he got kind of puzzled. Then he grinned, sort of, with a cigarette dangling from his mouth.

"Here, take a couple extra rations. They might help you grow into that helmet," he said.

I took them, even though I knew I wouldn't eat them after what Kaufman told me about throwing up.

"Thank you," I said.

"Don't mention it. And I mean it." He jerked his head at all the guys waiting.

When I put the rations in my pack, with the cigarettes inside, I could hardly close the top. My prayer shawl and baseball took up space too. It wasn't exactly a fighting man's knapsack, but everybody didn't have to know what was in it.

The orange in the sky was gone now, and all that was left was black. But a lot of lights were on along the docks and you could see smoke going up from engines that were running everywhere, from trucks going back and forth, and from the boats that had their motors on. I walked with Kaufman toward our boat. We didn't talk. Nobody else seemed to either.

The joking stopped. I guess it was time to get serious about where we were going. I could make out faces of men walking up the ramps and into the LCAs. The white lights on them made them look like ghosts. It was kind of scary.

"This is it, Sappy. Say goodbye to jolly old England."

The boat bobbed in the water every time someone stepped onto it. I watched Kaufman step down the rungs on the ladder and then jump the last couple of feet onto the deck. I tried to do it just like him, and it worked. When I hit the deck I didn't feel the bobbing everyone else made. Figures. I was even too small to do that. I looked around and it was like I was in a big box made of steel. I was one of the last people to get on. Everybody was still quiet, like they were waiting for something to happen. It was real cold too and everything was wet and clammy, even the steel walls.

"Makes you appreciate the Queen Elizabeth, doesn't it?" Kaufman said.

"It's going to be a long ride to France in this thing,"

"This is just a taxi, to the mother ship," Kaufman said. "That one will take us across the channel. Then, we get back on this one for our last ride to the beach. You're really lucky, Sappy, you know that?"

"I am?"

"Everyone else has been dealing with this stuff for six months, here in England, getting ready for tomorrow. You happened to find your way into a last-minute replacement company. We're sort of amateurs, a bunch of numb-nuts without enough training. That could be good, or it could be bad. Guess we'll find out soon enough. "

There was this loud whistle from up on the dock. Everybody looked up and saw the sergeant. He sort of chopped at the air with his hand. The guy who was going to drive the boat nodded his head and pressed a button on this box-like thing in front of him behind the steering wheel. That got the engine going, just chugging and coughing at first, and then it started this heavy roar and I could hear water rushing out from the back end. The driver wore a helmet bigger than an Army one. I found out later he wasn't a driver. A coxswain is what Kaufman told me he was. Only with all the noise I didn't get it.

"Cocksman?" I said. And that got a laugh out of Kaufman, who thought I was making a joke. I wasn't.

Whatever he was called, he slammed this big steel rod with a ball on the end forward. That obviously was the throttle, and it made the boat jump so much a lot of us either fell down or hung on to anything we could grab to stay up. When things settled down it actually felt good to be moving somewhere, anywhere, after all that hanging around in the camp. It was a short ride until we came to a bigger boat sitting still in the water. I guess I should call it a ship. It had big cranes hanging over the side and pretty soon I saw what they were for, when one of the LCAs like ours was being pulled out of the water and onto the ship.

Even though it was a short ride out to the ship, it was long enough and rough enough for a lot of guys to get seasick. I didn't, but when I smelled all the vomit sitting there on the deck, I almost did, just from that. It wasn't that they didn't want to throw up over the side. They couldn't get up high enough to the rail, so they just let it go where they were standing.

Kaufman said, "You're the only one who didn't turn green. Maybe I didn't, either. Am I still yellow?"

"You look O.K.," I said.

"How come you didn't upchuck?"

"I don't know. I just don't get seasick. Maybe it's all those fishing trips my father took me on."

When it was our turn to be lifted onto the ship, the swinging in the air on the way up didn't help things. A couple of guys started heaving again. We finally landed on the ship's deck with a huge, loud bump that felt like our boat might just break. And everybody started falling down again. Some of the guys were cursing at the coxswain, like it was his fault. He said, "Sorry about that, mates, but you'd best take up your complaints with the Yank on the winch."

When I heard his English accent, I wondered what he was doing driving an American boat. Then I remembered what Grigsby told me, about wanting to drive boats during the operation. I squinted at him in the dark, but I couldn't see enough of his face to know if it was him. Sure sounded like him, though. Maybe English guys were volunteering to do the jobs on our boats, sort of like getting even with the Germans who were bombing their country all the time.

"Wouldn't it have been easier to make the whole trip in the LCA?" I asked Kaufman.

"Are you kidding? You saw what happened just getting out here. Out in the open Channel, this thing would bounce like a little tin can. Maybe even swamp and go down. It would be like trying to take a rowboat across the Atlantic."

A siren went off on the ship, and it hurt my ears, it was so loud. And I heard a rumbling sound coming from up front. I knew what that was, an anchor chain dragging up from the water and across the steel deck.

"Looks like we were the last ones on," said Kaufman. "Come on, let's find the bar and have a beer."

"They have a bar?"

"We'd be lucky if they have toilets on this thing."

As it turned out, there were toilets. Long, metal troughs, actually, with wooden planks to sit on and seawater rushing through them. Not exactly private. They also had a mess hall, which looked too small for all the men on the ship but it was almost empty when Kaufman and I went down to eat.

"Don't think they're going to do much business in here," Kaufman said. "The last thing these guys are interested in is food. If they do eat, they'll just end up feeding it to the fish again."

"I think I'll try some of it."

"You can eat? Those must have been some fishing trips your father took you on. Where were they, Cape Horn?"

"No. Peconic Bay, mostly. Long Island."

"Sorry I asked," Kaufman said. "You go ahead and eat. I can feel the rolling already. I think I'll go up on deck. They say you don't get as sick when you can see the horizon."

"It's true," I said. "But it also helps if you can get some food down."

"I don't want to question your father, but it seems to me that what goes down goes up again when it gets rough. See you later."

I went up to the steam table and there was only one guy dishing out food. He had on a dirty white tee shirt and a chef's hat that was just as dirty. I held out my metal tray to him, but he didn't even look at me. He picked up two pieces of overdone toast and dropped them in the tray. He had a big scoop in his other hand filled with gravy about the color of his shirt. There were a lot of red flecks in the gravy, which I figured was meat. The gravy went plop over the toast. I didn't move away, and he must have thought I wanted more, which I really didn't, and he globbed another scoop of the stuff into my tray. It reminded me of what was left on the deck of the landing boat by the seasick guys.

I sat down at a mess table where there was just one guy, a private.

"They call it shit on a raft," he said, with a southern accent. "In the Army, it's on a shingle." Actually it did look a little like a raft. "You gonna eat yours?"

"I guess. You can get more, if you want."

"Why in hell would I want more? I don't want what I got. I only took it 'cause I felt for that guy who looks like he ain't gonna get rid of it. Figured I'd just dump it in the scullery when he's not lookin'."

Still, I was hungry, so I tried the stuff. And you know something? It wasn't that bad. Actually, it was pretty good. The little bits of red were like corned beef, which I always like anyway.

"You look as if you actually like that shit," the private said.

"You ought to try it."

"Let me ask you somethin'," the private said. "Where you from, in the first place?"

"New Jersey."

"Well, hell's bells. That explains why you could eat that. You're probably used to all kinds of different stuff that we just don't eat where I come from. Bet you never had you a bowl of grits, am I right? Or pork back."

"No, I guess I haven't. What's it like?"

"Well, it sure as hell ain't like shit on no shingle. I guess you're used to eatin' Yankee food, that's the problem. What kind of food does your momma make for you back home in New Jersey?"

Here it comes.

"Regular stuff, you know. Meat, potatoes, chicken, what everybody eats."

"What about foreign food?" the southerner asked suspiciously.

"Not at home. Sometimes we go out for Chinese food, or Italian."

Why doesn't he just come out and accuse me of being a latke lover?

"What are you, anyway?"

"I'm an American, from New Jersey."

"I got a feelin' that's moseying around inside me."

I'll bet he does.

"And it's not about anything Chinese or Eye-talian. Nosiree, I got this feelin' that, seein's how you're from New Jersey, maybe it's somethin' else." He paused for maximum impact. "You a Hebrew?"

I took a deep breath, wondering if I could handle myself in a fight with this strange guy. "The fact of the matter is, I am." All of a sudden I was back in the gym again, with Herbie Schoo holding a knife in his hand. Enough was enough.

"I thought you said you're an American."

Jesus, were there Black Cat Gangs on U.S. Navy ships? I'd had it. Something made me stand up and clench my fists. "I am American. A proud American. My parents are, too, and so is my brother. And if you don't like it, then you know what you can do about it."

I waited for something to happen. Like him standing up and punching me. But instead, the guy put up his hands and shook his head.

"Hey, fella, don't get me wrong. There's nothing wrong with your people being part of our country, too. Lord knows, there are a lot of you. The folks that own the general store in Henryville — that's where I'm from, Henryville, Alabama — they're Hebrews. Nice folks, too. It might be a surprise to you, but I happen to like Jewish food. In fact, I eat it all the time. Kosher dill pickles. Can't get enough of 'em."

Great. He thinks eating dill pickles makes him a friend of the Jews. What next? He likes bagels, too? That would get him a convert I suppose.

All of a sudden I lost my appetite and got up to leave.

"You ain't put out with me, are you? I hear you people can get real sensitive."

"No, it happens all the time," I said and took my tray to dump it in the scullery.

When I got back on deck, the air felt better than it did in the mess hall. Guys were all over the place, sitting on their gear with their legs stretched out, trying to sleep. And there were some standing at the rails and heaving, or trying to.

"Hey, Sappy, over here!" It was Kaufman sitting on a pile of gray rafts.

"How was the chow?"

"It was O.K. You-know-what on a raft, it's called. Didn't get to finish it, though."

"Get sick down there?"

"No. There was this guy, from the South, who started asking me a lot of strange questions about what my mother gives me to eat. Then he finally asked me if I was *Hebrew*."

"What a schmuck. Did you deck him?"

I just shook my head.

"Why not?"

"I don't know. Even if I did let him have it, what good would it do? The guy was like somebody who lived in the woods all his life, and he thinks we've got horns and tails. I'm surprised he didn't ask to see mine."

"You point him out to me if you see him. I'll be more than happy to show him my horns, if you know what I mean."

"We probably ought to forget it. He's just an oddball. Everybody else is O.K."

"Yeah, like the guy who called me Foo Man Jew?"

"Guess you're right. My father says there always will be some around. Even if we ever get into the clubs and the colleges, he says people will still treat us like we're not as good as they are. They just won't do it out in the open as much. Same thing with Negroes. Joe Louis is a real hero. Everybody says they love him, what he did to Schmelling and everything. But I'll bet if he tried to get in at the Waldorf Astoria he'd have a lot of trouble."

"Hell, *I'd* have trouble. They'd probably ask me if I was delivering for the Jade Palace," Kaufman said.

"Maybe that's one of the things that'll change when we win this war."

"I wouldn't bet any money on it. Remember what your father said. Oh, we'll hear that the end of the war means the end of persecution of people like us. But big changes? I doubt it. When all the parades are over, people are still going to need to see someone lower than them, someone they can feel better than. Maybe the Russians have the right answer."

"What do you mean?"

"Communism. I mean they built a whole system that's based on everybody being equal, working for common good. Nobody's richer than anybody else. If they are, they have to share the wealth with the workers. There's only one class of people, and everybody's accepted."

"Even Jews?"

"Why not. A lot of the guys who came up with the whole idea are Jewish. Marx, Lenin, and I think Trotsky, too."

"I don't know. My father says the Reds aren't any better than the Czars. He always makes fun of them. 'What's yours is mine, and what's mine is mine, too,' that's what he likes to say."

"Well, we're going to have to get along with them, whether we like it or not. They've been fighting the Nazis from the beginning. Lost millions of people doing it. You wait and see, when this is over, they'll be expecting us to divvy things up with them. And my guess is, that'd be fair."

"I guess. What do your parents think of the Russians?" I asked.

"They have no problem with them. Hell, they couldn't very well.

They're both members of a communist cell in Greenwich Village. The New School, where they teach."

"A cell? What's that like?"

"Not what you think. Not like something in a prison. It's a group of people who have joined the party, and they meet, like maybe every week for a few hours, and mostly talk about what's going on the world, how they can change it with these new ideas."

"I hear a lot of people don't think it's right for Americans to become communists," I said.

"Oh, yeah, that's true. They think it's betraying our country, especially when we're in a war. I wouldn't join the party, or a cell. I guess it might be going too far. But maybe if I was older, my parents' age, it would be more important to me. Right now, I want to see the Germans beaten, and beaten for good. Then, we'll see how America acts after it's over. If Joe Louis still can't get into a hotel, if Negroes still can't play professional ball, and if you and I still can't get into places everyone else can, well maybe I'll take a closer look at something different."

Then Kaufman stopped for a little and said, "Let's check out whether we can see anything," like he wanted to change the subject. "Looks like the clouds are breaking. I think I saw a couple of stars."

We walked up to the bow, which was good, because there weren't many people there standing at the rail.

"The sea's picking up," Kaufman said. Just then a big wave came over the bow and down the deck.

"Yeah. It's picking up a little."

"A little? If we hit waves like that in those tin boxes, I don't know how the hell we're going to get to the beach without being swamped, or worse."

Now an even bigger wave actually lifted the ship up in the air and dropped it again, with a big crash, and then a shuddering through the deck.

"What was that rumbling?" Kaufman said.

"The propeller was out of the water, just whirling around in the air.

Happens when the bow goes down far enough to lift the back end. That was something my father taught me on a very rough fishing trip."

"A wave that can toss us around like that must be pretty big stuff. Maybe dangerous stuff?" Kaufman said. That was the first time he sounded nervous to me about anything.

"It probably won't be as bad when we're in close to shore."

"But that's when these waves turn into breakers and we're in those little garbage cans trying to get on the beach. Don't like the feel of it one damn bit, I have to tell you."

I was wishing I could convince him there wasn't all that much to worry about. But actually, I wasn't so convinced myself.

"What time is it, Sappy?"

"Two-fifteen."

"We're getting close. I heard they're going to put us over the side at four, an hour or so before daybreak. We ought to try and get some sleep. Don't think we'll have much of a chance later on."

I looked around the deck area for a place to sleep, but didn't see anything in the dark. Kaufman said, "That pile of stuff over there looks like canvas. Come on."

All I could tell was it was a big pile of something covered with canvas and smelled like the tent again, oily. I pressed down on the top it was kind of soft. Kaufman banged on it and said, "Hey, not bad. Feels better than the things we've been sleeping on since we got here. Come on up, Sap."

I managed to get on top of whatever it was.

"You can just pull the top layer back, and get under it like a blanket."

That's what we did, get under the top part. It felt pretty good. I saw Kaufman had a small flashlight and was reading something.

"Hey, you know what this pile of stuff is?" he said.

"Life boats or something?"

"Try death boats. Ones that don't float, but just sink."

I couldn't figure out what he was talking about, but I didn't like the sound of it.

"Listen to this: Contents: Canvas. Burial at sea. 50 count."

"Do they really do that?"

"I don't think they'd have a stack of bags for it if they didn't, do you?"

That was all it took to get me off the pile in a hurry and back down on the deck.

Kaufman laughed. "Don't worry, it's not like somebody's going to put you in one. Unless, of course....."

"I'll just sleep on the deck here," I said, leaning against a bulkhead and using my knapsack for a lumpy pillow.

"Suit yourself. See you in a couple of hours," he said.

The problem was, I couldn't sleep now. I kept picturing myself in one of those white canvas bags, being slid over the rail and down to the water. What if I was still alive, and somebody made a mistake. How long would it take to drown? Or maybe get eaten by a shark first.

After a while I whispered up to Kaufman, "You awake?"

"I wasn't, until now. What do you want?"

"I was thinking about that number. That twenty per cent. And I figured out, there must be about two thousand people on this ship, right?" No answer. "And if twenty per cent are going to be casualties, that's four hundred of those canvas bags they're going to need."

"That's only if they get it here on the ship. Like we get hit by a bomb or something. If that's what happens, a lot of the bodies won't get found. And sometimes there's nothing left to pick up. Just dog tags maybe. So the fifty would probably be enough. Can I go back to sleep now?"

I tried to sleep, but it was hard, because I kept thinking about getting buried at sea and a bomb hitting us. Finally, I guess I dozed off. But then all of a sudden, a loud noise woke me up, and Kaufman, too. It wasn't a bomb or anything, but it was loud enough to hurt my ears and even the fillings in my teeth. It was like a horn, going *CAHOOGA-CAHOOGA-CAHOOGA* over and over.

Kaufman sat up and shouted to me. "This is it! We're stopping!"

I pointed to my glow-in-the-dark watch. "But it's only three o'clock!" I shouted back.

"So, we got here early. No traffic, I guess. Come on, before our ear drums bust open from that goddamn horn."

"What do we do now?" I said.

"Just get back in the LCA again and do what everybody else does."

I hoped that didn't include throwing up again all over the place.

"This is your last chance, Sappy. You can still sit it out. If you just don't board the LCA, nobody's s going to notice and try to figure out something to do with you."

"I'm not stopping now," I said. "Everybody on this ship has a job to do. Maybe I didn't get trained for one. But I can find one."

"You've got guts kid, that's what I like about you," said Kaufman. "You've got guts." It was a pretty good imitation of Humphrey Bogart.

CHAPTER

17

I guess I found out in a hurry what it means when someone says all hell broke loose. Those loud horns that woke everybody up were the signal for it. Big searchlights were turned on and lit up the ship, everyone on it and the water we were on. Men were moving fast in every direction, picking up rifles from racks along the deck. They checked over all their gear and gulped down tin cups of coffee that sailors were passing out. Some of them opened cans of rations, probably because they knew it was going to be a long time until they ate anything more.

Everybody was walking fast, even running, in different directions. There were sixty-five landing craft on the ship, Kaufman told me, but all the troops seemed to know where they were supposed to go. Everything, and everybody, started to look kind of reddish orange from the sun that was just beginning to show through the clouds.

The ship was rolling from side to side a lot, which would make it pretty rough in the LCAs when they hit the water. They would bang against the sides of the ship with a lot of clanging. Orders were being shouted over bull-horns by army sergeants and navy officers.

"Away number one-ninety-four! Easy on the winch....let her down slowly."

"Watch that swinging. Keep the lines taut! No, no, I said taut! No play in them!"

"Number two-twelve down. Hold her bow steady, men, that's it."

Then a whistle was blowing on the P.A. system and someone said:

"Now hear this: all remaining landing personnel who haven't reported to assigned boats for disembarking, report immediately to positions for boarding craft, on the double....Now hear this: before disembarking, secure all personal gear, check for loose ends that can foul in cargo nets..... Now hear this: all personnel possessing Dramamine, take a dose now."

I didn't have anything called Dramamine, and didn't know what it was. I asked Kaufman, "What's that?"

"Something you probably won't need, since you're just about the only one here who hasn't been puking. It's for seasickness. Mal de mer, they call it over here."

I figured the ride on the LCA now would be even worse than before, like Kaufman said it would. I thought maybe I should have some of the Dramamine just in case, even though I wasn't ever seasick And I reminded myself to find a place on the boat where I could always see the horizon but I didn't know if I could do that over the high bulkheads.

"Three-sixty-seven away!" a deck hand shouted out. I watched our landing craft go slowly down to the water, swinging back and forth. I saw the coxswain at the wheel. He looked up at where I was standing, and even though it was still pretty dark, I had a feeling that maybe this time it was Grigsby, the English chef, who was going to drive us. I waved at him, and he didn't wave back. He did nod, though, but I wasn't sure it was at me. I hoped it was him, and that he finally got his chance at some action, at least as a coxswain, if he wasn't going to be a commando.

"Three-sixty-seven down! Watch that bow, hold it off."

There was this big clang and the boat smacked into the ship, real hard, and then started bouncing around.

"Goddamn it, I said hold the bow off! On your toes down there, or someone's going to get hurt!"

Now I hoped it wasn't Grigsby at the wheel after all. I would have felt bad for him. Besides, the water was so rough, nobody could help it. Another voice yelled, "Let's go, down the net, soldiers. Watch where you step. Careful of the hands below you. Let's go, make it snappy, but make it safe!"

We went down to the LCA three at a time. They told us to face the ship and lower ourselves down a big, brown cargo net, which was a bunch of small squares made of rope. It was harder than it looked, with the big ship and the little LCA both bouncing on the rough water. But those guys must have practiced before. They knew what to do. Lucky for me, even though I didn't have the practice they did, I guess because I was lighter and did the rope climbing in school, I was pretty much able to keep up with them and managed not to step on anybody's hands. Which was also lucky for me. I didn't want to get bawled out in front of everybody.

I hit the deck in one last drop of about three feet, landing with my feet spread apart and my knees bent, the way I was taught in gym class. Kaufman had a little problem, though. He landed on his feet O.K., but another guy fell on top of him and they both went down. I thought Kaufman might get mad and yell at the other guy. But he didn't. He helped him get up.

"You O.K.?" Kaufman asked, holding on to the guy to steady him.

"Sure. Sorry about that. Didn't see you there."

That was when I realized something that changed. The joking around stopped, so did the complaining about everything. Now these same guys were caring about what they were doing and everyone else who was doing it. It was like all of a sudden, we were all on a mission. Which is funny, because that's exactly what it was, like General Eisenhower said. If somebody falls down, you pick him up, you don't step over him or laugh at him. If somebody is kind of scared of getting sick, you try and do something about it. Nobody cares what your last name is or what color you are or where you come from. You're just a bunch of guys standing in a boat that's bouncing so hard you can hardly stand up. Your stomach feels bad and you wish you didn't eat that food they gave you. You're cold and you're wet from all the spray that keeps coming in the boat. And you realize pretty quick that all those war movies don't show what it really feels like to be going to a battle. There's no music, nobody's singing songs about it. The fumes from the engine stink, and you think you do, too, because you can't shower any more. There's nothing nice about a war, except for one thing, coming home from it some day alive, and not ending up at the bottom of the ocean or on a bloody beach. Still, I wanted to be there. Or least I knew I had to be there. There's a difference, believe me. I tried to imagine forty men there on the boat who might not make it back, if Kaufman was right. All I could think to do was say a little silent prayer, and I did.

Please, God, let all of us make it through this, each and every one of us, and get to go home again to our families. I hope that's not asking too much, but I have a feeling it might be. Thank you, God. I realized that if all the men on my boat did make it back, then maybe another boat would have to lose eighty men, if that's what the law of averages is about, and it wouldn't be fair now, would it?

"Three-sixty-seven, shove off!" The order came from back up on the ship through a bullhorn. The coxswain checked everything on all sides, nodded and pushed the throttle hard to one side, and LCA367 was on its way with a big roar.

I was hanging on to keep from falling down, and I saw piles of stuff up in the corner of the boat. There was this gun kind of thing that I thought was a mortar or a small cannon. There were piles of rope next to it, with what looked like giant fishing hooks. Kaufman saw me staring at the stuff.

"That's how we're going to get up hundred-foot cliffs. Grappling hooks. We shoot them up with explosives. It's an idea they used back in the Crusades. Only they didn't have mortars. They threw them up, over castle walls. Not much changes in warfare. Just gets modernized."

It made sense to me. Shoot up a hook that sinks into the dirt and climb up the cliffs on it.

"Some of the other squads will be trying a different approach. Ladders. Not regular ones, but special ones for climbing up buildings that are on fire, courtesy of the London Fire Department, I hear. They're light enough for a couple of guys to carry ashore and put up against the cliff. But I'd rather use a rope. I hear those ladders can start swaying and can fall back into the water with guys on them. They'd be sitting ducks. Or dead ducks."

I tried to picture what Kaufman said and didn't like it at all. Then all of a sudden there was a huge explosion that shook everything, and everybody too. Then there were a few more, just as big, just as loud. It scared the crap out of me, and Kaufman could see it. Were the Germans shooting at us already?

"Don't worry. It's our guys on the battle wagons, bombarding the shore we're headed to. Sixteen-inchers. They'll be pounding away all morning."

Kaufman stood on a coil of rope to get a view over the side rail. I did the same thing. Then what I saw was something I never expected to see. It was actually all too big to describe. As far as you could see, for miles and miles, were ships, American ships, English and some I didn't know where they were from.

"Look at 'em," Kaufman said, and he whistled. "Destroyers, cruisers and the big babies lobbing shells at those cliffs we're headed for."

There were balls of orange flames and black smoke coming from the giant guns. Over and over, never stopping.

"Welcome to Normandy, Sappy," Kaufman said. "I heard this whole armada is the biggest invasion force in the history of war. And we're going to be part of it. How does that feel?"

"Good," I said. "A little scary, too."

"I know. Anybody who tells you he isn't scared is either a liar or crazy."

I figure I wasn't either one, just a kid who never saw anything like this in his life, and probably won't ever again.

For the first time I could make out land in front of us. There were a lot of cliffs, and I wondered which one we were supposed to shoot hooks and ropes up on. Then I could see hundreds of boats just like the one we were on, all going straight for the beaches and the cliffs. There was smoke coming up from the land now, and I figured it must have been from the shells coming over our heads. Now the only thing you could smell was that smoke, like somebody lit the whole world on fire.

"All right, men, gather round the best you can." It was a voice I didn't hear before. I saw it was coming from a man with one silver bar on his helmet. That would make him a second lieutenant, but I could swear he wasn't a whole lot older than me, maybe twenty-one.

The Rangers staggered away from the sides and let go of what they were holding on to. They walked very wobbly, like they didn't have their sea legs, and held onto each other to keep from going down. One poor guy hoisted himself up to the top of the bulkhead and vomited over the side. Nobody said anything, probably because they figured they might be doing the same thing pretty soon.

The officer had to talk loud with the motor and all the shelling making a huge racket. "We've been through it before, I know, but we're going to go over one more time what our mission is going to be. We hit the beach at o-six-hundred, when the air-cover starts. As soon as you feel that we've beached, grab all your gear and move forward. The coxswain will drop the ramp in what should be about two feet of water. Get down the ramp and into the water as fast as you can. We're expecting heavy enemy fire, aimed at the boat. So it's important to do two things: Don't be targets, standing in the boat or moving slowly down the ramp. Double-time it. The faster you move, the less of a target you'll make. The other thing, we need to unload the boat as fast as we can, so it doesn't become a sitting duck."

There were those words again. "The coxswain has to back off the beach and turn around — fast — so he can head back to the mother ship and pick up another load. He's not going to appreciate having to stand around while the German guns sight down on him".

"Mortar guys?" Four men nodded and raised their hands briefly. "You should get off first, and run like hell for the beach. As soon as you're on dry sand, get the charges loaded and the hooks ready to fire. Nobody can get off the beach until the hooks are up and the ropes are ready to climb. That's where there's the greatest danger of being a target. O.K.?"

Nobody answered.

"We go up the ropes one man right after another. No time to wait around for the guy in front of you to get up top. That means you have to hold on tight enough to avoid slipping back down on whoever's below you. And that brings up a problem we're going to have to deal with. It's been raining for two days here. It just stopped late after midnight. That means those cliffs have likely turned to mud. And wet mud is going to make the ropes slimy, hard to get a good bite on. Sorry, but you need to know what you're facing. We'll just have to make the best of it.

"Now, when we're on top, you know our mission: taking out the two big guns that are waiting in a concrete bunker. They're the biggest ones they've got, or anyone else has for that matter. And as long as they're operational, the Navy isn't going to be able to move in with the heavy stuff we need to secure the beach and the headlands. If we don't put those guns out of commission, this whole invasion could get bogged down. If we do get them, it can help us secure Normandy and move into France, then on to Germany. And you know what that means. The beginning of the end of this war.

"Now, make sure you've got all the grenades you can carry. Mortars alone won't do it. If you've got phosphorous grenades, save them for pill boxes and bunkers. And handle them very, very carefully. We've already had one accident, before we even left England."

He didn't have to tell me that. I could still see, and smell, that poor guy who caught fire from phosphorous grenades. I didn't have any, and didn't want any either, thank you.

"Any questions?" Maybe there were some, or even a lot of them. But nobody asked anything.

"This is what you've been training for the last six months. You're the best at what you do. Now, you're going to get a chance to prove it. Good luck, and God bless every one of you."

I was kind of relieved when the Lieutenant looked right at me and didn't seem to notice anything strange, like the way my helmet fit. But I was wondering where the captain was, who was supposed to lead the company into action.

I asked Kaufman, "That officer, the lieutenant, he's new. What happened to the Captain?"

"You didn't hear? He got hurt yesterday afternoon. A bad jeep accident. Roll-over. Guess he was driving down to the beach with more grenades that he requisitioned. Thought we didn't have enough. Some big-ass truck ran into his jeep, and he rolled a couple of times. The jeep landed on top of him. I hear he may lose both his legs. And he just kept screaming that he didn't want to be evacuated to a hospital. He had to go with his troops, he said. An awful way to get pulled out of action, before it even begins. Now we've got this green second-louie, probably right out of officer's school. Don't know if he has any idea about what a Ranger's supposed to do. Guess he'll find out soon enough."

I could see something different about Kaufman. It was the color of his face. It wasn't that almost-yellow, like a sun tan. It was almost all white now, maybe a little gray.

"You O.K.?" I asked him.

"I heaved my guts out. Well, maybe not my guts. Because I can still feel 'em. They hurt like hell."

I tried to change the subject, figuring it might help him. "How many ships you figure are firing their big guns?"

"Who knows. I doubt there's a single ship anywhere in the whole Atlantic that isn't here. Amazing, the fire power they're throwing. I don't know what France looked like before this, but I have a feeling it's going to look like the moon pretty soon, with all the craters that'll be there."

"Think maybe the Germans will just surrender now?"

"Fraid not. They're used to it, the bombing. They've been taking it for a long time. Besides, it's not even their country that's taking the beating. It's somebody else's. They stole it."

"Are you worried about what could happen to us?"

"Hey, I'm a Ranger, remember."

"Yeah, I know."

"But still, sure I worry. And wonder."

"About what?"

"If I 'm gonna die in the next second, or minute, or hour. You never know if it's going to happen, or when. You take your mind off it if you can. Think about how your finger's got to stop shaking long enough to squeeze a trigger. Your arms have to stop long enough to climb a rope. Of course, there's one thing that takes all the worry out of you, from what I hear."

"What's that?"

"Actually seeing the guy who's trying to kill you before you get him. I hear stories that when you see the enemy — I mean his face, not just a uniform and a helmet, but eyes and nose and everything — it's like some kind of potion. All the shaking stops, because you're looking right into the eyes of a guy who shakes and pukes just like you. But he also has to kill you. And you know you have to be steady enough to squeeze off a perfect shot. If you only have a knife, you've got to have enough strength to stick it through his neck or ribs. And if all you have is your two hands, guess what — you'll choke the guy to death with 'em. It's something that just happens, from what I hear. You're so worried you're not going to survive, that you *do* survive."

"But the other guy's going to do the same thing, isn't he?"

"Sure he is. But you know why he's going to lose, and why you're going to be the survivor, instead of him?"

I just shook my head.

"Because somewhere, in the back of his mind, even though he's had as good training as we've had, and he's got the same kind of equipment we do, and wants to live as much as anyone else, way back there, there's a little seed, real little. It's a seed of a question. He doesn't even know it's there. But at that one instant, when he has to stop shaking long enough to kill you, he's going to wonder, without even realizing he's wondering."

"About what?"

"About whether he's doing it, getting ready to die for something that's right. Oh, he's been told a million times that it's right, by his sergeant, his captain, his generals, his fucking fuehrer. But he doesn't know for sure, beyond a reasonable doubt, like they say in courts, that what he's doing is right. And in that fraction of a second, when he asks that little question, *BANG!* You put one right between his eyes. Because he didn't stop shaking long enough to put one between yours."

I thought about what Kaufman said, about the German he talked about. The war movies they show you in the theater on Saturday afternoon don't tell you about that stuff, about soldiers who have to stop shaking long enough to pull a trigger. Do the German guys actually believe that what they're doing is right? If they don't, do they maybe keep shaking on purpose so they don't have to kill somebody for something that's wrong? But that's suicide, isn't? Maybe that's really what war is. Kill me before I kill myself by shaking too much to shoot. That's crazy, I know. And that could be what war is about, too. Going crazy enough to kill people. No wonder everybody in it, like Kaufman says, is afraid.

I thought about the Twenty-Third Psalm, which the homeroom teacher usually reads after we salute the flag.

Yea, though I walk through the valley of the shadow of death, I will fear no evil.

Maybe not, but what about the stuff I can't see coming? Like a mortar shell, a machine gun round, a land mine?

Thy rod and thy staff, they comfort me?

I don't even know what a rod or a staff is. A big club, like a ball bat? A long pole, like to get things down from places? I don't know. What Kaufman said about the guy who isn't sure why he's supposed to kill you, I get that. But that other stuff, what stops that? What makes your foot go an inch to the left or right, so you don't step on the mine that's buried in the sand and that would blow your legs and everything else off you? Maybe I should ask Kaufman. On second thought, I don't think I should.

I felt the motor of the boat shift into high gear again.

"We're going in," Kaufman said. "It must be time."

"Do you know what a rod is?" I asked.

"A what?"

"A rod. And a staff. Do you know what they are?"

"What is this, Twenty Questions? We're going into a damn war, and you're asking me riddles. You're amazing, Sappy."

"No, it's not a riddle. It's a psalm. The twenty-third. Your rod and your staff, they comfort you. I was just wondering what that means."

"Well, I tell you what. If I get out of this thing, I'll find out for you. Meanwhile, if it's all the same to you, I'm going to depend on my own rod." He patted the rifle. "And my staff," he added, touching the bayonet he put on the end of the barrel.

I felt pretty stupid for bringing up the psalm business, but I thought maybe I could get my mind off the German trying to stop shaking.

"Sorry. I guess it was a dumb question."

"No, Sappy, nothing's too dumb to ask right now. Some guys are wondering why their mothers always put the peanut butter on the bread before the jam. Why didn't they do it the other way around? When you get as scared inside as some of these guys are, you really want to think about something else. Like, what did it mean when your girlfriend moved her leg over against yours in the drive-in? Were you supposed to take it is a signal to do more than just sit there and kiss her? What nobody wants to think about is what they think is going to happen to them. It's too scary. Peanut butter and jelly isn't."

Now something really scary happened. First there was a screaming whistle, and then a huge explosion that you could actually feel, like when thunder happens right over your head. And water sprayed all over us, like something huge fell in the water. It happened again, and again, even closer.

"Artillery coming in," the lieutenant shouted.

"Jesus, that was close," Kaufman yelled. "And big. They're shelling us from the shore, probably the guns we're supposed to take out."

The boat was rocking pretty bad from the waves that the big shells were making when they hit the water. I guess the Germans figured it was time for them to start shooting back and we were the targets. Sitting ducks. LCA 367 was only one of them. Most of the guys dropped down on the deck and put their hands over their heads and their ears. I just stood there, like I was frozen. Kaufman, too.

"All we can do now is hope," Kaufman said. "Nothing we can shoot at. Nowhere we can go, except to that beach, which'll probably be even worse."

Now the boat felt like it was jumping up out of the water. The coxswain was turning the wheel back and forth, left and right. We could hardly stand up, and just had to hang on the anything we could find.

"Evasive action," Kaufman yelled. And another shell hit the water pretty close, and we got another dousing. "Guess we're supposed to be a harder target to hit that way."

"Think it'll work?" I yelled back.

"Doubt it. My guess is they're just lobbing shells out here in our general direction, figuring sooner or later the law of averages will give 'em some hits. If they were actually aiming at something, it wouldn't be us, just forty guys in a box. They'd be going for the bigger stuff, like the LCTs, with the tanks and trucks, and a lot more people. Makes you feel like a sitting duck, doesn't it?"

"A zigging duck."

"Stand by to beach!" It was the coxswain shouting really loud. "Brace yourselves, lads!"

The boat came to a sudden stop, with a grinding sound, which must have been from the sand and rocks underneath us. I was still holding on to a cleat and managed not to fall down. Everybody else got up pretty fast. That was it, the end of the long trip from Teaneck, New Jersey to a beach in Normandy. I didn't know exactly what we were in for, and I don't think anybody else did either.

Then there was a clanging metal sound, and when I looked up at the front, I could see the big steel ramp dropping down, and then a thud when it hit the bottom. It was a like a drawbridge on a castle going down.

"Welcome to France, mates. Now kindly get your arses off my boat, so I can at least have a fair chance at getting away from this god-forsaken beach and back for more of you." It was the English coxswain again, sounding pretty excited.

Now the lieutenant yelled at us. "O.K., let's go. Grab your gear and hit the beach!" The sergeant slapped everybody on the back, for good luck, I guess, and gave a little push forward, too.

I was close to the last one to step on the ramp, right behind Kaufman. On the way out I heard this voice, with an English accent.

"Give 'em hell, New Jersey."

It was Grigsby, after all. I looked up at him, and he smiled and nodded, and then saluted. I saluted back, and felt a push behind me. It was my turn down the ramp, so I didn't have a chance to tell him I'd do what I would for his daughter Jenny.

There wasn't a whole lot of action going on in the sand that I could see in front of our boat. When I got off the ramp I went down in the water up to my chest. It was real cold, enough to get my teeth chattering. I didn't have a rifle to hold over my head like the guy in front of me, so I took off my knapsack and held it up, to keep my stuff dry.

"Holy shit," Kaufman yelled, and he pointed down the beach to the left. It looked like a living hell, maybe four or five football fields away. A bunch of boats were close to the beach, like ours was, but it was different. I could see guys falling down into the water, over their heads, and trying to swim. It looked like they got off in water that was too deep. Then I saw sand and water exploding. I could see dark things floating in the water. And I realized what they were. Bodies. Soldiers. Either they were shot or maybe drowned. The landing boats still kept coming, and the men still kept trying to get to the beach.

"It's awful," Kaufman said. "Look at the water down there. It's turning red. Blood, for God's sake." And I didn't say anything, because I couldn't.

The lieutenant and sergeant were already on the sand and trying to hurry everybody else to get there. They kept waving and pointing to this place that was like a cove at the bottom of a cliff that went straight up.

I was pretty sure it was the cliff everybody talked about, a hundred feet high, where the big guns were.

As soon as we got on the sand, we started running to the cove. I heard the sergeant shout, "Take cover there and stay against the cliff. On the double, let's go. Don't be a target."

Then it really got scary. Sand started to fly up on the beach and the same time you could hear machine guns shooting. I didn't know where they were coming from. It had to be on top of the cliff. Once we got to the cove, the guns couldn't reach us.

But then I heard some different noise. Engines, getting closer. A couple of guys pointed up in the sky, and you could see airplanes coming along the beach, real low.

"Strafers," somebody shouted.

There looked like maybe six or seven planes, and when they got near where we were, the sand started exploding even more. It was a long line along the sand.

"Messerschmitts," Kaufman said. Then he yelled up at them. "You lousy fucking Nazi bastards. Crash and burn. Die." They didn't, though. They just kept flying along the beach and shooting down at it. Then I heard an explosion that sounded real close.

"Grenade!" someone shouted and pointed up at the top of the cliff. Some of the Rangers took a few steps back on the beach to get a look.

"They're throwing 'em down on us. Get back against the cliff!" the sergeant barked out. Everybody listened and got right up against the muddy wall. A lot of them crouched down. I did the same thing, and so did Kaufman. It was a good thing. Because a second grenade exploded, pretty close. And a third one, too. It was so close I could feel sand coming down on me.

"We're never gonna be able to set up the hooks, with those goddamn grenades dropping on us," the sergeant said to the lieutenant. "They've got us pinned down."

"We can't just stay here on the beach, either," the officer said. "Something's got to give."

A whistling sound gave the warning that a shell was headed toward the beach where we were all crouching down. It sounded like it was coming from the ocean.

"It's one of ours. It's gonna be short!" somebody yelled.

Turns out it was short, but not enough to hit us. It must have been aimed at the big German guns, and the edge of the cliff. I guess it hit the ground at the top, because you could feel the dirt and stones falling down. Then there was a scream from somewhere up there. And something hit the ground with a thud in front of us. It was a body, a German one. You could tell by the grey uniform and funny-looking helmet they all wore.

"Dead?" somebody asked.

"No, look, he's moving," said another guy.

The German's uniform was all ripped, and had some blood on it. He just looked up at the sky and moaned. He had two leather belts criss-crossed on his chest, and they were loaded with hand grenades.

"That's the bastard that's been dropping grenades down on us," the sergeant said.

"Yeah, looks like he won't be throwing anything for a long time. Probably busted his arms up on the way down."

It must have been true, about him being the grenade thrower, because there weren't any more explosions in the sand.

"Somebody ought to check him out," said the lieutenant. "We have a medic here?"

"What for? He was trying to kill us."

"He's a prisoner now, that's what's for." A couple of guys groaned and shook their heads.

Somebody said, "The kid. He saved that burning guy back in England. Isn't he a medic?"   Everybody looked at me. "Hey, kid," one of them yelled. "Here's your chance to get your first German. Put a tourniquet, around his neck. Real tight."

"He ain't bleedin'," said another.

"I can fix that in a hurry," said the big New Yorker, Tiny. He pulled a big knife out of a holster on his leg and went over to the German.

"Never mind, soldier," barked the lieutenant. "That man's a prisoner of war now."

"We can't take any prisoners, sir," the sergeant said.

"But we've got one now. And the Geneva Convention says we have to take him into custody and give him medical treatment if he needs it. Now, somebody do something to help him."

"We don't have any medics with us," the sergeant said.

The German tried to get up on one elbow but couldn't. I could hear him gasping, trying to breathe. I knew that sound. I made it once in a football scrimmage at school, when someone rammed into my stomach with his helmet.

I figured nobody else was going to do anything, so I said, "I think he got the wind knocked out of him when he fell."

The guy stared up at me, looking scared, which was funny, because why would a guy with a chest full of grenades be scared of a kid like me? I helped him lie down again and straddled him. Then I reached under his jacket and grabbed his belt, like the coach did to me on the field that day. And I pulled up on it, then let go, and did it again a few more times. That got air into his lungs, and he started breathing again pretty soon.

"What the hell, the kid knows what he's doing. Look at that guy. His face ain't blue anymore. Just from pullin' on his damn belt."

The sergeant stood over the prisoner. He got down on one knee and started to unbuckle the two grenade belts. The German put his hands on the sergeant's, trying to stop him. "Get your hands down, damn you. You're a prisoner, and you're giving up those grenades and anything else you've got on you in the way of weapons. Got it?"

The German probably didn't understand the words, but I guess he didn't have to. He put his hands over his head and let the sergeant get the belt off. I counted twelve grenades, but they weren't like ours, with the pineapple bumps. They were like cans on the ends of sticks.

The sergeant said, "These might come in handy, if we start running short of our own. They work the same way as ours, but with these long handles that give you good leverage when you throw 'em," the sergeant explained. He turned to me. "What do you think, kid? Is he all right?"

"I think so."

"Let's find out. O.K., up on your feet."

The German shrugged and stayed put, which angered the sergeant, who pulled him into a sitting position, then stood and grabbed him under the shoulders and tried to make him stand. But the moment he put any weight on his legs, they both buckled at the knees, and he screamed out in pain as he fell back to the sand.

"Guess maybe he's *not* O.K.," the sergeant said. "Could be he broke a leg, or both of them, coming down. Well, at least he isn't going to take off on us."

I wondered what we were going to do with the prisoner. It's not like we could take him up the cliff with us or anything. The sergeant and the lieutenant finally propped the guy up against the bottom of the cliff, in the cove. They even covered him with a blanket that one Ranger offered.

"Somebody will get him. Either one of his people, or our medics when they come through later. At least he won't be shot at."

"Don't count on it," the sergeant said.

"Let's get going with what we were sent to do," the lieutenant said. "Position the mortar and the gang hooks. We've got to get to the top before they realize what we're up to, if they haven't already figured it out. For your information, this is Pont d'Hoc we're standing under. And the big guns are up there."

A group of guys dragged a mortar out on the beach a couple of feet and put it in position, aimed at the top of the cliff. They took the coils of rope and tied on the big hooks. Then they put the first one in the muzzle of the mortar. One guy sighted up at the cliff and waved his hand, like to say it was ready. .

"Fire away," the lieutenant said.

The mortar exploded with a puff of brown smoke and the hook shot up the cliff. The rope behind it uncoiled. When the hook went as far as it was going to go, it dropped down to the top of the cliff. But it missed the edge.

"Heads up. It's coming down!" the sergeant shouted, and anyone close to the mortar scattered away. The hook bumped into the cliff a few times and landed a couple of feet away from where they shot it.

"Let's go. Check your aim and fire again!" ordered the lieutenant.

The men didn't need the order. They were already re-sighting the mortar and pulled it back from the wall. Everybody held their breath when the hook shot up again. This time, it sailed over the lip and went out of sight. We all waited to see if would come back down again. But nothing happened. The sergeant grabbed the end of the rope and gave it a tug. It didn't give. He pulled again, harder.

"It's in," he said, like he was pretty proud of himself. "Let's get moving up there, on the double. And move the mortar over a few yards, so we can get another hook in."

While the firing crew was getting ready for another shot, a Ranger stepped forward, like he didn't have to be told he'd be the first up on the rope.

"Go get 'em, Bartholomew," the sergeant said, and patted him on the shoulder. Bartholomew grabbed the rope and pulled himself up. He jammed his feet into the wall, but the wet mud just slid down, and so did his feet. He kicked back into the cliff, cursed and pulled himself up a few feet. But then, his hands slid on the rope, which was wet and covered with mud. He slid down the few feet to the bottom again, cursed some more and tried once more.

"Come on, Bart, take a bite on that line. You can do it. Use your feet," one of his buddies said. Now he tried winding the rope around the heels of his boots. But then they slipped, too. I felt bad for him. He was one of the best climbers in the company a guy said.

The sergeant finally told the lieutenant, "It's too much weight to pull up with a wet rope. He's got sixty pounds on his back, plus his own weight. We never trained with a mud-slimed rope."

Another Ranger, Clausen, reached up and grabbed a hold on the second rope that was now in place. The veins in his hands bulged like they were going to pop. He'd stab his boots into the cliff, but rocks would pop out of the mud and so did his feet. Finally, after three or four tries, he just slid down the slimy rope to the bottom.

Finally the lieutenant said, "Hold it, soldier. It's not going to work this way."

Clausen looked at his hands, which were bleeding now. He said, "I'll make it. I just need to get a better grip, keep the rope away from the mud."

"We need someone a lot lighter, sergeant," the lieutenant said.

"They're all carrying the same load, sir," the sergeant answered.

"I don't think so. Not all of them." He looked at me and nodded. "He couldn't weigh much more than a hundred pounds. And look at that little pack on his back. Can he climb a rope?"

The sergeant was quiet, like he was thinking. Then he said, "Yes, sir, from what I've heard, he can probably climb a rope pretty well."

"Then let's get him up there. Send a rope with him. If he can secure it to something solid, a tree or a rock, we can work a pulley and haul system, take some of the load off people."

"Sir, he's just a kid. What if he runs into enemy fire?"

"What difference does his age make? He's part of the unit, isn't he?"

"Not officially, sir."

"What are you trying to say, sergeant? Time's running out on us. We've got to get up on top, while we can do some good. And you're talking double-talk."

"The captain knew about him, sir."

"Well, the captain isn't here. He's in a hospital somewhere. I'm here in his place. All I know about that kid is he rode in here with us after he saved a man's life in England, and that he can climb a rope, according to you. And you tell me he's not *official?*"

I figured I should probably say something. I went over to the lieutenant and said, "Excuse me sir. The sergeant's right. I'm not officially a member of this unit. It's a real long story. It started back on the Queen Elizabeth. A colonel told me to stay with this unit, until he could figure out what to do with me." He drew a deep breath. "I stowed away, sir."

The lieutenant's jaw dropped. He looked at me, and then at the sergeant, and finally out to the sea. He turned back and shook his head. "What the hell is this, the War of Eighteen-Twelve? Nobody stows away anymore. I can't believe this. But I don't have time to get convinced it's true. Whatever the hell you're doing here, you're here. And if you want to be part of this war that bad, I guess you're going to get your chance. But you'll have to volunteer. I won't order you to go up there. It's your choice. If you want to stay down here, you've got my permission to do that."

"I want to go up, sir. It's what I came here for."

"All right, then. If you're sure you want to take the risk," the lieutenant said. His voice was a lot softer than it was before.

"Yes, sir. I'm sure, sir."

"What's your name, anyway?"

"Saperstein."

"Any relation to the man who owns the Harlem Globetrotters? Abe Saperstein?"

"I don't think so. But a lot of people ask me that."

"Well, you've either got a lot of courage, or you're just pretty damn foolish. But I have a feeling you're not foolish. Good luck son."

I went over and picked up a coil of rope and dropped it over my head and one shoulder. It was heavier than I thought it would be, probably from all the water that got into it on the boat. Kaufman was staring at me, like he was kind of worried.

"What are you going up there with?"

"The rope," I said.

"I can see that. I mean, you don't have a piece, right?" I shook my head.

"How are you going to defend yourself if the enemy comes at you? Lasso them? Come on, you need to carry *something*."

"What do you think I should take?"

The idea of carrying a gun or, worse yet, having to shoot one, still bothered me a lot. I know that's strange. But I guess that's what I am anyway, strange.

"There aren't any extra pieces, I can tell you that. But I've got an idea," Kaufman said. He pointed at the German prisoner, who was watching me and eyeing the rope I was wearing. He got real nervous. I hoped he didn't think I was going to hang him with it or something. Kaufman walked over to him, and the guy sort of winced. But then Kaufman just walked past him to the pile of grenades in his belts that were on the ground. He leaned down and picked up the belts and came back over to me. The German looked relieved.

I stared at the strange-looking grenades, which seemed more like toys, something with a ball on a string that you toss up in the air and catch. But I knew they were deadly enough to kill people. Still I wondered what I was supposed to do with them.

"They're called potato mashers," Kaufman said. "That's what they look like, something your mother uses in the kitchen to make a kugel."

That was a really strange picture, my mother standing over a big bowl of boiled potatoes holding a hand grenade in her hand.

The sergeant was watching us and came over.

"What's this about? You giving him grenades? German grenades?" he said to Kaufman.

"He's got to have something up there. He could be climbing right into a whole nest of the enemy, unarmed. That's nuts," said Kaufman.

"Do you know how to use those things?" the sergeant asked me.

"I think so. You unscrew the cap and pull the cord and toss them. It takes about six seconds before they blow up, doesn't it?" I didn't tell him where I learned that, from one of my combat magazines.

"*If* they use the same timing we do. Anyway, until you pull that safety string, they won't go off. But once you do, you get rid of it. Not too fast, though. Sometimes they land with a few seconds left, enough time for the enemy to lob it back at you. When you get it back, it's out of time. And so are you."

I couldn't figure out what to do next. I guess Kaufman decided for me.

"Come on, hold out your arms. I'll put 'em on." That's what he did. Pretty soon I had the German's belts criss-crossed on my chest, with all those grenades. It was all pretty heavy and I wondered if that would slow me down. Or what would happen if one of the grenades got caught on a twig or something on the way up the cliff, and the cap would come off, and the whole bunch would explode. I'd be just a lot of pieces splattered all over the place.

"That's more like it. You're armed and ready now," Kaufman said. "Don't you feel more secure, like a Ranger?"

It was a question I didn't try to answer.

The lieutenant came over again. "Saperstein, if you make it up there and can drop a rope down, I also want you to look for that bunker, the one with the big guns. Don't try to do anything to it. Just check it out. If you can find out whether the guns are there, I want you to get over to the edge of the cliff and give us a signal."

"How?"

He thought about that a while, and then stared at the grenades. "I tell you what. When you think you're ready to let us know, unscrew the caps on the bottom of two grenades. If the guns are there, pull the rings out of two of them, one at a time, and toss them as far out, away from the edge of the cliff as you can on the count of four. In two seconds, they'll go off in the air. If the guns aren't there, just pull one ring and let the grenade go by itself, same way. Got that?"

"Yes, sir. Two if the guns are there, one if they're not."

"And give them a good heave. Like baseballs from the outfield." I kind of liked that idea, a peg from centerfield to home.

"Yes, sir." It was a real strange kind of code, one grenade or two, but I couldn't think of anything else to drop down the cliff. I only had one baseball, and there was no way I was going to give that up.

"If they're in that bunker, we can radio to the ships and give them the position to fire on. Understand?"

"Yes, sir."

"God be with you," he said.

I didn't want to tell him he usually is with me, that I talk to him all the time. That would really sound weird.

"And don't forget one thing. Those grenades. Make sure you're real careful once the rings drop out of the bottom. If they get caught on anything, well, you can figure that out."

"Yes, sir, I definitely can."

CHAPTER
18

So there I was, a make-believe soldier with a bunch of potato masher grenades strapped to my chest and a whole company of real soldiers watching me very close, probably wondering if I could actually get up the cliff, and then, what I could do if I did get there. Didn't they think I was wondering, too?

I stared at the rope and tried to picture what was up at the top of it. I saw concrete bunkers all over the place, with a lot of eyes, German eyes, watching for somebody to just try getting up there, ready to start shooting when they did.

"You can do it kid," one of the Rangers yelled out.

"Make mashed potatoes out of 'em," another one said.

"Yeah, and a *koo-gull* ,too." That was from that guy with the southern accent on the ship.

What was I supposed to say? That I wished I was home, taking a bite of potato kugel my mother made for the holidays instead of looking at a slimy, wet wall that I was supposed to climb to the top? So I just did one of those shrugs of mine and tried to smile, which wasn't the easiest thing in the world to do, I really mean it. I grabbed the rope and it had the same smell, kind of like tar, as the one in the school gym. I closed my eyes, took a real deep breath, and then I could see the sneer on Herbie Schoo's face, and the knife in his teeth. That did it. I was going to climb like I never did before, higher and faster, like there was a whole bunch of Black Cats after me, all with knives. I could feel the air slamming into my lungs and it made the grenades get tighter against my chest. I didn't try to use my feet, because I knew they'd just slip in the mud. I went up with hands only, and it made my arms feel like they were going to pop out of my shoulders. But they didn't.

Now I was maybe twenty feet from the top. My fingers were getting numb from the cold, wet rope. I could see blood coming running down to my wrists, but I couldn't feel anything in my palms, which I knew were bleeding and getting torn up. I just kept pulling. And praying.

Just a few more feet to go, and I turned my head to look back down for the first time. That was a big mistake, because when I stopped for just that second or so, I must have loosened my grip a little. I started slipping back. All I could do was kick into the wall, and hope it wouldn't start falling apart like it did with the other guys. A rock the size of a baseball plopped out of the mud and I watched it bounce all the way down, like I figured I was going to do.

Somehow, the toe of one boot managed to stick in, just long enough for me to get another bleeding grip on the rope and start up again. No more looking down, I told myself. Just up, unless I wanted a quick trip to the bottom like the German prisoner had.

Finally, the top was actually within my reach, that is if my arms could still go up ever again. Well, they did, slowly, and I was able to get my fingers into something I figured I might never see again. Grass. I stopped again before I tried to pull myself up there. I listened real carefully. All I could hear was the explosions from the big guns on our ships out there, and they seemed to be farther away. I didn't hear the machine guns, though, that were shooting down at everybody on the beach. It was a little spooky, because it just wasn't all that noisy any more.

I kicked into the cliff again, but at least I was holding on to the top, in case I started sliding. But I didn't. I was able to use my knees to help. And then with one push of every part of me, I got half of myself onto the grass and grabbed handfuls of it to get all the way over the edge.

I kept my face almost in the grass. It smelled good, like when my father mowed the lawn. I didn't want to raise my head up any higher than

I had to, just in case somebody had it in his gun sight. I saw this big, round concrete thing about a football field away, right at the top of the cliff. It looked like a fort. There was a very big steel door down near the ground, under these slits, which I figured Germans inside looked out from. Behind the concrete thing I could see railroad tracks that went back to some kind of shed. If the guns were there, in the bunker, that's what the guns on our ships were trying to blow up.

I saw the hook that was shot up and was sunk in the ground, behind a rock, which I guess kept it from coming loose. I sort of crawled like a crab to where it was. When I got there I got another whiff of something. But it didn't smell good, like the grass. Actually it was awful. Then I saw why. There off to the side of the hook and the rock, was a big cow. A dead one, laying on its side. It looked like someone pumped it up with an air hose and made it into a kind of balloon. As putrid as it smelled, I figured I should get over to it, so I could hide behind it while I got ready to attach the rope I brought up and drop it down to the Rangers at the bottom.

The closer I got to the cow, the more my stomach was acting like I was going to heave. But I held it in. I knew it was a good thing to hide behind, because when I got to it, I couldn't see the big bunker, which meant no one in it could see me. I couldn't help having a little talk with God again.

Dear God, how did I get myself into this? I'm hiding behind a dead cow in a woman's uniform that's starting to smell as bad as the cow and a helmet that comes down over my eyes. But thank you for letting me make the climb up here without falling back down. Or getting shot. Now, please just help me do what I'm supposed to do: Get the rope tied and down to them, so they can do something about those guns, if I can find them. Anything you can do to help me would be very much appreciated, dear God. Thank you.

I looked in the other direction now and saw a round stone tower, maybe about five stories high, without any windows and a bulge at the top. It looked real old, not like the bunker, which looked pretty new. The tower seemed like it was part of a farm, where they store stuff, but I don't know what. Maybe it was the farm where the dead cow was from. Farther away I saw a building made out of the same stone, kind of brown. It could have been a farm house or a barn. That was it, nothing else around.

I wondered if I should get the rope I brought tied down and dropped to the guys on the beach first, or try to find where the guns were before that. Dropping the rope would be easier, but if I did that first, somebody might see me and I wouldn't have a chance to check on the bunker to see if the guns were in it. So, I made a battlefield decision. First, look for the guns. If they were in the bunker, then I'd have the two grenades ready to drop, or one of them, if they weren't there. After I made sure the caps were on real tight, I didn't want to keep the guys on the beach waiting around any more, so I decided to make a run for the bunker and hope nobody saw me. That's why I went around the back, figuring I could get on top and find a way to take a peek in. I just hoped no German guy would come back from taking a leak or something and yell to the other guys that some kid with a helmet that's too big was running across the field, away from the dead cow. Maybe they'd think it was my cow, and I was looking for help. To do what? Deflate it?

I counted to seven. That's my favorite number, and I wear it on my baseball uniform and my basketball jersey, too. It was also the number of times I said my *Thank you, God*s whenever the Giants won a playoff game or Mel Ott hit one into the left field stands.

When I hit seven, I jumped up from behind the stinky cow and took off for the bunker. Half-way there, I stopped when I heard the whistling sound that meant there was a shell coming down. It got louder, and then stopped, and next there was a big explosion that made the ground shake, and me, too. It dug a big crater, like a lot of others that were around the field, and dirt and grass came down on me. I wiped some of it off my face and started running again, faster this time. When I got to the back of the bunker, I was breathing real hard and hoped no one could hear me doing it.

I couldn't figure out why I made it there with nobody seeing me. Maybe there wasn't anybody inside. Or maybe they could only see through the slits on the front, down the cliff to the beach.

There was one way to find out, and it wasn't going around the front where they could see me. I saw a ladder going up to the top of the bunker. I climbed up, real quiet, and saw a big piece of plywood there, like maybe it was covering something. When I saw busted hunks of concrete on the roof, I figured out what the wood was covering. A hole, probably from a shell that landed on the roof. A lucky shot from one of our ships, I guessed.

If I was real careful, I could try to hear if anyone was inside. As I tiptoed across the roof, I tried to keep the grenades on my chest from clanging into each other. Then, when I got to the plywood, I real carefully took out two of the grenades. Even more carefully, I unscrewed the caps on the bottoms and let the firing rings drop out, and held one in each hand, so I'd be ready to pull the ring on one or both of them, and make the toss over the edge of the cliff, and then make a fast getaway.

I stopped and listened. I heard a couple of voices. Even one guy was laughing about something. I don't know if it was German I was hearing, but I could bet it was. There were a lot of "ich" and "ach" sounds. Who else would be in there except the enemy?

Now I needed to find out about the guns. I stepped onto the wood, which felt soft and wet, probably from all the rain the last couple of days, to see if there was maybe a hole I could peek down through. And there was one, right in the middle, a small one. I squatted down, very, very quiet, and held the grenades up in the air so the rings couldn't get caught on anything, like me.

But then something totally crazy, and probably very deadly, happened. All of a sudden I heard this creaking noise from the wood, and it just cracked open like wet cardboard, and I fell through it. In one instant, I landed on a dirt floor, amazingly still standing and holding the dumb grenades in my hands. Four guys in grey uniforms jumped up from chairs and they looked like they just saw a ghost, of a kid, or maybe a short soldier, holding two grenades in the air. Nobody said a word, but they all just stared at me. I didn't say anything either. What would it be? "Excuse me?" Or "Sorry about that?" Which they wouldn't understand anyway. So it was just a crazy staring match that felt like it was going on for a long time, which it really wasn't.

I did see that the Germans all had silver bars on their collars, so they must have been important, like officers. Their bulging eyes weren't looking at me now, but on just two things: the grenades, with the white rings swinging just a little, still in my hands, probably from the shaking I couldn't stop.

It stayed quiet for a while. Then it came to me. Those officers must have thought some American maniac was on a suicide mission. I didn't know how to tell them I wasn't, so I tried to show them. I said, "Don't worry, they only go off if I pull this ring. Like this, see?"

I put a finger through the ring on one of the grenades, and said, "I have to pull this for it to go off."

That got them into a panic kind of thing. One guy, the one with the most bars and ribbons on his uniform, must have thought I was going to set the grenades off right there. He started saying, "Nein, nein," and he held his hands up like he was surrendering. Then the craziest thing happened. The other three guys all did the same thing. They raised their hands, too, slowly, like they didn't want to make a fast move or anything

I couldn't see any guns around, except for in the black leather holsters they all were wearing. The guy with the most bars real carefully opened his holster and pulled a pistol out. I figured this could be the end.

But he didn't aim the gun at me, like I thought he would. He slowly put it down on the table. He sort of smiled and pointed to the gun, like he was trying to give it to me and put his hands up. He was surrendering? To me? Did he think I would pull the rings on the grenades and blow all of us up?

The other three started talking to the guy who put his gun down, and were pretty excited. The one in charge, and without a gun, said something

I couldn't understand. It sounded like "Verr-ookt." He twirled his finger around his ear and pointed at me. "Er ist verr-ookt," he said. That didn't take a genius to figure out. He was telling the other guys I was crazy, probably crazy enough to pull the rings. I guess when I think about, I probably did look like I was off my rocker. Who else would come through the ceiling holding two grenades ready to blow himself and everyone else to high heaven?

The other three had a quick, nervous conversation. One of them pulled his gun out and pointed it at me.

"Nein, nein," the senior guy shouted. "Verr-ookt," he said again.

Another one put his hand on the guy's gun and motioned to give it to him. He wouldn't do it at first. The senior guy picked up his gun from the table, and now he pointed at the one who was pointing it at me.

Now if this sounds like some kind of Three Stooges movie, that's what it felt like. Here were German army officers, with guns, who didn't know who they should be pointing them at, and pretty scared, it looked like, that someone was going to die soon if they didn't do something.

Finally, they did do something. The guy who had his gun on me tossed it on to the table. Good thing it didn't go off when it landed. The other two officers shrugged, took out their guns and put them down, too. Now there were four guns and two grenades down there. Plus all those shells, too. It was pretty clear they didn't want to do anything that would make the "verr-ookt" kid go really crazy and pull the rings.

I tried to keep my voice from cracking and said, "Where are the guns?" I held my arms out to show them I meant the big guns that were supposed to be in the bunker. They winced when the rings wiggled around.

They all shook their heads and shrugged, like they didn't know what I was talking about.

"The guns. Where are the guns. One of the officers turned to the others. "Gunz? Vas is, gunz?"

"Verstait?" Another one said.

"Nein."

I had to send a signal pretty soon to the guys down below. It was time to do something instead of just standing there and scaring those guys. And myself, too.

I shook the two grenades and said, "Move." I nodded toward a door behind us. "Outside." I guess they got the picture, and the head officer moved back to open a steel door, which let light in from outside. He pointed at the door, nodding. "Outshied?" he mimicked.

The head guy moved his arms around and shrugged "Gunz? Nein Nein." Then he said, slowly, "Keine gewere." And the others all joined in, saying the same thing, "Keine gewere," over and over, and pointing around the empty room that must have held the guns, which would have been pointed through the big steel door on the front of the bunker out to the sea.

I motioned for them to go out the door and up the ladder I climbed to get on top of the bunker. They watched me real nervously, but did what I wanted them, too. They went up one on a time and stopped near the front of the roof, looking down at the busted up plywood and shaking their heads on the way.

Now they really looked freaked out, when I put my finger through one of the grenade rings, waited a little and watched their eyes get so big they looked like they were going to pop out. I pulled the ring, real quick, leaned back, counted to four, and let go the hardest throw I could. All five of us watched as it went over the edge of the roof and into the air and sailed down. Then came the big boom, my message that the guns weren't there.

The Germans must have thought they were safe from this crazy little guy now. So to make them forget about that, I pulled another grenade out of the belt and unscrewed the bottom cap to let the ring drop out of it. I waved it at them and motioned them to get down off the roof, and they got nervous again, which I was what I was hoping they'd do.

But now I had a problem. I had to get the new rope down the cliff, but I had four German officers who were acting like they were my prisoners. Sure, they could have tried making a run for it, but they probably figured

I'd be crazy enough to go after them with two potato mashers that would make them into one big kugel.

"I don't know if any of you understand me, but here's what we're going to do," I said. "I will let go of the handles." I made motions like letting go with both hands, as if I was dropping the grenades, which made these guys even more nervous. "Then, I will count to two. Ain, tsvei." I wasn't sure about my Yiddish, but figured it was close enough to German for them to understand. I heard the two languages are a lot alike. One of the officers nodded and the other three men just continued staring. "I drop the grenades like this," I said, making a dropping move with my arms over the hole I fell through. "Then, six more seconds – zecht – boom, boom. Everything blows up." More fear and amazement from the Germans. "Vershtait?" That's Yiddish, too, for understand. One nodded, then one more. "O.K., then."

I did one last silent message to God, *Please let this all work. I know it's crazy, but it has to work. Thank you, dear God.*

I went to the edge of the hole and forced my aching fingers, which, I was surprised, could actually move, to loosen my grip on the potato mashers, and pulled both rings at once, with my teeth, if you can imagine. I let go of them, into the hole, and started counting and jumped off the roof, with them following me now. "One-Mississippi, two-Mississippi, three-Mississippi...four Mississippi. We were getting pretty far away from the bunker. Five-Mississippi, Six-Mississippi, and I threw myself on the ground. The four of them did, too. We closed our eyes and put our hands over our heads. But nothing happened.

I sat up for about three more seconds, shrugged, and then a tremendous boom went off, shaking the ground. One of the Germans said something like "zehn, yah, zhen." The others nodded. Did I have some slow grenades, ten-second versions? Or did they have longer fuses? Who knew? Who cared? I didn't.

I got up and when the Germans looked like they might take off, and guess what. I pulled out two more grenades, held them up and said, "I wouldn't try that," like I was getting tough all of a sudden.

I pretty much knew what was going to happen next. And it did. It was like the Fourth of July in the bunker. All of the big gun shells inside started going off, and blowing through the roof and the walls. Smoke trails, flashes of light, all hell broke loose. They must have heard it down on the beach, because I was pretty sure I could hear some cheering all the way up there. The show lasted a good five minutes or so. Every time it seemed to be stopping and we started getting ready to walk away, another couple of blasts would go off.

Now I saw something I never expected. It was six men, it looked like, coming out of the trees and not in any uniforms, but carrying rifles. They came toward me and the Germans, pointing their guns at all of us. As they got closer, I realized it was only five men, and one woman wearing a heavy sweater and a cap. They just nodded their heads when they watched the last couple of shell explosions. It was a very unfriendly group.

The oldest man, who needed a shave, and a haircut, too, looked like maybe he was in charge. He came up to me and said something in French, which I didn't understand, of course, and neither did the Germans, it looked like. The guy moved his rifle up and down and I got the message. I put my hands up, like I was surrendering. The Germans didn't move their hands at all, which pissed off the French guy.

"En haut! En haut!" he said, gesturing again, and then, along with his comrades, bringing his rifle up to his shoulder in a totally threatening way.

The Germans must have thought better of their refusal and now lifted their hands above their shoulders.

"Sur le tete....le tete," ordered one of the others, pointing to his head.

I put my hands on my too-big helmet, which got pushed down lower when I did it. That made the woman smile, sort of. Now it looked like some local French people captured themselves four German officers and one kid that they didn't know who or what he was. "Excuse me, but I'm an American," I finally said.

The French people seemed surprised, looking at each other and shrugging.

"Americain?" one of them asked, then said something I didn't understand again. Whatever it was, it made the French men and the woman laugh. The woman came up to me and was sizing me up. She reached out and took hold of my helmet, pushing it up from my face, and then pushed it off all the way, making it drop to the ground with a clang. She burst out laughing and said to her friends, "L'enfant terrible!" They all smiled. Even the Germans did a little.

"I'm not an infant," I said. "I may be a little young, but I'm an American, with a Ranger company that's waiting at the bottom of the cliff for me to throw down a pull rope."

"If zat is so, are you old enough to wear zat uiniform zat does not fit you and wear ze German grenades?" One of the guys said in the kind of accent you hear in the movies.

"The Army thinks I am." It was only sort of a lie.

I started undoing the grenade belt, but then three of the Frenchmen cocked their rifles and pointed them at my chest. I guess they weren't convinced yet about who I was. "Hey, I just want to take them off and show you, these things are German, but I'm not. I swear to God."

"Do it very much wiz careful, if you do not wish to be shot," said the English speaking one.

I followed his orders, and did it, very carefully. But when I put the belts on the ground a couple of grenades bumped together and made a noise.

"I said *wiz careful*," the guy said. "I do not care if you blow to pieces zese pigs, and you, too, if you are one of zem. But not us."

"Sorry. Is it O.K. if I show you something?"

The man shrugged. "What is it you show us?"

"A baseball."

"Baze-ball? You want to play baze-ball now?"

"I want to show you I'm an American. O.K.?"

The man turned to his comrades and spoke in French again. They laughed. The man turned back.

"Show us your baze-ball."

I slowly opened my knap-sack and fished inside it for my autographed ball. I held it up. The English speaker stepped forward and took the ball, examining it, turning it in his hand.

"Mayel Ott? He make zis writing himself?"

"After he hit his last home run."

The man turned and tossed the ball to the young woman, who caught it easy in one hand. She examined it to. Then, she dropped her rifle to the ground and assumed a position resembling a pitcher, staring me down. She leaned back and with a kick of one leg like she was going to throw the ball in the direction of the burning bunker.

"No! Don't throw it, please!" I yelled.

She froze, her arm still cocked." Pour quois?"

"She wants to know why she should not srow ze baze-ball. It is not what a baze-ball is for? To srow?"

"It's very special to me. I carried it all the way from home. Please don't let her throw it away," Saperstein said.

"We will see. Give us more to prove you are American, not one of zem."

I reached into my jacket and pulled out my dog tag.

The woman approached me again, this time focusing on my jacket. She frowned and reached to undo the top button. She stopped, turned to the group and said, "C'est Francaise!"

Once again, my surplus woman's jacket came back to haunt me.

"You say you are American," said the English speaker. "But what you wear, it is not American. It is French. Ze buttons. Explain."

"It's not French. It's American. But for a woman." Now I was really getting embarrassed.

"It is what? For a woman? You wear clothes of a woman, and say you are American soldier, who carries baze-balls into battle?"

The man turned again to his group and spoke in French, getting more laughs.

"I came here in Operation Overlord. I have a letter from General Eisenhower. And I really have to hurry up and get all those Rangers up here," I said, fishing in my pocket for the folded Eisenhower letter and handed it to the English speaker.

The letter must have done the necessary convincing. I don't know if he understood the writing, but he finally said, "All right. Maybe you speak truth. If you do not, of course, we will shoot you. You understand?"

"Yes. But I have to find the guns they had up here. Do you know where they are?"

"Of course we know. But we have not something to blow up ze guns. No deenameet."

"I have something," I said, pointing to the potato mashers on the ground.

"Ah, I see. That was what you were to do wiz zose? Blow up ze guns?"

I nodded my head a lot, thinking I was finally getting through to these people. The English speaker went to his comrades and had a quick conversation with them. When he was finished he nodded and came back.

"All right. We will take you to ze guns. But we want to know, who made blow up ze bunker?"

"I did."

"How you do zat?"

"With the German grenades. We took them from a prisoner."

"And zese pigs. They were inside?" I nodded again.

"How you manage to take zem as prisoner?"

"I guess I sort of dropped in on them."

The English speaker shook his head, as if he either did not understand me or didn't believe anything I was saying.

The woman said something to the others, who turned and looked at the Germans. One of them walked over to the prisoners and motioned them with his rifle to lie down on the ground. The head officer wouldn't do it. The French guy who was doing the talking pushed him down on the ground and one held the muzzle of his rifle against the back of his head. It was pretty clear what he was ready to do. When the other three prisoners saw him go down, they followed suit and got on their knees and stretched on the ground. The leader looked at the woman and she nodded slowly, as he cocked his rifle.

I felt this panic. I was sure I was going to be a witness of a war crime.

"No. Please don't do that. You can't. It's against the rules," I said.

"Rules?" said the English speaker. "You believe zese people care about rules? I should show you rules zey broke in our town. They hang a girl of sixteen years from a tree, because zey believe she was spy for ze resistance." He turned to the woman and signaled her with a tilt of the head.

She moved to a position at the feet of the four prisoners, sweeping her rifle to point first at one, then the next, the third and the fourth one. I looked away, feeling sick, waiting for the first crack of the rifle. But I only heard footsteps and a succession of what sounded like epithets coming from the woman. I turned back and saw her rifle was on the ground and she was straddling one of the Germans. She wrapped a piece of rope around his wrists, and pulled it up to the on his back and made a knot in it. I think they call that hog-tying.

"We do not care of rules zat say we cannot tie prisoners like pigs and leave zem on the ground," said the English speaker.

"Oh, my God, I'm sorry. I thought you were going to shoot them," I said.

"Shoot zem? Zat is a very, very good idea." The English speaker turned to his comrades and spoke to them. They began laughing and nodding, while the woman finished tying all the other prisoners. "Zey sank you for making a good idea."

The rest of the French captors sighted down the barrels of their rifles, as though preparing to shoot.

"No, it was a terrible idea. Please don't."

The English speaker waved off the others, who continued to laugh and put their rifles back down by their sides.

"We were only making jokes with you. We will not shoot zem now. We need the bullets for sings more important. Someone else will decide how to deal with zem. Maybe someone from your army, when zey get here."

The woman got up and looked proud at her roping. The others made clucking sounds with their tongues. I guess that meant they approved. Then she took a long piece of rope from one of the men and wrapped it around the feet of each of the four prisoners, and looped it back through their arms, tying them together in a kind of neat package.

"Voila!" one of the others said. "C'est bon."

"Now, we take you to ze guns? O.K?" said the English speaker. And he led the way across the field, not back toward the cliff, but around what was left of the bunker.

We went past the inflated dead cow on the way to a clump of trees.

"You kill the cow?" the English speaker asked. "Zat is against rules, too, killing animals zat do not have guns."

"No. It was already dead. I just used it for cover."

You could hear the whistling sounds of Navy shells coming in, and then the explosions all around.

"Your ships, zey will make, what you say, Swiss cheese, of our beautiful Normandie. But zat is O.K. It will keep ze German pigs on ze ground, while your army comes to drive zem out."

When we got to the line of trees, one of the men stopped and pointed at them.

"Guns," said the English speaker. "And tracks, to take zem to ze edge of ze cliff," I followed them into the trees and we came to a clearing. I saw two canvas tarps draped over something big and long. Two of the Frenchmen pulled the canvas away, and there they were, the biggest guns I ever saw. The barrels must have been at least twenty feet long, and the muzzles were about two feet wide. Underneath were steel railroad wheels, and that's how they must have gotten in and out of the bunker, on the tracks.

"So, you are ready to use zose little bombs you carry up here?"

I nodded. I knew exactly what to do. They all did, too. They stepped back from the guns far enough to be safe. I stayed there and took off the grenade belt. I took the ten grenades that were left and, real careful, put eight of them into two piles, leaning against each other, under the back end of the guns. I kept two grenades out and hung on to them. The French guys were real quiet, just watching me unscrew the caps at the bottom to let the rings drop out.

I was ready. So I pulled the two firing rings and dropped the grenades against the two piles of the rest of them. And I ran like hell, over to where the French guys and the woman were. I even went past them for good measure. Then it got quiet for a second, and BOOM! Everything blew apart, just like it was supposed to. There were even fires coming out of the guns. And when the smoke died down, I could see both big barrels sort of broken and bent, pointing down at the ground, like a couple of limp, well you know what.

The French people came up to me and said a bunch of stuff I couldn't understand and looking pretty happy.

"You have done a good job," the English speaking guy said. "And you have saved many comrades from what zose terrible guns would do. Come, join us, and we will take zem on a ride, O.K.?"

The man bent down beneath the hulks of the guns and pulled a release lever beneath each of them. He signaled to the others, and they all got behind one of them. They pushed real hard, until the gun started to move slow. Then it picked up speed, and they were able to push it all the way down the tracks until it stopped at the big closed door on the back of the bunker.

Then they went back to the second gun and did the same thing. Finally both of them were up against the ruined bunker.

The French people rubbed their hands to celebrate. Then they saluted the limp guns.

"Vive le France," they all shouted out.

"And fuck ze Germans!"

I couldn't have said it better myself.

CHAPTER

19

When I finally tossed the long rope down, and made sure that this one was tied tight enough to a big boulder and wouldn't come loose, I was hoping the Rangers didn't give up on me. But I figured they probably realized the guns were up there after all, and heard the explosions that let them know what must have happened to them.

I felt three tugs on the rope and stopped letting it out. They got it, and the tugs meant everything was O.K. down there. I waited while I guessed they were tying the first and second ropes together to do the pulley thing they talked about. Then I watched the longer rope start to go down, and the other one started moving up. It was working. I pictured a bunch of guys down at the bottom pulling like in a tug of war. And pretty soon, I saw a hand come up over the edge of the cliff, and then another one. Then a helmet, and finally a face. I should have known who it would be. Kaufman.

"Sappy. Jesus, we thought they got you up here. Where the hell have you been?"

I reached out my hand. "It took longer than I thought it would."

"Well, you did it, and it doesn't look like anyone put any bullets in you." He was wiping away mud from his clothes, and from his face too. "They let me go up first. Guess they figured our kind stick together, don't you think?" He looked around at everything. "What the hell have you done up here? What happened with the guns?"

The English speaking French guy was standing there. "Your friend, he blow up by himself. He use, how you call it, ze potatoes?"

"You're shitting me. You did that by yourself?"

"Actually, I fell into the place, and these German guys were inside. Guess they thought I went crazy and was going to blow myself and them up, with all those big shells in there."

"See, zose are ze prisoners he take," said the Frenchman, pointing toward the four Germans tied together on the ground.

"You took four prisoners, single-handedly?"

"Zey are officers."

"Come on, Sappy, how in hell did you manage that, one of you, four of them?"

"I guess I surrounded 'em," I said, trying to sound like Gary Cooper in "Sergeant York." Only he captured a hundred Germans by himself.

A second helmet appeared at the edge of the cliff. The face under it was Tiny's, the huge guy from the ship who danced like a bear to the music we played.

"Hey, kid, we were worried about you. Actually, we were worried about us. Gettin' cold and lonely down there."

After almost everybody was up, it took maybe a half-hour or so, I asked where the Lieutenant was.

Kaufman said, "I guess he's not much of a climber. Probably didn't have time to learn in ninety-day-wonder school.'

"We can haul him up from here. He's a lightweight," Tiny said.

The sergeant came up after just a few other guys. He came over to me and said, "You O.K., kid?"

"Yeah, I'm fine. Sorry it took so long."

It was no big surprise when the lieutenant was the last man up. Actually, he looked like he was a pretty good climber, even if he did have to get help getting up there. And I thought he was a pretty good guy, too. I guess enlisted guys aren't crazy about new officers.

He came over to me and said, "I hope you know you're headed for a field decoration. I'm going to see to it." Then he began giving orders about taking custody of the German prisoners and interrogating them.

"What do we do with prisoners?" the sergeant said. He sounded impatient. "We're supposed to move out and hook up with the rest of the battalion."

"We're not going to leave them here, sergeant. Anyone we capture, we take to the nearest roundup point, which, in this case, should be at Saint Lo."

The sergeant didn't answer, just saluted and walked over to the French group.

"You guys with the resistance?" he asked them.

It was the woman who answered with a nod.

"Want to take the prisoners to Saint Lo?"

"Are you not concerned we would shoot them?" That was a surprise. She spoke English, pretty good actually. She could even pronounce 'th.'

"Not concerned at all," said the sergeant.

All of a sudden there was this cracking sound, like from a whip.

"Sniper!" shouted one of the Rangers, and most of them dropped on the ground. I dropped too, next to the sergeant.

"In ze tower!" shouted the English speaking guy, pointing his rifle toward the top, where there was a skinny slit.

"He's been hit. Kaufman." My God, no, not him. Not my friend. Please God, no.

I got up and ran to where he was lying on the ground, not moving. Then there was another cracking sound, and a hunk of dirt jumped up just a few feet away.

"Get down, kid, get down!" the sergeant yelled. He turned around and fired a bunch of shots up at the tower. Other Rangers started shooting too. Little chunks of stone flew off from the tower.

"Don't waste your ammo," yelled the lieutenant. "We're not going to penetrate that stone with rifle fire."

I got down on the ground next to Kaufman. He wasn't moving or even breathing. His eyes were open, but they weren't seeing me or anything else. In the middle of his forehead was a round, blue-red hole, maybe the size of a penny. He must have died right away, when the sniper's bullet exploded in his brain.

I felt like crying, but I didn't, except maybe inside. I only knew Kaufman for about ten days. Still we got to be friends, good friends. He made me laugh, and he made me feel good when I could have felt real bad. He watched out for me, and he worried about me. Now he was gone. One second he was laughing and celebrating what I did there on the top of the cliff. The next second he was a casualty, one of the twenty per cent he told me wouldn't make it back.

Death wasn't something I wasn't expecting to see, or touch. What was I thinking I'd see? Just a lot of guys doing what they were supposed to do to win the war, without getting killed? If that's it, I was pretty stupid. Or maybe just not grown up enough to understand what war is all about. Whatever it was, it hurt, real bad. I kept looking at Kaufman's face. It was actually kind of peaceful. I thought I even saw just a little hint of a smile, very little, in both corners of his mouth, like he was starting to laugh at something, at me, maybe, when that bullet stopped everything in his body, even a smile, and sort of froze it there. I had a problem with his eyes, though. They should be shut, not open, because he couldn't see anything with them anymore. They should look like he was asleep. So I put my hand down, gently, and closed each eye. I was surprised at how easy it was, as if it was O.K. with him.

"I'm sorry, kid. He was a good soldier," said the sergeant, who I didn't see standing over me.

"He was a good friend, too." I said, and I felt tears start coming out of my eyes. I tried to keep them in, but I couldn't.

"It's O.K. Let 'em come," the sergeant said. "People really liked him. Sure, they kidded him, but they were glad he was with them."

"Even the ones who called him Fu Man Jew?"

"Yeah. Even them. You get into a war, and you end up being close to the kinds of people you never knew before. You make some mistakes about them. But it doesn't take long to figure out they're pretty much the same as you. They can fight like you, hurt like you, bleed like you. They get scared like you. And they die like you. He did. And there isn't a guy here today who doesn't understand he was as good as any man in the outfit, and better than a lot of 'em.''

I could taste the salty tars when they reached my mouth. "How do we bury him?" I asked.

"We don't. It's not the way we do it. We make sure his tags are on him, and leave him for the medics to move out when they can get here."

"How long will that be?"

"I wish I knew. They're picking up a lot of men down there on the beach. Too many. Then they have to find a way up here. But eventually, they'll get here, and take care of him."

I didn't like what he was saying. I couldn't stand the idea of Kaufman lying there in the sun for who knows how long. And I reminded myself that when a Jew dies, even a half Chinese one, he's supposed to be buried pretty fast, like in twenty-four hours.

So I said to the sergeant, "There's a law that's maybe more important than the army's rules about this."

"And what's that?"

"He has to be buried by tomorrow."

"Who's law is that?"

"The Talmud."

He squinted down at me, as if he had an idea of what the Talmud was, but wasn't quite sure.

"It's the Jewish book of laws. Actually a lot of books. And it says a person who dies has to be put in the ground by the next day."

"I don't know what to tell you. But I see a problem here that doesn't have anything to do with this Talmud, or army procedure. It's just plain decency. I don't like leaving a body out here in the sun, with the birds, the insects and all. It does something to the honor of what he did for his country. Got any idea of what we can do?"

"A funeral."

"We don't have a chaplain."

"We don't need one. I can do it. Just a simple one. And we can dig a grave here. The dirt's pretty soft."

"No coffin, though."

"A sack is O.K.," I said.

"It says that in the Talmud?"

"I'm pretty sure. But even if it doesn't, I think it would be O.K. Can we do it?"

The sergeant looked at his watch. "What the hell, go ahead. He deserves at least that. So do you. The lieutenant may not like it, but don't worry. Anyway, he's real busy trying to interrogate those prisoners. You ought to hear him try to talk in German. But see the corporal over there, the one with the big pack? He's got a folding shovel, and some body bags they kept on the ship. I'll tell him to give you a hand. But I want you to wait for one thing. I can't take a chance on people standing around in the open with that kraut sniper still up there. You'll be like clay pigeons for him."

The sergeant called out to another Ranger, who stood next to a partially-disassembled mortar that had been used to shoot the gangling hooks up to the top of the cliff.

"Bring any shells with you, or just those charges for the hooks?" the sergeant asked.

With a big grin on his face, the soldier said, "Hey, I figured we might have to take out a tank or somethin'." And he reached into a green box and pulled out a shell and held it up.

"Think you can take out the top of that tower?"

"As long as I'm shooting live rounds, and not big fish hooks, yeah I think maybe I can do that."

"Then go to it. We've got things to do here before we move out," the sergeant said.

The soldier went to work in a hurry. Another guy helped, and they were sighting the mortar at the tower pretty quick.

"Where you want it, sarge?" asked the man with the mortar. "On top?"

"He had to be shooting from that slit about five feet down. Think you can get close to it?"

"Shouldn't be too hard," he said, looking through olive-green binoculars. He called out co-ordinates to the other man and leaned back on his haunches.

"Clear!" he called out, and then slid the shell he was holding down the round tube, and he and the other man leaned away, placing their hands over their ears. There was an explosion, more of a loud whoosh, and the shell was on its way.

In about a second and a half, the shell hit the stone wall of the tower, about two feet to the left of the slit. It just did minor damage.

"Got a little wind from the south," said the mortar man, calling out new co-ordinates, and the other guy twisted a dial.

"Clear!" And another shell was dropped down the muzzle. This time, it hit about a foot below the slit, not doing much more damage than the first shot. "Damn, not enough vertical."

"You only have two more shells left?" asked the sergeant.

"Yeah. But this time, I think I'll quit foolin' around and just put one through the little old slit."

"A six inch slit? You think you can put one inside?" the sergeant said.

"Hey, these shells are only three inches around. Plenty of room."

"Yeah, well good luck." And I said the same thing, but to myself.

"Clear!" Everybody waited, looking up at the tower.

Whoosh. And another explosion. This time, there was a more hollow sound from the tower, and big pieces of stone exploded.

"Jesus, he did it. Went right in through the slit!" Tiny shouted.

As the puff of smoke settled, all you could see was the slit was gone, plus a couple of feet of the stone wall. But when more smoke settled, you could see something else, half of a man's body, the upper half, hanging out of the jagged hole. There was a rifle hanging on a strap from his shoulder. The rifle must have been the one that fired the shot into Kaufman's head.

"You got 'im. You knocked off the sniper," the sergeant said. "Nice shooting."

"You must have stepped in some horse shit today," said Tiny. "That's one hell of a lucky shot."

Sure, I felt relieved, like everybody else, seeing a guy wearing a German helmet dangling from the tower. But I felt a little bit of sadness, too, at the sight of another killing. I knew the guy killed my friend, but that was his job in the war. Revenge is supposed to be sweet, but I didn't really feel it that way.

• • •

This was a first for me, and I hope the last, too, doing a funeral. It wasn't anything like the one I went to last year, for my grandfather, in a quiet cemetery in Fairlawn, New Jersey. There were birds singing there. And there weren't any huge guns firing shells in from the ocean, or of machine guns going off in the distance, and planes flying over.

It was my grandfather's prayer shawl that I brought with me that I put on around my shoulders, with the white tassels flapping in the wind like little flags. The sky was dark, with no sun, which seemed right for what happened. Everyone who came in on the landing craft was there, standing behind me. In front of me, on the ground, was the white canvas sack, with my friend inside it.

When one of guys took off his helmet and bowed his head, the soldier next to him nudged him in the ribs and shook his head. The guy put the helmet back on when he saw me wearing a white skull cap. I was holding a white card that was in the blue velvet bag with the shawl. It said, In loving memory of Isadore Saperstein, who passed from life December 18th, 1941. Underneath that was the mourner's kaddish prayer in Hebrew and English. Considering that there were probably only one or two Jewish guys in the whole company now that Kaufman was gone, I decided on the English version.

Magnified and sanctified may His great name be, in the world He created as He wills, and may His kingdom come in your lives and in your days and in the lives of all the House of Israel, swiftly and soon, and say all Amen!

And they all did say amen. Some of them had tears running through the caked mud on their faces

The prayer goes on to say God's great name should be blessed, praised, glorified, raised, exalted, honored, uplifted and lauded, to bless Him above all blessings and hymns and praises and consolations that are uttered in the world, and to say all Amen.

And they all did say amen again, the forty-three of them, together.

May a great peace from heaven – and Life – be upon us and upon Israel, and say all Amen.

And they all did, once more. A few of them put their hands on the shoulders of whoever was next to them.

May He who makes peace in His high places make peace upon us and upon all Israel, and say all Amen.

I felt like I needed to do one last thing. I went over to the deep, narrow hole Tiny dug. It was Kaufman's final resting place. I bent over the white bag and zipped it open part way. Then I took off my grandfather's prayer shawl, and my yarmulke, too. I folded the shawl and put the yarmulke on top of it. I bent over and put them both on Kaufman's chest, and zipped the bag closed again.

"Is that the custom?" the sergeant asked.

"I don't think so. But it's the only thing I know to give him, to comfort his soul."

"He'd appreciate what you did," the sergeant said, real quiet now. Then he got back his regular big voice and said, "O.K., as soon as this is over, get ready to move out. We're going east, to hook up with the battalion and airborne. Then we're headed for Paris, to throw these bastards the hell out of France."

When it was over and Tiny shoveled the last earth back on the grave, the soldier with the southern accent, the one who bragged that he liked kosher pickles, came up to us with a rifle in his hand.

"It was his," he said. "He deserves to keep it, don't y'all think?"

Tiny shrugged. "Guess so, country boy."

"You think so?" the southerner asked me.

"If nobody will get in trouble, sure, I think it's a good idea."

"I'll make sure no Nazis can use it." And the southerner quickly tore down the firing mechanism, until there was nothing left of the rifle but the wooden stock and the steel barrel.

He jogged over to the edge of the cliff and heaved the parts as far as he could. Then, he trotted back and forced the muzzle into the fresh earth, letting it stand upright, as the only grave marker Kaufman would have, at least in France. I picked up Kaufman's helmet and placed it on top of the rifle butt.

"Goodbye, my friend," I said. My voice wasn't shaky anymore.

"See ya, Kaufman. Hope you didn't take no offense to the jokes about you. You did good," said Tiny. He did a quick salute to the rifle and helmet.

"May the good Lord protect and keep you, no matter which Lord you're gonna be with," said the southerner, making Tiny and me look at each other in a funny way.

The sergeant came over to me.

"I just talked to the lieutenant. He says you can't go with us."

My mouth dropped all the way open. "Why?" was all I could say.

"You're still a technically a civilian. He thinks the army won't want to be taking the responsibility for you. It's too risky."

"But the colonel – "

"I know what the colonel said, about staying with us, about giving you some kind of induction. But he's not here to give us any orders to take you into any more battle situations. You shouldn't have been in on this one, according to the book. But the truth is, you did enough to earn a chest full of medals today. And I hope you get 'em all."

"I don't care about medals." I said.

"You probably don't. But the army runs on rules. And the lieutenant says we can't keep on breaking them. Look, what if you got killed? Can you imagine what everybody back home would say about an army that lets a thirteen-year-old kid get killed in the front lines? They'd think we were as bad as the guys we're fighting. The Germans, they pull kids out of school and put guns in their hands. They don't care if they get their heads blown off. It's for the fuehrer."

"Nothing's happened to me so far."

"That's right. And it's lucky for you, lucky for us. Let's leave it that way. Now the lieutenant talked to that one Frenchman who speaks English, and the woman. All six of them are resistance fighters. They know how to get around this countryside better than anyone. The lieutenant told them about you, and that you need to get back to one of our ships out there in one piece. They said they'll do their damndest to get you there. They're all grateful as hell for what you did to that bunker and those guns."

"I was hoping to see Paris. I hear it's really a terrific place."

"Yeah. But not right now. The Germans got it. Once we liberate it, sure, it'll be a great place again, if they don't blow down the Eiffel Tower and everything else. Maybe you can go see it some day."

"I could still help. You know, with some climbing, maybe?"

"I imagine you could. I get the feeling there are a whole lot of things you can do. But it's out of my hands."

The English speaking man came over to us now and waited. The sergeant saw him and nodded.

"Well, kid, I guess this is the goodbye part. I want you to know something. Every last one of us is proud as hell to have been with you on this operation. We're all damn grateful for what you did. If you hadn't, we could still be down on that beach, stuck there, waiting to be picked off, one by one, once they found us. So, thanks, and take care of yourself, O.K.?"

"O.K.," I said, feeling really sad. I never did like goodbyes much. When the sergeant got to the two columns of Rangers who were waiting to move out, he stopped.

"Attennnn-shunnn!" he bellowed. The men snapped to attention.

"Huh-bout-faaace!" And they pivoted around, to face me.

"Right hand salute!" And every last one of them, even the lieutenant, snapped their right hands smartly to the edges of their eyebrows, and held them there for a while. I returned the salute, and they all dropped theirs.

"All right, Rangers, we've got work to do!" shouted the sergeant, and they all turned to the east and started marching away.

I watched them march off past the stone tower, with the German sniper still hanging there. I guess nobody thought he should have a funeral. And I felt bad for his family.

The English speaker came up to me. "O.K., my friend. Now we must see about getting you back on ze ship."

"Yeah, I guess."

CHAPTER
20

Let me tell you about something that happened back in Teaneck, New Jersey, around the same time as the funeral for Kaufman. I found out about it later on, after all this stuff was over.

My parents weren't regular moviegoers. But once in a while they liked getting away from the war, and from worrying all the time about me. So it was on a hot June evening, June tenth, I guess, five days after D-Day, that this amazing thing happened in the Teaneck Theater.

My father convinced my mother to go with him to the air-conditioned movie house to see "Sun Valley Serenade," even though he wasn't crazy about movies with a lot of singing and dancing in them, but he knew my mother liked them. Still, she didn't feel right going out to have a good time, with the war on and still not knowing where I was and whether I was O.K.

"Dear, give it a try. It'll take your mind off things for at least a little while," he said. She finally agreed that getting out of the hot house and being in a cool movie theater might be good for both of them. It wasn't just the heat wave that was getting to them, it was seeing something that reminded them of me everywhere they looked.

My father bought my mother a box of Nonpareils, her favorite movie candy. She liked to lick the sweet, pebbly coating away from the chocolate wafer, the same thing I did. Guess I got it from her.

They settled back, and probably felt good with the breeze from the air conditioning. The red velvet drapes were still opening when the Movietone

News name came on, with the big movie camera turning around until it was pointing right at everybody, with marching music playing. They called it the Eyes and Ears of the World.

The first story was about the war, like it always was. This time it was about the invasion of Europe, D-Day, on the beaches of Normandy. My mother really didn't want to hear anything about the war. It made her too sad and nervous. She looked away from the screen and down at her box of Nonpareils. My father knew how she was feeling and squeezed her arm, gently.

The voice of the newsreel came on.

"Southampton, England, where the combined Allied might gathers to launch the largest military invasion in history, Operation Overlord. Thousands upon thousands of valiant young men patiently await their turn to board the boats that will take them across the English Channel to the coast of Normandy....to drive the German armies out of occupied France...in an operation that remained top secret until now."

My father's grip all of a sudden got much tighter on my mother's arm, making her wince and look at him.

"Look," he whispered. "There, that soldier, the short one, talking to the Oriental-looking one."

She looked at the screen, squinting to find what he was talking about. And then she got a quick look at this short, very young-looking soldier wearing a helmet that was too big.

"Oh, my God!" she said.

And the black-and-white picture ended as quick as it started. Now it was just movies of the huge fleet of landing craft moving out to sea.

My mother jumped up and started yelling like a crazy person. "Stop! Turn it back!" she shouted. "That was him. Our son. Oh, my God, he's over there, in the war."

A few people made *shushing* sounds. One man muttered, "Stop shouting, lady." But nothing stopped her.

"I know that was him. Tell them to stop and play it again," she said to her husband. "My God, I can't believe it. Our baby."

"It doesn't work that way. They can't stop it and play it again. It's a newsreel," he said.

Somebody shined a flashlight on my mother and father. It was an usher wearing white gloves and a blue uniform with a black bow tie. "You'll have to stop talking, folks," the usher said. He was only about seventeen.

"It's our son. He was up there," my mother said.

"He went up on the stage?" the usher asked? "That's not allowed."

"No, for God's sake, he was in the newsreel. In England."

"Well, ma'm, that's nice. But you can't disturb other people."

"Come on, Dear," my father said. He took my mother's arm and said, "Let's go talk to the manager."

After a lot of explaining, the manager agreed to have the projectionist replay the newsreel after the last showing of "Sun Valley Serenade," which would be at ten-fifteen. If they didn't not want to sit through two showings, they could leave and come back. He offered to refund the dollar they had paid for tickets, but my father, with his usual pride, wouldn't accept the offer. They decided to go home and come back again at ten-fifteen. It was a very long, and very hard two-and-a-half hours they spent, watching the clock tick slowly in the kitchen

At nine-fifty-five, they were back at the theater, asking the usher to tell the manager they were there. The usher looked at his watch and shook his head, saying something about overly-proud parents.

"I've arranged to have the film stopped whenever you give me a signal," said the manager, sitting in the row behind them in the empty theater, twenty minutes later. He was a friendly man, dressed in a brown pin-striped suit and talking like a doctor or an insurance salesman, to show he cared about people.

"When you see the person you think is you son, speak out loudly, so the man in the booth up there can hear you. All right?"

My mother said, "I don't *think* it's him. I know it is."

"Fine, Mrs. Saperstein. I've also arranged to have the film reversed, and then played again."

"Can you stop it, in a still picture, when we see him?" my father asked.

"Oh, I'm afraid that would be impossible. The heat from the exciter lamp would burn the film. It could even start a fire in the projection booth."

"I understand."

"But I can have the scene replayed at slower speed. Perhaps that would help."

And it did help. By the time it was all over, my mother had him play the scene back three times, in slow-motion.

The first time, she got all excited and said, "That's him. God in heaven, that's him." The second time: "He's lost weight. And his face is so filthy." And the third: "We have to call somebody, right away."

"Who do you wish me to call?" the manager asked.

"*Some*body. The police. The G-men. I don't know. President Roosevelt. They've got our son, over there, in the war, in a helmet, and everybody has guns. My God, it's terrible. Please, do something."

It took a whole lot of talk, and tears, too, from my mother to convince the manager to do another showing of the newsreel the next morning, before the theater opened for the Wednesday matinee. And that was only after the manager had a meeting with the theater's owners, an old couple in Hackensack who hardly ever came to the theater any more, mainly because they both couldn't hear now and only watched silent movies.

It took even more convincing to get a kind of committee to come to the showing to see if they agreed it was me in the newsreel. There was the chief of the Teaneck police department, the Bergen County agent in charge of the FBI, Captain Loewen, the officer in charge of Army recruiting, who I had talked to a couple of times about enlisting, and Miss Vale, the principal of the junior high school. She could probably do the best job of making sure it was me, because I was in her office so many times.

My father got my mother to try and keep herself from yelling out things like, "My God, that's him," and from talking about my dirty face and weight I lost. He said it was to make sure the people watching the newsreel weren't distracted, but I think it was probably something else.

After three more replays of the scene, the manager turned on the lights and everybody waited for somebody to say something.

Finally, Captain Loewen broke the silence. "Mr. and Mrs. Saperstein, are you absolutely sure it's your son?"

"I know my son. That couldn't be anyone else in the world. It's him."

"The helmet is a little big for him, and hides part of his face," the captain said.

"Not enough to fool me. I could pick that face out in a big crowd."

"Yes, that's actually what you did, ma'm."

My father said, "She's right. There's no doubt in my mind either. That's our son. It's not just what he looks like. There's something inside you that calls out when you see your own flesh and blood. Believe me, he could have had even more of his face hidden, and we'd know it's him."

"Miss Vale, do you agree?" the army captain said.

She nodded slowly. "Yes, I'm inclined to say that's him. There's something in his eyes, something I always noticed at school. An innocence, perhaps."

"I don't know," said the police chief. "If he managed to get all the way over to England on a troop ship without being detected, I'd be hard pressed to describe him as innocent."

"Wait just a minute," my mother said. That made her kind of mad. "Are you saying our son is guilty of something?"

"I said he doesn't seem all that innocent," said the chief. "I mean, after all, if he stowed away on some ship going into the war, that takes some doing. That means he's a pretty shrewd kid, that's all, not guilty of something."

"Actually," added the FBI agent, "stowing away on a ship, without paying for passage, is against the law."

"Excuse me," my father said, "I don't think all the thousands of soldiers going over to Europe buy tickets to get there, do they, Captain?"

The captain chuckled at the thought. "You have a point there, Mr. Saperstein. They don't exactly book passage."

"Well, this whole argument about whether he broke any laws doesn't help us find our son," my father said.

"There *is* the matter of impersonating a member of the armed forces," said the FBI agent.

"And a thirteen-year-old is going to be put in jail for that?" my mother said.

"No, that's not what I said. Someone raised the question of whether any laws have been broken, and I represent law enforcement," the FBI man said.

"So do I," said the police chief.

"Look," said Miss Vale, "I don't want to offend anyone, but I really think this discussion is getting too far afield to solve our problem. There's a boy in England, or maybe even in someplace far more dangerous, and there's only one thing we should be concerned about, and that's getting him out of danger and back home to his family."

"Thank you," my mother said, calming down now. And my father smiled politely.

"I think the responsibility rests with the United States Army," the captain said. He sat up straighter in his chair, like he had a mission to volunteer for.

"Well, my agency reports to the White House," said the FBI agent.

"And?" the captain asked, but it was more like a challenge.

"I'm just reminding you that matters of national security are dealt with by the Bureau."

"Do you think a thirteen-year-old boy who wants to serve his country in time of war is some sort of threat to our security? I should think it's a contribution to it."

Now it was the police chief's turn. "My department doesn't report to the White House, just to Town Council. But there's the matter of a missing persons case."

"Which seems to have been solved, wouldn't you agree?" said Miss Vale.

"As far as we know at this time," said the captain, "we have an underage boy who somehow got himself to England and is in the company of the invasion forces of Operation Overlord. That means he could be in harm's way and –"

"*Could be*?" my mother interrupted."Did you see all those guns?"

"Yes, ma'm, I saw them. Soldiers have to carry them," the army captain said.

"And do you know where they were all going?" she asked.

"Yes, ma'm, I'm very familiar with where they were headed. Not the specific location of where that one group landed, but I have a general idea. It *is* an invasion."

I guess it got pretty quiet now, from what I heard about it.

The captain spoke up again. "All right, here's what I think we should do. The Secretary of War, who also reports to the White House," he said, looking at the FBI man, "must be notified of the situation immediately. It will be my recommendation to the department that an alert be sent to every command in England and with our advancing forces in France. We can get a picture from the newsreel film and have copies dispatched to Europe and posted there as quickly as possible."

"You mean like those signs in the post office to catch criminals?" My mother said.

"Dear, he's not saying it's like looking for a criminal. He just wants to help us get him back," my father said, staying calm, the only one besides Miss Vale who was.

"Thank you, sir," said the captain. "I'm sure, if we can just locate him, it will be an easy matter to get him back here. Our troop ships operate in both directions. After they drop off their passengers, and deliver the wounded they have to come back to pick up more."

That wasn't exactly the best thing to talk about in front of my mother. She proved it by gasping like she might pass out when she heard the word "wounded."

"Mr. and Mrs. Saperstein," the captain said, "We will do everything within our power to return your son safely. The United States Army doesn't let children go off to war."

Everybody just looked at him, like they were thinking, "But wait, isn't that exactly what you did?"

Then, there was a knock on the door, and a very serious-looking guy in an army uniform came in. He told everybody who he was, some kind of important person in the War Department. He just got to Teaneck from Washington (he drove all night, I guess) with something very important to tell the people there. Of course, my mother got really scared. And everybody got real quiet and most of the eyes there got real wide. Here's what they were told:

> The Secretary of War heard about the newsreel and all, and sent this guy to the theater to say that nobody, and he meant nobody, could talk about what happened in Normandy with me. For some reason, it was a big military secret, and he talked about the terrible things that would happen, during wartime, if what went on over there got out. It was something about undermining the war effort, whatever that meant.
>
> So everybody in the room went out of it promising, even signing some kind of paper, that nobody would say a word, not one word, about the whole story and me, not while the war was still on. You can imagine how tough that was going to be for my mother. After all, she does like to, well, express herself. She agreed to sign, though, only after she got the War Department guy to swear (she actually wanted it on a Bible, but nobody had one there) that I'd get home very soon, safe, in one piece, and with not a scratch on me.
>
> Like I said, I wasn't there, and I wish I was, but I heard all about it later. In secret, of course, crossing my heart and everything else.

CHAPTER 21

So, back to France again, where I still was, in that town in Normandy.

"You do not know my name. It is Jean," the English-speaking Frenchman said to me.

"I'm pleased to meet you John," I said.

"No....Zshon. But that is O.K. You say it as you wish. And zis is Arlette," He gestured toward the young woman who called me l'enfant terrible.

"Bone-joor, Arlette," I said, wishing I had a better French accent.

"She will take you to Arromanches, when it is safe. Perhaps tomorrow. Zere will be American boats to take you back to England, so you can go home. For now, it is O.K. to be here. The Germans gone away from the cliff, since zeir big guns have been destroyed. Zey are preparing – how you call it, attack counter? — a few kilometers east. I must go with ze ozers now and prepare."

"But how will we speak to each other?"

Jean grinned, turned to Arlette and spoke to her, in French, of course. I couldn't make out any of their fast talking. But I noticed the smiles both of them had on, and Arlette was looking back at me and nodding. Jean said something that made her laugh out loud, throwing her head back. I had a feeling that whatever he said probably would have been embarrassing for me.

Jean said, "She tells me it is always possible zat people who do not speak same languages find ozer ways to speak. Especially when one is a man and one is a woman. Understand?"

I felt myself turn so red, the color probably came through all the grime on my face. "Yes," was all I could manage to say. I did like, though, that they thought I was a man, and not that "enfant" the woman called me.

"All right. We leave you now. You did very brave things today. As a Frenchman, I sank you. I hope we meet again some day. Perhaps here, when France is free. Or maybe in New York. You take me to a baze-ball game. Yankees, maybe, no?"

"Yes. You and your friends are very brave, too. I wish to thank all of you. Would a Giant game be all right?"

"Are ze hot dogs as good?"

"Better, actually."

"It is agreed. Ze Giants, it will be, my friend," Jean said, turning to speak to Arlette. I saw her look surprised at something Jean said, and she gestured about something big with her arms. I guess it had to do with Giants.

"She thinks you take me to a place in America where giant people play a game. Maybe you can somehow explain baze-ball and Giants, O.K.?" Jean said.

"I'll try. Thank you for everything."

"Be safe, Saperstein." he said, and he walked away, with his rifle over his shoulder and waving at me without turning back.

"Allez," said Arlette, pointing to the farm house on the other side of the field. I could at least understand that much French, and followed her.

"Ici. Vous etes a chez mois." It sounded like words from a French song, what Arlette said when she stopped at the wooden door of this small farm house.

"Does someone live here?" I asked.

She shrugged, either because she didn't know, or because she didn't understand me. She pushed the heavy door open and went inside. I waited outside. Pretty soon she came back to the door and looked at me, as if she was asking why I just kept standing there. So, I went inside to what looked like a living room, or a least the main room. I could smell wet concrete and feel the cold in the air. It must have been a very old house, without heat. There was a big fireplace with a pile of ashes. It probably was the only way to heat the whole place, and it looked like it hadn't done any heating in a long time.

Arlette lit a match and held it on the bottom of a glass lamp. It got bright enough to show just about everything in the room. The heavy furniture looked like somebody carved it out of tree trunks. Arlette sat down at a big wood table and nodded at one of the four chairs, where I guessed I was supposed to sit down. I did that but didn't know what I was supposed to do next.

Then Arlette did something that made me pretty uncomfortable. She reached her hand across the table and put her hand on my cheek, smiling at me. There was a woodsy kind of smell coming from her heavy wool sweater, which made me think of pine forests in Maine, with brown needles covering the ground.

"Quel age avez-zous?" she asked. Of course I didn't understand the question. "Moi," she continued, pointing to herself, "Vignt." And she held up all ten fingers, then clenched them back, and opened them up a second time. "J'ai – vignt – ans." she said.

"You are twenty?" I said, slowly, like maybe she wouldn't understand me.

"Oui," she said. Then she pointed at me. "Et vous?"

I thought I might as well get the embarrassment over with. "Thirteen." I held up ten fingers, then three more.

She seemed surprised, even though she called me an infant when she first saw me. "Mon dieu. Treize?"

So that's how we tried to talk to each other, with hands, pointing and hoping there were words that meant something in both of our languages. And while that was happening, I began getting a strange, and, actually, kind of nice, feeling. It was like what happens when you go outside of a movie theater after seeing a scary or sad movie into the bright afternoon sunlight, and you realize what you saw in the dark didn't really happen, or maybe it did, but it was over and behind you. Friends were waiting to shoot some hoops, and there was a Saturday night dance at the Little Brown Jug to go to.

Well, there weren't any hoops to shoot or a dance to go to, but the awful things I saw on top of that cliff were, like a movie you can't forget, behind me. And in front of me was this woman. She was as pretty as anyone I would have danced with at the Jug, even though she was a much older woman, seven years older to be exact. The way she touched my cheek and smiled at me gave me that afternoon sun feeling. Good thing she couldn't read my mind, because I was getting some pictures of her, like with that cap off her head and her long brown hair falling down to her shoulders, and we were dancing. Sure, dancing. Where? In a musty, cold farm house with no music? Great, Saperstein, just great.

"Voulez-vous quelque choses a manger?" I figured that question out, the way she brought an imaginary fork up to her mouth a couple of quick times.

I nodded and said one of the two French words I knew, twice: "Oui, oui." Then I used the other one: "Meer-see."

Then she said something that sounded like a town in Connecticut, Darien. I guessed it was how you say you're welcome.

She got up and made a meal for me on a blue and white metal plate with flower designs. She used stuff that was in the cabinets to make a sandwich of some spicy meat, kind of like corned beef, on really good crusty bread, and a hard-boiled egg that was from a jar with water in it. She also gave me a glass of what looked like red Kool-Aid. I was pretty thirsty and took a swig out of the glass, but it wasn't what I thought it was. It was red wine, and I had to fight the urge to spit it out, which would have made me look like the world's biggest jerk. I swallowed it and tried to act like I liked it. Don't get me wrong, it wasn't the first time I drank wine, but it was very different from what my parents and grandparents served on religious holidays, Manischewetz, which is a lot closer to Kool-Aid.

After the meal, Arlette tilted her head and put her cheek on her hands and closed her eyes. I got that one pretty quick. She was talking about sleep. I did the hands and eyes thing back to her. Then she took me by the hand, which, I have to say, suddenly got me feeling pretty warm inside. The wine helped too, I guess. She led me up these narrow stairs to some kind of loft that you could see down to the main room from. There was a thick mattress on an iron bed, with a patchwork quilt and a couple of pillows on it.

She acted like she was showing me a hotel room, pointing at the bed. She said something like da-coor, which sounded like a question. I guessed that meant, "Is this all right?" Or maybe, "I hope you like it." I just grinned and nodded my head and said, "Da-coor," back. And she went back downstairs.

I sat down on the bed, which felt pretty terrific and all. Everything on it smelled like clean laundry, nice and fresh. It seemed like it was an awful long time since I slept in a real bed, which made me feel even better about everything.

Arlette came back up the stairs. She was carrying a white basin, with a pitcher in it and a grayish-purple bar of soap that smelled almost like perfume. It was actually more like some flowers in a field, kind of girly, not like the Lifebuoy I used, but that was O.K. She didn't say anything but just smiled and went back down the steps again. I used the water from the pitcher and the soap to get off as much of the grime and mud as I could. I didn't think there was a bath tub or a shower there, but it still felt good to get cleaner than I was. Finally, I stretched out on the bed and fell right to sleep, because I really needed it.

The next thing I knew I was dreaming that I was in a big bed and could smell that soap again. And there was somebody next to me, touching me, actually a woman I couldn't really see, but I could feel.

Then I woke up and said to myself, "Holy crap, this isn't a dream." There really was someone next to me. It was too dark to see who it was, but I didn't have to. I could smell that flowery soap coming from her, and the wool of her sweater. It was Arlette, if you can believe it, lying there next to me. In the bed. I could feel my heart beating like crazy. After all, it was the first time in my life that I was sleeping with a woman. Well, I mean, like just sleeping, not making out or anything.

"Bon jour," she said. Her voice was sleepy.

I sat straight up and said, "Hi."

"Hi," she said, imitating me.

Some blue light came in from a small window over the bed, and now I could make out Arlette's face. She was smiling at me. I didn't know what to say, or how to say it, of course. Then she slid her hand around my neck and touched my cheek, like she did down at the table. She put her other hand on my other cheek, and tried to nudge me back down on the bed.

"It's O.K.," I said, and didn't move back down. "I don't think I could sleep anymore."

She giggled, like she probably understood the dumb-ass thing I just said. "L'enfant – l'enfant tres terrible," she said and definitely pulled me down next to her, pretty firm about it, too.

Now she sat up. But it wasn't to get off the bed. She was on one elbow and just looked at me for a while. Then she leaned down and kissed me, a gentle, soft kiss that felt different from any kiss I ever had playing Spin the Bottle or on a hayride. It wasn't a French kiss, but it was from a French woman, which probably made the difference. I could taste salt on her lips, and there wasn't any of the pressure you felt from girls, like you should hurry up and do what you're going to do before somebody finds out.

Her mouth opened, just a little, and the tip of her tongue poked in and just sort of flicked around. Maybe it was a French kiss after all. She propped herself up again and ran her hand through my hair, which must have felt pretty filthy. But she didn't seem to mind it.

She slid her other hand down the front of my weird field jacket and stopped at my belt, which she started to unbuckle. Then it dawned on me what was going to happen next, and I sat back up, real straight. "You can't do that." I said.

"Qu'est-ce que?" she asked, wrinkling her brow and looking pretty surprised.

"We can't go all the way."

"Awl ze way? Ahh. Oui. I'm gonna love you awl ze way," she sang, in a poor imitation of Frank Sinatra. And she started to kiss me again.

"You don't understand." Of course she doesn't understand, genius. She's French. But she knows the words to that dumb song. "I mean, I respect you. I couldn't do that. If we got married, then it would be great. I mean it, really, seriously great, the way you kiss and smell and everything."

Come on Saperstein, she still doesn't understand you, and it's a lucky thing. You sound like the world's biggest moron. And a pansy, too.

"Mah-reed? Moi? Vous? "

Oh God, she understood the word. She thinks I asked her to marry me. Actually, it's maybe not such a bad idea.

But then I wondered if it was such a good idea, when I noticed the silver crucifix dangling from the chain around her neck, shining in the blue light.

I have to say, I was about as totally confused as I've ever been. And turned on, too, more than I've ever been. I figured at that point that the only thing to do was get out of the bed. I stood up, forgetting the big bulge in my pants, and leaned back, in that close-dancing bend, to keep from stabbing a girl. But Arlette saw it and covered her mouth and giggled, looking at what she did to me.

"Excuse me, but I have to go to the bathroom," I said, as if I knew where it was, or whether there even was one in the old house. And I went down the steep stairs, starting to feel the pain that made me suffer so much on the bumpy bus ride home from the camp dance last summer. There was only one thing I could do to stop it.

I didn't find a bathroom, though. I wondered if there was one outside, but I never got to look. I was sitting at the table, very straight and trying not to move much, and Arlette came down from the loft.

"O.K.?" She asked in the accent I was really getting to like.

"Yes." I nodded, hoping she didn't notice the pain I was feeling. "Oui."

She leaned over and kissed my forehead. Like the other kisses, it felt really good. She sat down next to me. Maybe she did know about the pain, because she took a quick look down there. Then she slowly slid her hand down my chest, past my waist and between my legs. And she started this slow, gentle movement, up and down, in a circle, too. I didn't want it to end, but, well, maybe just the pain. I was in kind of a trance, and I started feeling like I was lifting off that wood chair and floating up to the ceiling and just going in circles there. She didn't say anything, and I didn't either. Then, my whole body started shaking, and I just stayed up there on the ceiling until an enormous shudder went through me like one of those grenades, or actually a dozen, or maybe a hundred of them going off at once.

And the pain stopped, and I came down from the ceiling, looked into Arlette's eyes and said, in a very hoarse voice, "Thank you. Mare-see bow-coo."

She smiled and kissed me one more time.

"Is O.K.?" she asked glancing down there. I just nodded and watched her go to the sink to get another basin. She filled it with water and handed it to me with a small towel. She said nothing more, but kept smiling. I didn't want to look down at my pants and just waited until she walked back upstairs, so I could be by myself to clean up a little.

I was probably the most embarrassed male human being in the world. But I was also the happiest one, if you can imagine.

• • •

When the first light of the morning was coming into the house I looked down from the loft and saw Arlette getting ready to leave. She put on her boots, a muffler and her hat, and loaded her pockets with rifle ammunition.

She must have noticed I was watching her from up there, and she looked at me but didn't say anything. She just lit a cigarette that was dangling from her lips. Then she moved around, putting stuff away, like she didn't want anyone to know, mostly the Germans, that she spent the night in the house. I figured they'd really like to find the kid who blew up their big guns and the resistance fighter who was hiding him out.

I came downstairs after I straightened up the loft. I even made the bed, so Arlette wouldn't have to ask me if I did.

She opened the door and looked in both directions before she stepped out. She motioned to me to follow her outside. I closed the heavy door behind me and looked around. I didn't see anything or anybody. And it was very quiet, too. The shelling must have stopped. I could even hear a couple of birds chirping. That felt pretty good.

I had to catch up with Arlette because she moved quickly, while I was stopping to look around at all the craters the shells dug up. She had her rifle slung over her shoulder and looked a lot tougher than she did the night before. She was all business now, a fighter looking out for her enemies, ready to shoot her way through them if she had to.

We walked along the narrow dirt path on the top of the cliffs for maybe an hour, to a high spot that looked down on a small town on the water. What we saw was amazing. You could hardly see the water because it was so filled with hundreds and hundreds, maybe thousands, of ships, small ones, medium ones and huge ones. It looked like you could step across them and get a long way out to sea. Then we saw something very sad, down on the beach. Soldiers with red crosses on their helmets were moving around bodies in the sand. Some of them were still halfway in the water. They never got to set foot on French soil, but got mowed down before they could. There were a lot, maybe hundreds, of men still alive but wounded, lying on stretchers, or just sitting on the sand, waiting for medics to patch them up. It was the part of war they don't show you in the newsreels, but probably should, instead of just all the pictures of happy guys waving at the camera and smoking cigarettes.

Arlette shook her head like she couldn't believe what she was seeing She turned to me and said, "l'Americains, l'Englaise...tout."

Then she motioned to me to follow her down a path that wound back and forth down to the town. The streets looked like mid-town traffic in New York, only instead of cabs and cars, it was a sea of green army trucks, bumper to bumper. They stretched all the way back to the edge of the water and were still coming off the big transport ships. We walked down along the sidewalks that were jammed with local people waving at the soldiers. And the soldiers waved back, like they knew they were welcome, really welcome. When Arlette and I walked by them, a lot would smile at her, obviously liking what they saw. Then they'd look at me and roll their eyes like they were wondering how I got lucky enough to be walking around with her.

"Didn't waste any time, did you?" an infantryman said to me. Another one said, "She have a sister?"

Arlette knew she was getting all the looks, but she didn't pay any attention to them. Either she was used to the looks, or was too busy thinking about shooting Germans with that rifle over her shoulder.

At the town post office, or at least what was left of it after a direct hit by a bomb or a shell, Arlette stopped to talk to an older man who carried a rifle like hers, slung over his shoulder, as if he were on a hunting trip. She pointed at me, and then back to the cliffs. I guess she was telling him what happened to the guns and the bunker. The man kept shaking his head and laughing. Then he came over to me and said, "You are ze one who destroy ze bunker, who make capture of ze Germans, no?"

I felt kind of silly, because I wasn't a real hero, just an accidental one. But I didn't know how to tell him that, so I just shook my head like he probably had the wrong soldier.

"American officer soldier, he ask me if I know where you are. I tell him no, but if I see, I will go to him. So, now, if we can find officer soldier — many, many soldiers here – I take you. O.K.?"

"Yes, sir. Thank you."

"You wait here?"

"Yes. I will wait here."

The man spoke again to Arlette. She shrugged, as if saying she probably had to wait there with me, and I could tell she wanted to get going. But when she turned back to me, she smiled again, that great smile like the one when she was lying next to me on the bed. Even though I was ready to start my long trip home, which I knew I had to do, I knew I would miss her. I couldn't ever tell anybody what happened in the farm house. I mean, how could I tell my friends, or my brother, or, God forbid, my parents, that this great older French woman was ready to have sex with me without even getting married.

I did have this image, though, of me standing next to her on the steps of a synagogue — even though she wasn't Jewish — and she wasn't wearing the wool sweater and the hat, or carrying a rifle. She had on a white wedding dress and was holding flowers. I came up to her and took her hand, but then there was a tremendous explosion.

But it wasn't in my daydream. It was real, down on the beach. I looked down there and saw a puff of black smoke, and then heard another blast and saw more smoke and a half-track on fire.

I heard somebody yell, "They're shelling the beach! Heads up!"

Without thinking, I grabbed Arlette's hand and moved toward a door that was open in the post office. Inside, there was just a lot of rubble on the floor. The sun came through a big hole in the roof. Stamps and papers were all over the place.

"Hey, soldier, no time for that. At least wait until the shelling's over," someone called from outside, laughing. It was a good thing Arlette didn't understood English. But maybe she did, because she smiled at me and raised her eyebrows.

The shelling lasted only a few minutes, and then things started moving again on the street. When we got outside, I saw a jeep working its way through the traffic jam, with the horn honking. A corporal was driving and next to him was an officer, a captain, wearing an MP arm band. In the back seat was the old Frenchman who talked to me on the street, pointing at me.

The jeep stopped and the captain got out. He looked me over and then looked at Arlette.

"Is your name Saperstein?" he said.

"Yes, sir."

"A lot of people are looking for you. You know that, don't you?"

254 THIS BOY'S WAR

"I guess so, sir."

"I don't know what all you did to get here, and I guess it doesn't matter. What does matter is that we get you back on a ship and headed home as fast as we can." He turned to Arlette. "Are you with him, Miss?"

She used her hands and a tilt of her head, which I thought was pretty cute, to let him know she didn't speak the language.

"She take care of him," said the Frenchman, who got out of the jeep. "She see him do all zose things, when he blow up ze bunker, and make prisoner ze Germans."

"I think the command here is going to want to talk to her," said the captain.

"I do not know if she can wait for zat," the older man said. "But I will ask."

He spoke to her, and she got pretty worked up, pointing to the hills beyond the town.

"She say she must go now. Comrades wait for her, zen to go and do something to tracks for the train where ze guns were," he said to the officer. "Blow up...poof."

"Well, I can't order her to stay, obviously."

"Yes, it is true."

"O.K., Saperstein, let's get you down to the beach and assigned to a boat. I'm also told to put someone with you, just in case you get any ideas about going back and capturing any more Germans. Hop in."

I went closer to Arlette, and it felt like I was in a movie. I didn't plan what came out of my mouth.

"I guess this is goodbye." I knew the words were really corny, but I didn't know what else to say. From the look on the captain's face, he thought they were corny, too.

"Au revoir?" she asked.

"Yes. Oh-revoor. I'll think of you a lot."

She smiled, but didn't say anything, until the older man said something to her in French. She said something back to him.

"She say she miss you too, much," said the interpreter.

"Would you tell her, please, that I would like to write her."

The man did not understand. "What is that you say? You write what?"

I pointed to a mail box that dangled from the post office's damaged wall. "I want to write letters to her, mail."

"Ah, yes," the man said, and turned back to Arlette again, explaining. She smiled, nodded and picked up a piece of paper from the street. It was a used, stamped envelope. She reached in her pocket and got a wooden pencil. She went down on one knee and wrote on the envelope on her thigh. The captain and the private, too, watched closely. When she finished, she stood and handed me the envelope.

In addition to an address, I was able to read a line written above it: "Pour m'enfant terrible, avec amour." I knew the soiled envelope would take its place next to my prized baseball and autographs, and swore to myself to keep it forever. I didn't want to leave her, but I knew I had to go. I felt sad, with a little bit of happiness mixed in. For a half a second, I wondered what would happen if I grabbed her hand and started running for the hills with her, which was a completely crazy idea, I knew that. How hideous it would be if the captain and the private came after me in the jeep and handcuffed me in it like a prisoner, so all the soldiers there could see what happens to a schmuck with too big of an imagination.

Arlette finally turned away, after one last look, and started walking up the sidewalk, with that quick step that meant she always knew where she was going, and would get there no matter what. I drifted into one of my little unwritten letters in my head.

Dear Arlette, it was very hard saying goodbye to you in Arromanches. I watched you walk up the winding street and wanted to run after you, but I knew it would be a bad idea. Here I am on a ship going home, but I'm not so sure I want to go home. Something makes me wish I could have stayed in France, and I guess I have to tell you, in all honesty, what I am thinking. It's about us, maybe, some day. I can't tell you how much it meant to be with you, even though you are a lot older than I am, and we couldn't talk to each other.

The captain interrupted my mind-writing. "Don't worry, she'll be here when the war's over," he said. Did he really think she would be? Probably not. But it made me feel good.

• • •

In less than an hour after saying good-bye to Arlette, I was on board a landing craft again, bouncing over choppy waves toward the armada of ships that were anchored a little ways from shore. Most of the others in the boat were injured and various parts of their bodies were covered with bandages. A few of them stood with crutches or canes, some of them sat, and the rest laid on stretchers. Two medics were also in the boat and, at one point, they eyeballed me, like they were wondering why I wasn't wounded.

"Hey, buddy, where'd you get hit?" asked a soldier. He had to tilt his head back to see out of the one eye that wasn't blocked by a bandage that covered his head and most of his face.

"Nowhere" said Saperstein.

"No kidding. How come you're goin' back?"

"Orders," was all I said.

"You didn't turn tail, did you?"

I shook my head. I didn't try to tell him the truth, but felt bad that he thought I ran away from the battle, especially the way he was all bandaged up.

When I got on the bigger ship that was headed back to England, I tried to find a corner someplace where I wouldn't stick out without any bandages or crutches. When I was standing at the rail looking out at the sea, I heard a familiar voice, with a New York accent.

"Hey kid, you goin' home now?"

I didn't have to turn around to know it was Tiny, the big man with the loud voice. He was lying on a stretcher, with one of his hands sticking up, all covered with bandages. One of his ears was covered, too

"Tiny. What happened?"

"Some kraut son-of-a-bitch shot me. Twice. Knocked off most of my ear with the first shot. The second one took three fingers."

"God, I'm sorry."

"Yeah, I am, too. Won't be able to pick my nose as much now. Too bad for the guy who shot me. He wasn't good enough to put one between my eyes and finish me off. I was still able to squeeze one off with my left hand. Got him in the gut. Then I saw he was still breathing. So I decided to fix that."

"You shot him again?"

"Shit no. I stood on his throat, all two-hundred-and-eighty pounds of me, until he stopped breathing, for good. Oh, well, that's war, ain't it?"

I wondered if that's what it was supposed to be. I spent the rest of the trip back to England sitting next to Tiny, trying to find something to make him comfortable. I offered to go get him food or water. But he just wanted to lie on his back and talk about all the things he was going to do when he got home, including several things he had been planning with his girlfriend, Louise. He told me his favorite way of making love to her, where she wore her roller skating costume, with a very short skirt and nothing under it, and her skates, too. I didn't find anything sexy about that, but Tiny did, and that was O.K. He deserved it. I acted like I really enjoyed hearing it all.

When I stepped off the gangway back in England, after making sure all the wounded troops got off first, an officer, this time a young lieutenant, was waiting for me. He seemed like he knew who to look for. I guess it was easy. It wasn't like there were other thirteen-year-old kids getting off the ship.

"Are you Saperstein?" he asked me.

"Yes, sir, I am."

"You're to come with me."

I followed the officer to a jeep and climbed into the passenger seat.

"Am I going on another ship?" I asked him.

"I don't know. All I know is I'm taking you to meet with the General."

"What general?" I felt a shiver run all through me. Was I in that much trouble? The lieutenant braked the jeep to a jolting stop and looked at me.

"You're kidding, aren't you?" I shook my head ."They didn't tell you?"

"No, sir, nobody told me anything, except I was being sent home."

"Tell me something. Did you ever hear the name Dwight D. Eisenhower, who just happens to be Supreme Allied Commander?"

Sure I heard of him. Everybody did. We all got that letter from him before we left. But the real question was, why would he have heard of me. And why he did he want to see me. He had all those thousands of troops to worry about. And I wasn't even a troop, at least not a real one.

The lieutenant started driving again and shook his head like he couldn't believe me. But that was O.K. It seemed like a lot of people couldn't.

We stopped in front of a building that looked like it just got built. It was painted green, like everything else in the war, and there were guards with rifles all around it. Two sergeants with MP arm bands stood at attention on the sides of the door into the building. When we walked past them to go inside, they both snapped to attention and saluted the lieutenant, like they knew who he was.

In the hallway, another sergeant saluted the lieutenant and looked me over.

"The General's expecting him," The lieutenant said.

The sergeant pivoted and stepped to a big door that had five gold stars painted on it. He knocked and waited.

"Yes?" It was a firm voice that came through the door, the voice of a busy person.

The sergeant opened the door just a little and peered in. "The lieutenant and a young, ah, enlisted man, it would seem, sir, to see you."

"Right. Send them in," was the answer. The lieutenant nodded at me, and I stepped through the doorway into a pretty big room. At the back of it was a long desk covered with papers and books. There was a big conference table in the middle of the room, surrounded by chairs.

The walls were covered with large maps of what seemed like most of Europe. Of course I knew who was behind the desk. It was him, General Dwight Eisenhower, looking sort of kind and stern at the same time. Actually, he reminded me of my grandfather, but younger. He was mostly bald, and his eyes looked like they could see through a wall if he wanted to.

"Are you the one they call Saperstein?" he asked me.

"Yes, sir, I am." My voice cracked, like I was afraid it would.

"Come in son. It's David, isn't it?" I nodded. "That's my middle name, did you know that?"

"No, sir, I didn't."

"Have a seat," he said, pointing to a brown leather-covered arm chair. He leaned back behind the desk and held up a sheet of paper and studied it. Then he looked over the paper at me.

"Thirteen, are you?"

"Yes, sir. I'll be fourteen pretty soon, though."

"And you wanted to get in this war so much, you got your own uniform, left home and stowed away on the Queen Elizabeth."

"Yes, sir, it's true."

"And do you mind telling me why it was so important to get over here, to put yourself in that sort of danger, five years before you'd be of legal age to enlist?"

"I guess I feel responsible."

Ike's eyebrows went up. "You think that was a responsible thing to do, impersonating a member of the military?"

"I don't mean responsible that way, sir. I mean that I feel responsible for things that have happened."

"What things?"

"Things that Hitler is doing. Killing people because of their religion. My religion."

"You think it's your fault, the way that madman is trying to bring the world down in flames?"

I had trouble coming up with an answer. Finally, I said, "Well, sir, I used to hear in school, every day, that the only reason America went to war was to protect the Jews from Hitler."

Ike's voice dropped got quieter, and softer, too. "Son, do you think when colored people got lynched by people in white robes it was their own fault?"

"No, sir, I don't."

"Well, the idea makes as little sense as yours. You have to understand one thing about this war. It's not your fault. It's not France's or England's fault. It's not even exclusively Hitler's fault. No, the fault lies with every person in Germany who didn't have the courage, or the wisdom, to turn away from the evil that Hitler represented. No one can launch the war machine that he's managed to launch without a nation unified behind him. Somebody's going to have to find out why his own people didn't refuse to follow him into the flames. Until then, we've got to fight this war with every ounce of energy, with all the will we can muster. It's a crusade that must not fail."

"Yes, sir, I know that."

"Well, enough of that. Right now, we've got to do one thing with you: Get you home to your family. They're worried sick about you. And I don't blame them one bit. But before we do that, I want to talk to you about what you did over there in France."

I wondered if the general could possibly have heard about Arlette, and what happened in the farm house.

"Those were some incredibly brave things you accomplished. I got a full report. You climbed that cliff, without any help. Then you captured four Germans all by yourself.."

"That was kind of an accident, the way I captured the Germans."

"I don't much care if it was. The fact is, you did it. Then, while you held them captive, you blew up the guns they would have used, plus all the shells for them, against our troops. Now, that's the stuff that earns medals, like the Silver Star, the Bronze Star, even the Distinguished Service Cross."

My eyes got bigger. It all kind of scared me.

"I think you deserve all of those medals. But the truth is, I can't let you get a single one, as unfair as that might seem. You know why? Because you're not even in the Army. You're a civilian. Besides that, you're under-age. And we absolutely cannot let it get out that the United States Army let this all happen, at a time when we need support of the people at home more than ever before. We just can't let America, and the rest of the world, know that we're that sloppy, that we'd let a boy of thirteen slip through our security measures, infiltrate a top-secret mission and go into battle. It would do more harm than we can withstand right now. Do you understand that?"

"Yes, sir. I do."

"I can't make you do what has to be done now. But I'm going to ask you, in the interest of your country, of all those men who are fighting to free France and the rest of Europe, to keep silent about what you've done, at least until this war is finally over. I mean every detail, from stowing away, to your heroic actions, for which I, the rest of my command and the President of the United States – and he has heard about this, I can assure you – will always be grateful. But we must be grateful in silence. Can you accept that?"

"Yes, sir, I can."

I thought about the poster I saw in New York, LOOSE LIPS SINK SHIPS, but I wasn't sure how talking about what happened would do that. I wasn't going to take any chances though, believe you me.

"I'm glad you understand. In the meanwhile, to me, you'll always be the boy who turned into a man at Normandy, and quite a man at that. You have a bright future ahead of you. Who knows what you might choose to do. You could go into the military when you're actually old enough. Maybe go to West Point, like I did. We never know where our actions will eventually lead us." He chuckled. "For Pete's sake, some politicians back in Washington told me I should run for President some day. Now that's absurd, of course. But the point is, anything's possible."

I thought about what he said, joining the army when I'm old enough. Would that be re-enlisting? I didn't know, and I guess it really didn't matter.

"Now, about getting home. Let me ask you something. Done much flying in airplanes?"

I squirmed in my seat. I didn't really want to admit it. "Actually, sir, I've never been on an airplane."

"Well, that's even better then. Because that's how you're going home. You're going to get a ride on a U.S. Air Corps transport plane, along with some of my officers who are going back to brief the White House on our initial progress. It'll take off from just outside Southampton at daybreak tomorrow. Your parents will meet you in Washington, I'm told. And I have a feeling they're going to keep a very close eye on you. My aide will find you a place to sleep tonight, and scout up some clean clothes for the ride home. By the way," he said, looking curiously at my jacket. "Does that field jacket button the wrong way?"

"Yes, sir, it does."

"Well, it's not important. Now, before you leave, since I can't give you those medals you deserve, and since no one can know about your, ah, journey, is there anything I can personally do for you, to show my thanks?"

"Yes, sir, there is one thing."

He waited while I reached down to my knapsack. I laid it on my lap and pulled out my autographed baseball with all the signatures of the Giants, all except one, of course. I held the ball out to him, and he looked it over, like he was impressed.

"Would you autograph it?" I said.

"Well, I'm not a Giant," he said, smiling for the first time, and taking the ball. "Why would you want my name on there, with Mel Ott and the others? They're stars."

"I think you're going to be famous some day, sir."

"Why, thank you. I'll certainly try not to let you down." And he scribbled his name on the ball and started laughing to himself and shaking his head. "Famous," he said.

He stood up and did something I'll never forget, along with a lot of other stuff that happened over there. He actually saluted me. That's right. A general, the Supreme Allied Commander, saluted me, a kid who wasn't even in the Army he was in charge of. All I could think about doing was salute him back. And I did.

I guess war can make pretty crazy things happen, when you think about it.

CHAPTER

22

On the second Monday in September, the first day of the new school year, I stood three inches taller than I was at the beginning of vacation. I guess that sounds hard to believe, but it really happened. My father said, "You shot right up through the top of your own head this summer."

Looking in the mirror one last time before heading for school, I thought I saw another change. I checked my new blue and white striped polo-shirt, which almost seemed like it was bulging just a little around my chest and arms. But it must have been my imagination. Or the shirt.

Before leaving the house, I kissed my mother goodbye, like I did every school morning of my life. Of course she held me tighter than before, ever since I got home from the place I wasn't supposed to talk about. But I let her squeeze me as much as she wanted. It was the least I could do, don't you think?

My father wasn't there to say goodbye to me. He had to leave the house at five-thirty every morning because of all the work he was doing at "the place" for the Army and Navy, making insignias and stuff for their uniforms, instead of lace underwear for women civilians, which I liked a lot better. But he would tiptoe into my bedroom before he left and just smile at me. He even looked like he might have been crying one time, while he was smiling at the same time, but I didn't let him know I was awake and saw him.

When I was ready to head for school, I was worried about a look in my mother's eyes after she gave me that crusher hug. Something was bothering her. I got the idea that she wanted to drive me to school, instead of me walking. But I knew she wouldn't try to do that, as much as she wanted to. Not with an eighth grade student who lives less than a mile from school. Talk about being embarrassed.

I felt really different when I walked out the front door, because things were different. Sure, there was still a war on, but I knew it was going to be over pretty soon, and all those brave soldiers, the ones who made it through everything alive, would be coming home. My uncles, too. Especially my uncles.

I stopped and looked up at the front window. The flag with the gold fringe was still hanging in the window, the one the brick got thrown through. At first I didn't notice the difference. But then I saw it. There were three blue stars on it now instead of just two. I guess my mom and dad and my brother knew I was going to come home again after all.

When I turned the corner at Ramapo Road to walk the last half-block to the entrance of Teaneck Junior High, I saw something familiar, something that always meant nothing but trouble for me. There they were, the Black Cat Gang, all of them, back for another year. They had summer tans, but it didn't look like they grew much, the way I did.

They stood at the edge of the school lawn. One of them spotted me walking in their direction, and nudged a pal, who broke into a big fat grin, then said something to the rest of the gang. Now they all grinned, watching me come up.

But I didn't stop or try to walk around them. I felt too different to do that. It wasn't just the three inches taller I was. It was everything that happened during my summer vacation. Good things, bad things, even funny things. And I couldn't say a word about any of it. That's what I promised Ike.

I tried to imagine what Arlette would think if I avoided those kids. Or Kaufman, or Charlie, or Tiny, or Grigsby the Englishman and the French guys. So I just kept walking right toward them, instead of around them like I used to do, standing straight as I could, and headed for the front door of the school. No detour today, no way.

When I reached the gang, something pretty strange happened. I stared at them, the fearsome Black Cats, Herbie Schoo and all the rest that had hounded me every single day, all year long, with those stupid grins.

But the grins disappeared when I looked at them. Maybe it was the way I sort of half-smiled, something I guess they never saw me do before. A few of them looked away. Something was making them uncomfortable. One of them looked up at the sky, shading his eyes with his hand. The sun seemed a lot stronger than usual. I almost felt like it was shining a little brighter on me, but I'm sure it wasn't. It just felt that way.

"Good morning," I said as I walked by them. They made room for me. That's all.

No one answered me. No taunts, no name-calling. It just seemed like it wouldn't be such a good idea for them to do or say anything.

And so it turned out to be just another opening day of school, with one difference, a big one. Those guys who made every day of my life as miserable as they could must have changed too, not the way I did, but different, almost like they didn't want any trouble. I guess that's how it is with bullies, don't you think?

Well, there you have it sports fans, as Frankie Frisch always says on the radio at the end of another Giant game. The whole nine innings of how I really spent my summer vacation.

Maybe you won't believe it. I wouldn't blame you. Sometimes I can't either.

ACKNOWLEDGEMENTS

A writer's life is said to be a solitary one, which is why it is so important to have the company of others along the way. I am particularly grateful to a band of authors I have known, at the ready to offer counsel, support, and even deserved questions like, "Are you really sure you want to say that?" Special thanks go to Sandra Dallas, Wick Downing, Carol Essner and Harry MacLean, along with proof reader Chris Murata for being there.

My thanks also go out to the team of the very creative designer Rudy Ramos, who gave this book a cover that came alive off the page.

And I shall always remember one of America's most loved actors, Christopher Lloyd, who took the chance to star in my first feature film, and, sensing my jitters on the first day of filming, assured me, "Relax, I've got your back."

269

ABOUT THE AUTHOR

Arnold Grossman began his writing career in New York at *Redbook* and then *Good Housekeeping* magazines. He continues to write novels and non-fiction, published in U.S., United Kingdom and Japanese editions. He also writes and produces for the stage and screen.

At the same time, he developed a strong interest in politics and, for a number of years, served as media consultant to senators, governors, mayors and House and Senate candidates.

His deep concern for the plague of gun violence gripping America also led him, in the aftermath of the Columbine school massacre, to co-found SAFE COLORADO (Sane Alternatives to the Firearms Epidemic),which helped pass a statewide initiative to close the gun show loophole. It also led him to write the book, *ONE NATION UNDER GUNS, AN AMERICAN EPIDEMIC*.

He still calls Denver, Colorado, home, where, in his words, "I'll never cease searching for any just cause that could help ensure a safe and happy future for my five grandchildren and for everyone else's on this fragile planet."

www.ingramcontent.com/pod-product-compliance
Lightning Source LLC
Chambersburg PA
CBHW052036240626
47153CB00006B/2110